By Allison Winn Scotch

The One That I Want
Time of My Life
The Department of Lost & Found

THE DEPARTMENT
of
LOST & FOUND

Allison Winn Scotch

wm

WILLIAM MORROW
An Imprint of HarperCollins*Publishers*

This book was originally published in hardcover in 2007 by William Morrow, an imprint of HarperCollins Publishers.

THE DEPARTMENT OF LOST AND FOUND. Copyright © 2007 by Allison Winn Scotch. All rights reserved. Printed in the United States of America. No part of this book may be used or reproduced in any manner whatsoever without written permission except in the case of brief quotations embodied in critical articles and reviews. For information address HarperCollins Publishers, 10 East 53rd Street, New York, NY 10022.

HarperCollins books may be purchased for educational, business, or sales promotional use. For information please write: Special Markets Department, HarperCollins Publishers, 10 East 53rd Street, New York, NY 10022.

FIRST WILLIAM MORROW PAPERBACK EDITION PUBLISHED 2011.

The Library of Congress has catalogued the hardcover as follows:

Scotch, Allison Winn.
    The department of lost and found / Allison Winn Scotch.—1st ed.
        p. cm.
    ISBN 978-0-06-116141-4
    ISBN-10 0-06-116141-1
    1. Cancer in women—Fiction.   2. Self-perception—Fiction.
3. Psychological fiction.   I. Title.
PS3619.C64D47 2007
813'.6—dc22   2006051512

ISBN 978-0-06-116142-1 (paperback)

11 12 13 14 15 OV/RRD 10 9 8 7 6 5 4

For Lizzie. I still hear you roar.

The Department of Lost & Found

ROUND ONE

• • •

September

· ONE ·

*D*ear Diary,
    And so I begin. Janice, my cancer therapist, suggested that it might be healthy for me to channel my feelings onto paper instead of channeling them inward and sitting around feeling sorry for myself, which I've spent a great deal of time doing in the past few weeks. So I'm going to give this diary thing a shot. Though, really, who can blame me for moping? I was diagnosed with wretched cancer, my boyfriend dumped me, and the office won't return my calls.

    Of course, when Janice suggested this little hobby, I told her I had nothing to write about: My cancer was certainly out—spending hours in a darkened bedroom with a pen in hand mulling over my mortality wasn't an option. But then, I was lying on my couch staring at the ceiling, hearing the radio but not really listening, when I heard Jake's voice come over the airwaves. Jake. He of my all-consuming love. He was singing about lost love, and I sunk into the pillows and pulled the chenille throw blanket over my legs and wondered if he were singing about me. When the DJ spun a new song, I sat up with a start. Inspiration.

You see, Diary, in the weeks since Ned up and dumped me, it has occurred to me that I'm not entirely sure what went wrong between us. And when I further pondered this situation, I realized that I wasn't sure what went wrong in just about all of my prior relationships. And when I pondered this one step more, I realized that I must lack any or all bits of self-awareness. I mean, what sort of person walks away from a relationship and doesn't even devote a moment to the root of its ending? Sure, I spent time mulling over the ending itself—the overdramatic epitaphs, the wasted tears—but not necessarily the why behind it.

So with that, Diary, I'm off to retrace the steps and missteps of my past: Yes, I'm going to track down the five loves of my life and see what I might glean, who I'll be, where I'll end up. Who knows where it will lead? But you'll be along for the ride, Diary. Wish me luck.

THE ELECTION WAS in six weeks and counting, and admittedly, being out of the action was beginning to take its toll. Ever since law school, I'd only known one thing: work. Higher, stronger, more. Which is how I'd ascended to my pivotal position as the great Senator Dupris's senior aide. All by the age of thirty, which

I turned in early September, just before the world as I know it otherwise imploded.

Before said implosion of my world, I was a woman about town. I'd be parked at my desk by 7:30 A.M., already having run four miles, chatted up the Starbucks barista, and scanned the morning headlines. The next twelve hours would be a blur: The day would be spent cajoling aides, seducing lobbyists, caressing the media, or demolishing anyone who stood in the senator's way. If I were lucky, in the evenings Ned and I would split Chinese takeout around nineish, and after checking my e-mail one last time, I'd crash on my four-hundred-thread-count sheets, only to start it up all over again the next morning.

Now? Well, here's an example of what I did today.

8:27   I wake up.

8:28   I consider vomiting, so roll back over onto Ned's side of the bed and pull my sleep mask back down.

8:31   I can't ward off the effects of Friday's chemo treatment any longer, despite my heavy use of the antinausea drugs that Dr. Chin, my oncologist, prescribed, so I rush to the bathroom just off my bedroom and lean over the toilet while my body rebels against the very medicine that's trying to save it.

8:35   I brush my teeth, wipe the sweat off my brow, and climb back into bed, swearing that I've never hated anything more in my life than this cancer, which, if you were privy to several of my professional entanglements,

says a lot about my distaste for my current condition.

9:26   The phone rouses me from bed, and I assure Dr.
Dorney—well, Zach, I should really call him (or
Dr. Horny, as my friend Lila, the one who ended up
dating him for a year and a half before unceremoniously dumping him on the grounds that she couldn't
stand dating a man who looked at vaginas for a living, liked to call him)—that I'm fine and don't need
anything, and please to not stop by. I sit up in bed
and catch my reflection in the closet mirror on the
opposite wall: my matted hair, my three-day-old pa-
jamas, my sallow skin. No, I tell him firmly, you should
most definitely not drop by.

10:06   My eyes (and brain, perhaps) glaze over as I become
entranced with Bob Barker and his lovely bevy of
beauties.

10:11   The antinausea tea that I've quickly grown to rely on
winds its way through my system, so I nibble on a
banana. It's only been three weeks (or one chemo
cycle), and I've already lost five pounds.

10:54   Despite feeling rather bulletproof with my *Price Is
Right* expertise, I lose the vacation to the Bahamas
and the Ford Thunderbird in the showcase showdown. Now what do I have to live for?

11:02   Time to e-mail Kyle at work.

From: Miller, Natalie
To: Richardson, Kyle
Re: What's Up with Taylor?

Kyle—

   Saw the paper this AM. What's up with the leaks about
Dupris's tax returns? You know that Councilman Taylor
will do anything to win this election and put her out of the
job. He's a slimy bastard—and a state councilman at that!
Where does he get off? What are you guys doing for damage control?
—Nat

11:54   I check e-mail.

12:03   I check e-mail.

12:11   I check e-mail.

12:34   I realize that my BlackBerry will alert me to my e-mail,
        so decide to take a walk.

1:37   The flukishly mild late September air warms my body
        from within, and as I sit on a bench in Central Park,
        I'm surprised to discover that I am not overcome with
        a fit of shivers. The chemo has turned my skin into
        virtual Saran Wrap, as if the drugs aren't just killing
        the lethal cells within me, but eating away at my pro-
        tective coating as well. I inhale the sunny air while
        watching a group of new moms "strollercize" in front
        of me and wonder if I'll ever have kids. The pit of my

stomach rises up, as I remember that Dr. Chin told me that the odds of a Stage III cancer patient maintaining her fertility are not high. I then further remember that the odds of survival aren't that high, either—about 50/50, give or take—so I push the ruinous, devastating thoughts from my mind and pour my energy into walking the half mile home.

2:07   I finish the banana and become embroiled in the disturbingly weird plotline of the soap opera *Passions*, which involves a witch, a puppet, and a long-lost sister.

3:11   Plodding to my computer, I e-mail myself to ensure that my e-mail and BlackBerry are working properly.

3:24   Nap time.

4:55   The phone once again shakes me awake, and I groggily say hello to Sally, my best friend, who has returned from Puerto Rico, where she is planning to marry next spring. I assure her that I'm feeling fine; I'm just a bit stir-crazy. Senator Dupris mandated that I take time off from work during the first few chemo cycles so that I won't run myself ragged, but it's not the cancer that's killing me, it's the boredom. Thus my *Passions* addiction. I fill Sally in on my diary plan and ignore her when she states, "Returning to the scene of the crime is almost always dangerous. I wrote an article on this once, and psychologists say that revisiting history can do more damage than good." I respond that despite the fact that she is a freelance writer (primarily for women's magazines) and thus well versed in just about every subject and study known to man, she does not, in fact, know everything, and therefore, I'm planning on completely ignoring her sage counsel. She doesn't argue, instead saying that if she has to write one more insipid story on lipstick, she's going to jump off a bridge.

5:12   I pick my cuticles.

5:16   I pick my pimples until my face is both puffy and splotchy.

5:34   I apply a cooling Kiehl's mask in hopes of undoing the damage of my picking.

6:02   I check e-mail.

6:27   I make Lipton's Chicken Noodle Cup-a-Soup and sit down on the plush white couch in my living room to watch the evening news.

6:34   My blood pressure palpably rises, and I nearly blow a gasket when Brian Williams introduces a segment on Dupris's "checkered" tax returns. When I sense that my cheeks are getting unhealthily red, I try to breathe in through my nose and out through my mouth, as Janice taught me, in an exercise to ward off stress, but discover that I don't have the patience to count to five on each exhale, so I quickly abandon this so-called calming exercise. Barely hearing the end of the segment, I race, well, move as swiftly as possible under the weight of my blue puffy slippers and terry cloth robe, to my pine desk that overlooks Columbus Avenue and serves as my home office.

6:38   I dash off a semifrantic note to Kyle.

From: Miller, Natalie

To: Richardson, Kyle

Re: Have you seen the Nightly News???????

K—

Haven't heard back from you. The tax return shit is everywhere. The third story on NBC tonight. What the hell is going on??? Why haven't you responded??? Does the whole office go to hell when I'm not there??? You need to act on this ASAP.

I'll be up for a while. Call.

—N

7:11   I rush to the ringing phone on my nightstand and feel a wave of disappointment when Caller ID comes up as my parents, not Kyle. Falling back on my bed, I stare out the side window while I absorb my mother's daily stoicism masked as a pep talk—that my strong will can beat this disease and even if my grandmother succumbed to it, that I shouldn't let that affect my attitude and outlook. She'd been offering up these mantras ever since she and my dad headed here from

Philly and hunkered down at the Waldorf to nurse me through my first chemo blast, as if tough love were all that I needed to beat cancer. I flatly tell my mother that I wasn't even thinking of my grandmother at the moment, but thank you for reminding me that this disgusting disease has already put its pox on our family tree.

7:52   Relief washes over me as my mother finally says goodbye. My wave of nausea passes, so I nibble on a semi-stale bagel.

8:23   I survey the damage of my zit picking in the dim light of my white-tiled bathroom, and then halfheartedly brush my teeth. Why bother? I think. Morning breath is the least of my worries.

8:31   I check e-mail.

8:45   I strip off my cherry red tank top and stare at my breasts in my full-length closet mirror. I stare and I stare and I stare, while I wonder what I did to cause my body to turn against me, to ever deserve this mutiny. I cast my eyes upward and realize that in the blackness of my bedroom, illuminated only from the closet light above, I almost look like an angel.

9:12   I check e-mail. For a faltering moment, I consider adding Ned's name to the mailing list for the penis enlargement drug I received. Instead, I hit delete.

9:54   I fall asleep on my couch while watching Animal Planet
        and wondering how it might feel to have an uncondi-
        tional best friend who smothered my face in slobber
        even when poll numbers were down, even when I
        hadn't showered for three days, and even when my
        face resembled a pepperoni pizza from Ray's.

So that's my day. Sure, just one day, but really not so different
from the rest ever since this cancer set up shop. Now be honest, if
you were me, wouldn't you need a hobby, too?

· TWO ·

It all happened very quickly, which is why, I think, I still felt so shell-shocked three weeks after my diagnosis. I mean, one day, I'm prepping the senator to launch a major initiative on birth control, and the next, I'm donning a paper-thin robe, sitting in Dr. Zach's cloyingly pink-walled examination room, watching his face fall as he feels my right breast and rolls the lump over and back and over again underneath his fingers. So you have to understand that in the span of less than a month, my (disloyal, scum-sucking) boyfriend of two years dumped me ("I can't handle this" is how he put it, right before I threw a vase at his head, which, surprisingly enough, because he wasn't much of an athlete, he actually managed to duck); my job, which previously had been my lifeblood, had been pared down to admittedly semidesperate e-mails; and my health, my mortality, something that I'd never even given a flying fig of a thought to, was suddenly in total jeopardy. So it's not hard to see why I was coming more than slightly undone.

It didn't help that with nothing much left to do, I had to pack up Ned's clothes. After finally honing in on the cues that I had no intention of returning a single phone call of his ever again, he resorted to e-mail.

From: Sanderson, Ned
To: Miller, Natalie
Re: My stuff

Natalie,
    I understand why you aren't calling me back. Surely, I could have chosen a better time to tell you the truth about Agnes and I. I'd like to talk about this with you. When you're ready, please let me know. In the meantime, I need my clothes. Please let me know when I can come by and get them.
Love,
Ned

I sat in front of my computer screen and snorted. *Idiot*, I thought. It's *"Agnes and me." Half-wit*. How I ever considered dating him, no, *loving* him, seemed truly beyond the realm of possibility. Because Ned, nonathlete, evident coward, grammar whiz inextraordinaire, was not the man who one might dream of when one dreamt of men. Since he left me two days after discovering the burrowing lump of insidious cells while feeling me up during ho-hum morning sex, this might go without saying. As if to prove this point, I took a sip of my chamomile tea and hit reply to his e-mail. *I'll show you how ready I am.*

I swirled the lukewarm tea around in my mouth and clicked my mouse to insert a table into the blank white space underneath the e-mail header. On the left side, I typed "why I loved you," and on the right, "why I didn't."

- *Idiot*

- *Makes a lot of money at a job that a chimpanzee can do*

- *Tendency to stare too long in the mirror to the point of vanity*

- *Not good-looking enough to have the right to pull off above behavior*

- *Your moles*

- *Boring—I never missed not having dinner with you because it was a snoozefest*

- Tiny *penis (note to readers: this isn't necessarily true, but surely, he didn't know that)*

- *Amazing ability to drop your blue-blooded family's name into any conversation with important people*

- *Insecure twit*

And that was just the right-hand column.

In the left, I put a question mark, but conceded that we had, indeed, dated for two years, so that didn't seem entirely fair. So instead, I hit the delete key and wrote:

- *Has good decorating taste*

- *Makes decent pancakes*

Both of the characteristics were true. When we first moved in—actually, when Ned moved in with me, which is why I was the one who got to kick him out—Ned didn't rest until our one-bedroom was sharp enough to nearly be photographed for *Architectural Digest*. Ebony floors. Rich leather headboard. Deep crimson foyer. And yes, he did make a mean weekend breakfast. On the rare Saturdays when I was in town and he wasn't toiling away as a vice president at Goldman Sachs, he'd wake up before me and serve up the most perfect silver-dollar pancakes that a girl could ever dream of.

But before I got too wistful, I realized that these two attributes also meant that I could tick off another trait in the right-hand column.

- *Aforementioned domesticity would lead me to the conclusion that you should, perhaps, examine your sexual preference.*

And then I thought of one more.

- *Leaves cancer-laden girlfriend for ridiculously named hussy*

It was true. If *Ned* and *Agnes* were to ever procreate, their kids had no chance at being cool. This was a fact.

I went to press Send, but then remembered the very purpose of the original e-mail. "I'll leave your clothes with my doorman by 5:00 tonight. I don't want any future reminders of you around to stink up my karma."

Send.

THIS WASN'T THE first time I'd been faced with packing up my romantic history. And certainly, if it hadn't been for the nuclear drugs coursing through my body and the diabolic cells they were trying to stomp out, this wouldn't have been the hardest. No, that title fell to Jake. So as I pulled out Ned's seemingly endless amount of staid blue pin-striped suits and threw them—literally threw them, he could have *Agnes* iron them for him—into a duffel bag, it was hard not to think of Jake.

I met Jacob Spencer Martin when I was twenty-five. I'd moved to the city only three months before, fresh out of Yale Law, to join Dupris's first election campaign, and given the clip at which I worked, I wasn't looking for anything romantically. To be more precise, I wasn't looking for anything. But on a damp October evening, Sally begged me to join her for a girls' night out. "We haven't seen you in a month," she said, and she wasn't incorrect: I'd been holed up in my crappy cubicle in midtown making last-minute calls encouraging people to get out and vote. When she put her figurative foot down and told me that if I didn't come out, she'd never speak to me again (she has a knack for exaggeration), I caved. I placed the cap on my highlighter and tucked away my list of phone numbers and met Sally, Lila, and a pack of other sorority sisters at a bar in the East Village. I didn't even bother changing out of my entirely too-geekish suit. I can assure you that I was the only one there in pumps. And hose. And we'll leave it at that.

Around 10:00, a band, the Misbees, one that my friends made a point to see every time they played in the city, hit the stage. Maybe it was the wine, or maybe he really was a fucking great singer, but either way, I couldn't take my eyes off the blond, tousled-hair guy behind the microphone. His voice hummed out low and deep, and when he sang of pain and betrayal and love and lust, I believed him. And I wanted to know more. Our eyes locked toward the end of the set, and I felt my pulse speed up and my stomach tighten.

When the Misbees finished their set, the singer wandered over to the bar directly next to my perch on a stool and ordered a beer, and when he took a step backward, he somehow missed the fact that said leg of the stool was in his way. Which is how he wound up tripping and dumping at least half of his Heineken on the Donna Karan suit my mother had bought me when I accepted the senator's offer. Maybe that should have been a warning sign—an inauspicious start—but when he patted me down with a napkin and apologized with his hound-dog eyes, I was hooked. Line and sinker. Sinking fast, actually. . . .

I heard the microwave timer ding, and shaking off my memory, I placed my feet firmly into the existence that now comprised my reality. I stared at a pin-striped shirt and snorted. *Ned*. As if he'd ever compare to the great love of my life. As if he were anything more than filler. *Maybe I'll e-mail him again*, I thought. *Just to let him know.* I plodded out of my walk-in closet, dropping Ned's dry-cleaned Armani on the floor and stepping smack on it. I might have even let my foot swivel a few times before I actually took a step forward.

I'd programmed the timer to remind me to take my medicines: the antinausea, the anticancer, the pretty much antieverything. It dinged four times a day, subtle reminders of my altered existence just in case I should ever be lulled into a false sense of reality. The antinausea drugs were the worst: so large I didn't see how it was possible for a gorilla, much less a human, to swallow them. I'd swing back a gulp of water and the prickly pill would hang in the curve of my throat, daring me to dry heave or cough and start all over again. You'd think after three weeks, I'd have mastered this, but there are some things you just never get used to.

I went back to the closet and picked up Ned's Armani. My hands dove into the side pockets: I figured that if he had any spare cash, I might as well line my own wallet. I'd already found $31.57, and I was only half done. I pulled out a receipt from an Italian restaurant in the West Village, dated the night of the day that Ned discovered the lump. *Bastard. He told me he was in Chicago.* I threw the Armani onto the duffel bag on my bed and kept the receipt. Ammunition in case things ever got dirty, I figured. *As if they're not dirty enough,* I thought. But I'd learned that on the job: Keep whatever evidence necessary to burn the opponent and shred whatever evidence might be able to be used to bury you.

I reached up to the top shelf for his T-shirts. His lacrosse shirt from Harvard. I tossed it over my shoulder into a garbage bag. After all, it was his favorite. Not that he actually played on the team, you understand. But he managed them, so I guess he felt entitled to don it regardless. And not that he actually got into Harvard on his own merits. As I've already mentioned, he's one step above a complete twit. But his family practically dates back to the Mayflower, and the admissions committee seems to look fondly on ancestry that has enough cash and leverage to donate a new library or two.

From that same shelf, I pulled out a Martha's Vineyard T-shirt. THE BLACK DOG, it read. Ned and I had spent a week there earlier in the summer. He started in on me in April to set aside a week in July for "just the two of us," and given the desperation in his voice, maybe I should have sensed that the lives we were carving out around, not with, each other, weren't enough. He brought it up again when I was dashing out the door to begin a weeklong trip through Europe with the senator, and in my haste, I agreed, which is how I found myself begrudgingly enjoying a lazy week in a quintessential beach house on the Vineyard. That week, I boiled lobsters for dinner because they were his favorite, I indulged him in renting a kayak, and I stayed up far later than I liked just to sit on our rented porch and listen to the lapping of the waves and hold his hand and stare at the stars.

I held the Black Dog T-shirt out in front of me and almost tasted the homemade donuts that we'd eaten each morning that week. Tangy, sweet, cinnamon, soft, and crusty. Ned would dunk his into his black coffee, and I'd eat mine slowly until it literally melted in my mouth. Maybe I should have savored more than just the donuts, it occurred to me just then. I pulled the shirt into my face and inhaled, as if I might still be able to smell the salty air or breathe in the hazy sunsets or capture those moments—the moments of my former life—in the deep gasp of my breath.

But there was nothing. So instead, I wiped away the solitary tear that had weaseled itself out of my right eye and careened down my cheek, and with sheer brute force, grabbed the neck of the T-shirt and tore it right down the middle. It would make a good dust rag, I figured, when I needed to do some cleaning up.

•   •   •

From: Miller, Natalie

To: Richardson, Kyle

Re: Please Call Me

K—

   No word from you. The *Post* has this splattered all over the front page, of which I'm sure you're well aware.

   Call ASAP.

—N

It was hardly an ideal thing to wake up to: your boss's dirty laundry airing out for all to see, complete with the headline, "Dupris Is Duplicitous." Lovely. The truth was that I didn't know the particulars of this sticky tax problem. And as her senior adviser, I probably should have, but even I, future Madame President, wasn't immune to the occasional dropped ball at work. And besides, dirty laundry is simply part of my job. In politics, it's not the dirt that bothers us, it's the chance that someone might pick up our reeking scent. If you can manage to wring everything through the laundry without the evidence being spotted, well, hurrah to you.

In the early spring, Kyle, who was my age but still a notch below me in seniority, which didn't always foster the warmest of relationships, brought the senator's endless list of gifts—including a Fabergé egg from a Russian diplomat and carved ivory elephants from ambassadors—to my attention.

"I don't think this is legal," he said, taking a deep sip of the grande coffee that I wasn't sure I'd ever seen him without. "Have you ever looked into this? I mean, she gets thousands of thousands of dollars of gifts. And I think it could be an issue."

"Go away," I said, waving my hand and squinting at my computer, dismissing him in the way that a queen might shoo a fly. I stopped to readjust the elastic band in my hair and pulled my highlighted brown locks into a bun at the nape of my neck.

"Natalie, I'm serious. I think that this campaign might get ugly, and I really think that this could be an issue. I took a look at some of the stuff that she's declared in the past, and . . ." He paused. "Not everything is there."

I rubbed my eyes. "*Everyone* fudges, Kyle. *No one* reports everything. Not our senator, not anyone else's. *No one* cares and *no one* gets caught. It's just SOP." I sighed and softened my voice. "Look, I'm fucking dying here trying to write this proposal for the birth control bill—those assholes from Mississippi are threatening to block it—as if offering women the right to insured birth control is somehow a threat to their own testicular power. So I trust that you can handle this. I handled it for years before you, and I'm sure you can handle it now. If you have further concerns, call Diane in

Senator Kroiz's office; though she'll be relatively hush-hush about it, she'll tell you this is SOP, too."

I turned back to my computer just as I saw his face turn perfect cherry tomato red. Despite his tailor-made suits, crisp pocket handkerchiefs, and polished Prada shoes, Kyle was not nearly as composed on the inside as he was on the out, and his emotional constitution was perhaps his one weakness. After all, in politics, you never let them see you ruffled. (Unless, of course, it helped your poll numbers, in which case, they saw you ruffled, rattled, and rolled.)

"Fine." He huffed dramatically, his voice registering about two decibels louder and dripping with disdain. "But you heard it here first. I think this is a red flag, and I *thought* that, you know, as her *senior* adviser, you'd want to know."

"Yeah, well, I don't. It's never been a problem in the past, and I'm sure it won't be now. So clean it up however you need to. Alter the returns, fudge this year's gifts, whatever." I kept typing.

"So that's your final word? Do whatever I need to do?"

Rather than answer, I flicked my hand in his direction as his cue to leave.

I heard him snort as he spun around to leave, and under his breath he muttered, "Senior adviser. *As if.*"

"Kyle?" I called after him, ceasing my work and looking up at him. He swiveled his neck over his shoulder rather than give me the courtesy of turning. "I'm sorry. I'm just overworked and on a deadline, and I truly can't deal with this right now. I'm putting it in your court, so handle it."

He raised his eyebrows. "You? Natalie Miller. Sorry? I don't buy it for a second."

"Fair enough," I said, half-smiling. "I'm not really sorry. But I figured that you'd stop bothering me and go about getting your job done if you thought that I was." I turned back to my computer. "So go get it done. And keep me out of it."

So really, as I stared at the *Post* and popped the first of my morning pills, I could hardly blame him for ignoring me now that his theory had hit the fan. Turns out, I'd preemptively ignored a very large and seemingly looming time bomb. I flipped on the TV. *The Price Is Right* was coming on in fifteen minutes and even though I never envisioned a time in my life when this would be part of my daily scheduling, there it was.

I dropped the remote on the couch and went to the kitchen to prepare a bowl of oatmeal. If there were any good news of the day, it was that I was actually feeling semidecent. When I first met with Dr. Chin, when I sat in his dignified mahogany-walled office decorated with Persian rugs and leather chairs, he had told me that there were three stages of chemo recovery. The first week, you feel like your insides are on fire, like the chemicals rushing through you might kill you if the cancer doesn't. The second week, you sense that you might survive; it's not that you feel normal, but you feel the absence of the afflictions that plagued you the last week, so in that way, it's like you won the lottery. And the third week is the one where you can't believe that you ever felt like such a steaming mound of shit. Chemo? You're thinking. That's the best you can dish out? Because that, my darling cancer gods, I can take without blinking an eye. The sick part of this pattern, which I'm sure you've already figured out, is that just as you're on the cusp of returning to your everyday life, right as you press your nose up to healthfulness and start going about your business as you did before the disease mowed you down, you have to start it all over again.

At the time, Dr. Chin flipped through my chart, ignoring his assistant, who kept paging him over the intercom, and explained that we'd be doing six or seven months of chemo, a round every

three weeks, and based on my reaction to this treatment, we'd proceed from there. At some point along the way, either in the middle
or at the end, they'd perform a mastectomy. They would take my
breasts from me.

He also spoke about what I could expect: fatigue, nausea, and
the thing that I dreaded most—hair loss. "The aim of chemother-
apy is to kill the fast-growing cancer cells," he explained. "But
what also happens as a result is that healthy cells are killed as well.
So, for example, your hair follicles are, in effect, shut down. Fortunately, the human body is resilient and smart enough to know how
to grow them back when we're done." He said all of this in the
kind of tone that he'd clearly perfected after years of treating depressing cases such as mine. He was firm yet still reassuring, regretful yet still commanding. I sat in his office and stared at his
numerous diplomas and awards and medical society memberships,
and I simply nodded my head, a small acknowledgment of the in-
evitable, of resigned acceptance. It's not as if I had a choice.

What I didn't tell Dr. Chin, when he asked how I felt, because
surely he was referring to my physical maladies, not the emotional
ones, was that I was gutted. That the fear that ran through me was
nearly paralyzing. That the sheer terror of his words, "you have
cancer," caused my breath to leave my body, and that nodding my
head in resignation was all that I *could* do. Anything more simply
would have been impossible, because, you see, I was frozen.

I was thirty. I was the future ruler of the free world. And
yet . . . this. *I was thirty, and I had cancer. I was thirty, and I had cancer.* I replayed it over and over again in my mind because it didn't add
up; it *couldn't* add up. This. Could. Not. Be. My. Life. And yet . . . it
was. So I sat in his office, and I tasted the horror that comes from
discovering you're not invincible, and maybe it was the cancer, but

more likely, it was the spine-chilling terror of my diagnosis, but I literally wanted to curl up and die. Because the sum of Dr. Chin's words led me to believe that I might just do that anyway.

Before I got up to leave, he pressed a card into my hand. "At some point, you might want to go see her." I looked down and read *Mrs. Adina Seidel. Master Wigmaker.* Dr. Chin offered me a thin smile. "She's the best that there is. And many of my patients find the process cathartic." I met his eyes and wondered how a pile of fake hair could ever make someone feel more complete. But rather than reply, I took the card into my shaking fingers, thanked him for his time, and told him that I'd see him in a few days. As I left his office, I remember thinking that I couldn't feel my legs. That I was walking, yes, surely, I was shuffling down the linoleum-covered floor and through the dimly lit corridor, but how I was doing it, I don't know. I remembered back to high school biology, when my teacher, Mr. Katz, lectured us on the "fight-or-flight" syndrome: that when an animal is put in peril, any unnecessary part of his brain function shuts down, that his body responds in a purely visceral way, doing what it must to survive the threat. But my own body, when faced with such a threat, was seemingly retreating. Rather than gathering its army to face the hell to come, it was already abandoning me. Already shutting me down. My legs were just the beginning.

But now, as I wrapped up the last few days of my first chemo round, things were indeed looking up. At least as far as my vomit/nausea/exhaustion/dizzy problems went. That, I supposed, was something.

I stared at the *Post* while stirring my oatmeal, waiting for it to cool. I reached for the cordless phone on my white Formica counter and considered calling Kyle but figured that I could at least wait until the end of *The Price Is Right* to harass him. (I was getting quite adept at homing in on the prices of nearly all of the electronics the contestants had to bid on, though admittedly, the groceries still threw me off my game.) Besides, I rationalized, Kyle was probably in his morning meeting. He'd definitely e-mail me as soon as he was done. So instead, I dialed Sally, who promptly agreed to meet me for an afternoon walk. Dr. Chin had recommended that I stay as active as possible without crossing the line to where I actually did more damage to my weary body.

By the time Bob Barker had awarded the showcase showdown (a vacation to Tahiti! Was this really just an excuse for *The Price Is Right* girls to wear bikinis onstage? I wondered), there was still no word from Kyle. There was, however, word from the senator. Or her assistant, Blair, to be more precise.

> From: Foley, Blair
> To: Miller, Natalie
> Re: The BC bill
>
> Hi Natalie!!!!!
>   I hope you're doing well!!!!! We're all keeping our best thoughts with you and know that if anyone can beat this, it's you!!!!
>   Anyway, the senator asked me to alert you that she is no longer moving forward with her push for the birth control bill. She told me to thank you so much for all of your hard work (she'd tell you herself, but she's about to dash up to Albany), but that she doesn't want to get into it with the Mississippi contingent, and she also said "I don't think this matters very much right now," in case that helps you

understand. I think she meant that in the nicest way possible!!!! As in, we don't need to worry about this for now!!!!
Great news, right?

   Hope you're feeling great!!!!!!!!!

Blair

From: Miller, Natalie
To: Foley, Blair
Re: re: The BC bill

Blair—

   Please ask the senator to hold off her car to Albany, I'm
coming into the office. And tell Kyle he better get his ass in
gear: I expect to speak with him when I'm there. Tell him
those words exactly.

—Natalie

I surveyed myself in the mirror. This wouldn't do at all: the
ratty, thinning hair, the pallid, blotchy skin, the protruding cheekbones that resembled Kate Moss at the height of her drug habit.
Shit, I muttered, standing in my now much more spacious closet
and looking for a magic suit that would somehow make me look not
even polished but merely presentable. I'd settle for presentable. I
grabbed a tweed skirt suit, tugged on my nude hose, and slipped
my tingly feet (a side effect from the chemo) into my alligator-skin
pumps. PETA would have a field day in my closet, despite the fact
that Dupris (and thus supposedly her staff), at least on paper, was
staunchly pro-animal rights. However, I suspected that if PETA
took a closer look into Dupris's wardrobe, they'd find it even more
egregious than mine. A rabid fan of just about any accessory that

required an animal skinning, she wasn't quite the poster child she was thought to be. I took a more tempered approach. I loved dogs more than anything, tolerated cats, and only ate red meat when I'd already gulped down a minimum of two glasses of wine. Anything fewer, and I was a part-time vegetarian.

I splashed cold water on my face and gingerly applied a layer of Stila concealer underneath my eyes. I stared into the mirror and saw myself for what I was, or at least what I looked like to the outside world: an exhausted, disheveled, thrown-together mess, nothing that even touched a reflection of who I was a month earlier. I stared until tears started to well. *Hold it together, Nat, hold it together,* I whispered to myself as a wet drop slithered down my cheek. This wasn't who I was. This wasn't who I should be. I focused in on my moist eyes and wondered if there would ever be a day again when I'd come close to being the person of my former life. And then I realized that my bruised-looking eyes aside, today could be that day. I, Natalie Miller, was going to the office. To get something done. To make a sweeping change to protect the uteri of women across the nation. And with a rush of adrenaline, I stuck my hand back into the pot of concealer.

When one layer wouldn't do, I slathered on another, then another, and then remembered a trick that Sally had written about for *Allure*: dotting the insides of your eyes with white eye shadow to make them pop and look more awake. I dipped my finger into a packed tub of shadow that sparkled like a field of morning snow and dabbed my eyes. I'm not sure I looked more alert or more like a dressed-up fairy on Halloween, but I didn't have time to remedy it. The senator would be leaving any minute. I pulled my still somewhat tolerable, though slightly thinning hair back with a headband, slid on rosy pink lipstick and thick, black mascara, and dashed downstairs to a cab. *Christ.*

Sally. I dialed her from the back of the taxi and told her I'd take a rain check for tomorrow.

"You're not going into work, are you?" she asked. "I thought you'd committed to taking it easy for a few months."

"Emergency, Sal, emergency." I put my hand over the mouth-piece and told the cab driver to cut down Central Park West to avoid the traffic. He ignored me and turned up the hip-hop station on the radio.

"Fine." She sighed. "I'm working on a ridiculous story on infidelity, anyway. God, what I wouldn't do to be able to actually cover a story that really matters." She paused, refocusing on me. "Wait, Nat, define emergency."

"A situation in which I control the power to single-handedly save the future of your reproductive rights."

"Single-handedly?" I heard her sigh again.

"More or less, yes."

"Correct me if I'm wrong, but you're not the actual *senator* are you?"

"More or less, Sally. I don't think she could survive without me."

· THREE ·

It had started raining by the time I made my way through midtown traffic, so I pressed ten dollars into the cab driver's hand and dashed to the revolving doors, leaving wet handprints on the glass as I pushed through. The elevator doors were closing, but I shouted "Hold it," and bolted there just in time, sticking the tips of my fingers through and pushing back the doors. "Thanks," I muttered to the lunch crowd, to really no one in particular, and offered a thin smile.

When the senator won her seat after a fierce campaign six years ago, just after I'd come to work for her as an assistant, one of her first tasks was to purchase office space in midtown Manhattan. She liked to be "among the people," as she liked to say, though her brushes with "real citizens" were usually limited to her walks to and from The Four Seasons for lunch or Frederick Fekkai for highlights. We sat on the thirty-first floor—too far above to hear the raucous din of the taxi horns or the clangs of construction or the buzzing of the pedestrians, and certainly too far aloft to make out any of the pedestrians' faces or to see their problems or assess their woes.

In fact, though my office had a sweeping window with a decent view of Third Avenue, most of the time the blinds remained firmly shut. If the sun bore down and spread its rays across my desk, I'd find myself missing the fresh air that I wouldn't get to taste for another twelve hours. So generally, the blinds did the trick, casting an illusion of my insulated world, as if the only thing that mattered was the policy I was crafting on my computer, not the people below whom the policy might actually affect.

I hadn't been back to the office in the month since my diagnosis. Although I'd practically begged the senator to let me keep working, she personally fielded a call from Dr. Chin, and when she explained my long hours and my incessant travel schedule (and, I assume, my insatiable appetite for the office), they both agreed that I should tone it down a notch (or two) while my body acclimated to the chemo. Even my mother agreed—my mom who once decided, back when I was eleven, that she wanted to run the New York marathon, just to test herself, to see how far her body could sustain the pain (and most likely insanity), and thus trained for all of five weeks, and managed to cross the finish line at just under four hours. So it wasn't as if my mother's sympathy chip was finely honed.

My parents had driven up from Philly for my first round of chemo. "You don't have to," I'd told them on the phone, wiping away the snot that poured from my nostrils after succumbing to a crying fit over Ned. I couldn't remember the last time I'd wailed so loudly; surely my neighbors thought that someone had died. But then I did remember it, of course. It was when Jake cut a wedge so deeply into my heart that I feared I'd never be able to successfully breathe, much less relish the life that comes along with that breath, again.

But my parents arrived just three hours later, and my mom sat and squeezed my shoulder as I reclined in a blue recliner and watched *General Hospital* while liquid toxins filled my bloodstream. "That wasn't so bad," I told my mom in the cab ride home, and she rubbed my back and pulled my head to her shoulder, something she probably hadn't done since I was about five.

My parents stuck around through the weekend. Although Dr. Chin had warned me of the symptoms, sometimes words do little to warn you of the oncoming storm. Within a day, getting out of bed to pee seemed too big a task. To say that the fatigue felt as if I'd been plowed, flattened, pancaked by a Mack truck would be close to the truth. To say that the effort required to lift just my pinky or my little toe or even to crack open my eyelids felt Herculean would also be accurate.

And of course, the pesky part of dealing with the exhaustion is that within twenty-four hours, I was also battling nausea. So the little energy I did have in reserves was spent running back and forth to the bathroom with the threat of constant vomiting. Finally, my mother matter-of-factly placed a stainless-steel bowl, one that Ned and I had bought at Bed Bath & Beyond when we moved in together, at the right side of my bed. What had been purchased with the thought of spending lingering hours whipping up gourmet delicacies as a new cohabitating unit now served to receive the pure bile purged from my stomach; it wasn't as if I had the appetite to eat anything to barf back up.

Five days later, I slowly emerged from the cocoon of my first chemo treatment, and my parents checked out of the Waldorf, ready to return to their now semialtered lives. I was gingerly stepping out of the shower when they stopped over to say good-bye.

"We'll be back in a few weeks," my dad said, ignoring my damp hair and pulling me into him, as I clung to the top of the towel rather than return his embrace. He kissed the top of my head, and I heard his voice crack.

"I spoke with your boss," my mom interrupted, as I pulled back from my father. "She's agreed that it's best if you work from home— or really, don't work at all—for a few weeks or even months."

"What? Who gave you the right to do that? We're headed into the election, I'm not taking any time off." I walked into the bedroom to get dressed.

"Natalie, this isn't negotiable," she said to my back.

I slung on a sweatshirt and pajama bottoms and reemerged with the towel wrapped around my head. "I can't believe that you did this!" I was sixteen all over again and my mother had just called my swim coach and told her that they were pulling me from the team so that I could focus on my SATs. It's not that I loved swimming, and truly, it wasn't even that I didn't *want* to focus on my SATs (after all, no one became president with lousy SATs . . . or so I thought at the time), but it was all so typical: her making decisions about me, *for* me, whether I wanted to quit swimming or not.

My mother eyed me coolly. "The senator and I both spoke with Dr. Chin. And this is how it's going to be, so don't waste your energy screaming at me. You need to preserve what you have right now."

"Why are you butting in?" I pulled the towel off my head, throwing it on the couch. "This is totally ridiculous. It's *my life*. I know what's best for me, and cutting myself out at work is *not what's best for me.*"

My mom moved forward to kiss my cheek. "Honestly dear. I really don't think that you know what's best for you." And then she took my father's hand and walked out the door, leaving me there shaking from rage, damp hair, and the side effects of chemo.

A month later, with nothing much to show for my time off other than accumulated knowledge of *The Price Is Right,* I knew with more certainty than ever that my mother barely knew me, much less knew what was *best* for me.

Now, back at the office, as the gold-mirrored elevator doors opened, the first thing I noticed wasn't the buzzing of the junior aides in their cubicles or the pulsing of the incessantly ringing phones. No, it was a foul, fetid rotting smell. I gulped down a pocket of air and tried to breathe through my mouth as I made my way through the maze of cubes to the senator's office at the opposite end of the floor. When we first moved in, Dupris had attempted to make the space look luxurious—I convinced her that it certainly wasn't illegal to allocate the extra campaign money for renovations—but regardless of how she dressed it up, it still looked like a drab, lifeless void . . . except for the toiling of the actual live bodies. Staid white cubes were laid out like honeycomb; bluish-grayish carpeting hid linoleum tiles on the floor; fluorescent bulbs glared down from above, highlighting our omnipresent purple under-eye circles.

Blair was laughing into her earpiece when I reached her desk. She pushed her blond bob behind her ears, then held up a finger and mouthed, "One second," when she saw me. "Love you, too," she said, before she clicked off. "Sorry." She looked up at me and beamed. Clearly a new boyfriend.

At twenty-two, fresh out of Georgetown, Blair still had the naïveté to be caught up in the throes of young Manhattan love, which would inevitably get stomped into the ground as soon as one of them got too drunk one night and made out with another twenty-two-year-old in a basement bar with pulsing music and far too many candles to legally pass any sort of fire code. "I told him not to call me here, but, you know how it is . . ." She waved her manicured hand in front of her.

"It fucking reeks in here. What the hell is going on?" I peered down, ignoring her idealistic romanticism.

"Oh, gosh, I'm sorry. Yes, yes, I know." The blood drained from her face. "Um, a pipe burst three days ago, and um, water seems to have gotten underneath the carpet. So, um, it seems to have, um, mildewed. The cleaners are coming tonight after work."

"Whatever." I sighed and looked toward Dupris's door. "Can I go in?"

Blair bit her lip. "You just missed her actually." Her voice rose an octave, as she jumped out of her chair and tripped over one of the legs. "Natalie, I'm so sorry! I tried to tell her that you were coming in, but she said that she couldn't wait, and I tried to delay her, but . . ."

I pushed open the door and slammed it behind me before she could finish. Dupris's office looked jarringly different from the hovel in which we plebeians toiled. Rich forest-green drapes hung from the picture windows, lush cream carpeting welcomed my pumps. Her deep ebony desk had been a gift from an Indian ambassador: He claimed that his son had made it so she didn't have to refuse it as a potential bribe. And of course, for the senator, there were no fluorescent lights with which to highlight the damage from the previous evening's all-nighter. Just brass lamps scattered throughout. If you didn't know that you were in the office of one of the most powerful women on the Hill, you might have thought you'd inadvertently walked into an Ethan Allen catalog.

I pulled out her chocolate leather chair and sat down, grabbing the gold calligraphy pen that was perched on the right corner.

Senator Dupris—

I'm sorry that I missed you. I know that you don't check e-mail, so wanted to leave you a note. I strongly urge you to re-consider your stance on the birth control referendum. I know that we can avoid the Mississippi contingent—I looked into it and have some tactics and information to quiet them.

Please keep this in mind.

—Natalie

PS—Thanks for the orchids last week. They are wonderful and thriving in my living room.

"Good God, Blair," I said as I left Dupris's office. "How can you even work with this rancid smell?"

"You get used to it. I can't even smell anything, actually." She burrowed around in her purse. "Want a piece of gum?"

"No. Thank you." I craned my neck around to peer into the cubes. "Where's Kyle? Did you give him my message?"

She folded the piece of gum into her mouth and turned the color of a spring beet. "Um, I forwarded your e-mail to his Black-Berry, but he hasn't been in all morning, and he didn't write me back. I wasn't sure what to do."

I inhaled and exhaled just like Janice told me to do. But this deep breathing thing really didn't seem to be working. So after three goes of it, I slammed my hand down on her desk and stared until she pressed herself as far back as was humanly possible to press oneself into a swivel chair without actually becoming one with it.

I started to open my mouth, to chastise her for a job so inadequately done, but all at once, I was exhausted. Bone-crushingly exhausted. Crawl-under-the-desk exhausted. I broke my gaze from Blair, massaged my temples with my now-stinging hand, and leaned back into her desk.

"Natalie, are you okay?" Blair asked meekly, cocking her head to the side and putting on a worried face.

I blew out my breath and stood up straight, tugging at my jacket to ensure that I didn't wrinkle.

"Fine, Blair. I'm fine." And with that, I turned and walked toward the elevator before it became apparent to anyone besides me that I wasn't fine at all.

ROUND TWO

• • •

October

· FOUR ·

I had the dream again. The same one I had during the first week of my first cycle. I was at a deserted amusement park at dusk, and when I looked out from my perch atop a roller coaster, I saw that the only people left on the grounds were the clowns. Thousands of them. Bright red wigs bobbing up and down, silly plodding shoes leading their way. I sat on the roller coaster and at once felt my car, one in the very back, lurch forward, and soon I was flying so fast that tears unwillingly came to my eyes. The car slowed as it approached the big incline upward, and suddenly (because this can happen only in dreams), I was squished in my seat by dozens of clowns. Overflowing even. Pressed like sardines up against me with a saccharine smell of cotton candy. I tried to undo my seat belt to jump, to release myself before my claustrophobia set in, but it was as if the ride itself wouldn't set me free. We reached the top of the climb, and I felt it—the panic that comes right before a dead drop, the kind that I imagine pilots sense when a plane has gone into a nosedive.

"Please," I shouted to the clowns below. "Please, pull the lever and make it stop!" But all I heard was merry-go-round music, oompa-loompaing in the background, my voice bouncing off it and echoing back. And besides, it was already too late. We'd crossed the hump of the hill, and gravity was already pulling us down. I tried to grab hold of the clown pressed up to my right, but my grip went right through him, like he was an apparition and bore no weight. The car was flying, and I was going with it. We went fast, faster, faster still until we tore off the track, skidding against the paved grounds and leaving smoke in our wake. We landed on a mound of sand, a flattened beach in the middle of the park, and though I should have felt relief, what I felt was only increasing panic. Because all at once, like a tentacle around my calves, a sucking force pulled me down, deeper, deeper until I was in the sand up to my thighs. I frantically flailed over crimson clown wigs, oversized buttons, and suffocating cotton candy, but no matter how much I willed it to be so, I couldn't gain solid footing. And I couldn't make it stop. Just as I was about to give up, just as I was about to surrender to my fate, a hand reached out and pulled me up. I tried to see who it was, see who saved me, but all I saw was a faceless shadow, and then, even that was gone.

I WOKE UP on my couch with the ladies from *The View* yammering in the background, and moved my hand up to feel my pulse nearly beating through my neck. Gingerly, I swung my legs to the floor, wiped the film of sweat off my forehead, and reached for my Nikes. The waves of nausea had mostly passed, at least for this week and this round, so I propelled myself out the door. Dr. Chin had urged me to be kind to my body, not to push it, but also to keep it vibrant, let it know that it was still living. My four-mile-run mornings were out, but walking, breathing in the throbbing vitality of the city all around me, I could do.

October had set in, and it had always been my favorite month: the one where the air still captured the warmth of the previous season but also hung with the promise of the fall chill. When the light on Seventy-third Street turned red, I stopped and nuzzled the wet nose of a black lab standing beside me with his owner, and in exchange, he lapped my face in a warm bath. I wiped down my cheeks and smiled. As I cut over to Central Park, the sun bounced off the crimson and golden leaves, and other than the passing dog-walker, it was just me, the nutmeg-scented air, and the autumn hues.

When Jake first moved in with me, we took lingering walks each weekend. It was our thing. Some couples play poker, some love to bowl; we loved to explore the park like we might have when we were nine: It was our private playground. We'd stumble over the roots in the Rambles, roam up to the ball fields and watch Little League, or sit on the swings at dusk and split a bottle of merlot.

Eventually, our buzz for each other faded, as one's buzz inevitably does, and I spent more weekends holed up on the thirty-first floor, and he spent more weekends racking up frequent flier miles, in hopes of becoming the next Mellencamp or Petty or Clapton or whomever he'd deem cool enough to emulate that month.

Today, because I was on the slow upswing of my chemo cycle, I felt well enough to follow the looping path down past the ice rink and around the carousel. I stopped and watched the little kids, mostly with their nannies, grab the fiberglass horses as tightly as their tiny fists could hold, and squeal with delight as they went up, then down, then back up again.

That summer, the one before Jake and I came down from our heady romantic tornado, he'd convinced me to sneak into the carousel after dark.

"This can't be a good idea," I'd said, citing the potential political damage to the senator if we were arrested. "I can't imagine that bailing out one of her senior-most aides will be looked kindly upon in the papers."

But he grabbed my hand and picked the lock and led me in anyway. And it was amazing: It was truly as if we were three or four or five, like those kids I saw today. It was a cloudless night, and though you can't see the stars in New York City, in the darkness of the park, it's almost as if you can. We sat on the jester-colored horses and stared up at the sky, watching the lights from the skyscraping buildings bounce off the clouds and listening to a nearby Summerstage reggae concert. We didn't speak for nearly an hour, and then Jake slipped off his perch on the horse and circled around mine and kissed me. And then we fell into each other in ways that we definitely wouldn't have if we were five.

This afternoon, the carousel slowed to a halt and the music wound down. As the kids scattered and a few cried, I took my cue to exit as well, pushing my hands into my pockets and wrapping my scarf tighter around my neck. I wasn't sure if the sudden chill were noticeable to anyone but me. Or if there were a sudden chill at all, really.

I was nearing the park exit when I heard my name echoing behind me.

"Natalie? NAT? Is that you?"

I spun around to see Lila Johansson, my sophomore- and

junior-year sorority roommate, and by more current definitions, my second-best friend after Sally and a fellow bridesmaid in Sally's wedding, waving at me from beneath a towering maple tree. With her crisply straight, perfectly highlighted blond locks, dark denims that just skimmed over her gazellelike legs, and her man-crushing stilettos, Lila was the embodiment of a celebrity, even though the only place she was famous was within our inner circle. And she was really primarily famous for putting those stilettos to use. And often. We first met our freshman year. We'd sat down next to each other after receiving our bids from our sorority and were promptly assigned to go to lunch together. I looked down at my monogrammed turtleneck and fingered my pearl bracelet and wondered what on earth a girl like me would have in common with a gal like her. Turns out that over chicken kung pao we discovered that hair color and inseam length have little to do with the true testament of who you are. True, she would happily desert you for a glass of wine with a budding Armani model, but her faults were clearly laid out from the get-go. At least those I could see.

"Oh my God, I thought that was you!" Lila ambled closer. "What are you doing out in the middle of the day? I was on my lunch break and . . ." And then she blanched. "Um, how *are* you?"

I forced a smile. Clearly, Lila's gut instinct to hail me down took hold before she thought of the consequences of having to actually *speak* to cancer-riddled me.

"I'm fine." I nodded. "Really, I'm fine." I looked down and kicked some crisp leaves with my foot.

"I'm sorry," she said, as she pulled me in for a hug. "I should have called. Sally told me a few weeks ago, and I've been on the road for work, and . . . oh *shit*. There's really just no excuse."

"It's okay. Honestly, it is," I replied into her cashmere-blended wool scarf and then stepped back.

"I just . . ." She raised her arm and let it drop. "I just didn't . . ."

"Know what to say? I know. Really, it's okay, Li. A lot of people haven't called. In fact, most haven't. You're not the only one." I shrugged and looked down at my sneakers. Breaking news to friends that you had cancer wasn't in the etiquette guidebook—truth be told, I'd reached out to as few people as possible. Consequentially, supporting said friend when she's diagnosed with life-threatening illness isn't exactly a paint-by-numbers situation, either. I'd told Sally that she was allowed to spread the news to a few choice people, but that they wouldn't be hearing the ghastly info directly from me. Besides, other than an intimate group of friends, of which Lila was a part, true enough, I hadn't exactly been stellar about keeping in touch over the years. So it was no surprise that, since I faded out of my old friends' lives, they weren't exactly bounding to get back into mine.

"Oh God," she whined. "Now I feel even more horrible. I just, I don't know. There's no excuse. But I was just worried I'd say the wrong thing or make it worse or somehow look like an asshole."

I grabbed her hand. "Lila, really. We're okay. Come on, walk with me. I was thinking of going around the loop one more time."

Lila and I had nearly finished my second lap when the wave of vertigo overtook me. I felt the pavement tilt below me, and suddenly the trees stood on a diagonal. I clenched her arm to keep from falling, but it didn't help much. Instead, I dragged her down with me, both of us just barely landing on the dying grass just off the sidewalk.

"Oh my God, should I call someone?" Lila panicked and reached into her leather buckled Prada bag for her cell phone. "Nat, look at me, look at me! What's wrong?" Dr. Chin had warned me about dizzy spells and about pushing myself too hard. As Lila rubbed my back, I stuck my head between my knees, something I remembered from high school first aid, and muttered at her, "No, no, this is just a side effect. I'm fine."

I'm not sure how long we sat there, my friend and I, in the autumn glow of a perfect New York afternoon, but when my breathing evened out and my eyes seemed to steady, I slowly rose and told her I wanted to keep going. I wanted to finish what I'd started, even though it was just a silly walk with my old friend five weeks after I'd been diagnosed with cancer.

"Nat, you're too exhausted. Your face is, like, the color of my walls. Let's just hail a cab." She put her arm up to nab a taxi as it cruised through the park.

"No," I said firmly. "I'm walking home."

"Natalie, don't be ridiculous. You're going to pass out on Central Park West. We're stopping. This can't be good for you!"

"Don't tell me what isn't good for me! And don't tell me to stop," I screamed, as Lila took a step back. "How the hell can anyone know what's good for me! I mean, I work out, I eat relatively well, I'm not a bad person, and it appears that none of it, none of it, is good for me! So how the fuck does something like this happen to someone like me?" Without warning, I squeezed out fat teardrops that fell as if from the storm earlier that week. Lila pulled me close and held me up until I stopped shaking.

"I'm sorry," I said, lowering my eyes. "You're just trying to do right by me, and I act like a crazy person."

"Oh please, this is nothing compared to how you reacted when you found out that Brandon was cheating on you sophomore year. Remember that? If I can handle that, I think I can cope with this." She laughed and handed me a tissue from her purse. "Okay," she conceded, "we won't stop." She squeezed my hand and started walking.

"Did you hear that, 'cancer'?" I replied, mustering up a grin. "I'm not stopping until you prove me unstoppable."

• • •

Dear Diary:

The good news is that I barely think of Ned at all anymore. And when I do, it actually doesn't occur to me to head down to Modell's and buy an aluminum bat with which to bash his brains in. So that's good news, right? I mean, I sort of get it. Why he left. No. Let me amend that. I will never GET why he did what he did WHEN he did it. But in the larger picture, I mean, I think I might get it. The truth is, Diary, we didn't have much of a relationship going, even if we thought we did. And I know this now because my life hasn't changed so much since he left. I still eat most of my meals by myself, I still confide more in Sally than in him, and other than my rage, I still don't miss him much when he's gone. Huh. So go figure. Maybe if I get around to it, I'll listen to his side of the story, too. But that's my peace for now.

And of course, as life would have it, as soon as I've made peace with one thing, another battle arises altogether. See, Diary, I've been thinking about Jake. A wee bit too much. And I also think I might have a teeny, tiny crush on Zach. Oh, who I haven't told you much about. See, the fact that he's my ob-gyn should, I know, be enough to skeeve me out for, like, forever. I mean, Lila jokes that he's been in more vaginas than the entire NBA (and she would know since she broke his heart into a billion pieces this spring when she up and dumped him without any warning). But he bears a striking resemblance to Patrick Dempsey, and, well, he calls a few times a week to check up on

*me, and when he does call, it's like I almost forget that I have
cancer—which I know is stupid, since that's the only reason he's
calling to begin with—but still. Let me be clear here, Diary:
Zach looks nothing like your gynecologist, nor does he look anything like your previous gynecologist. In fact, with pools of green
eyes, a lean runner's body, and wavy hair that curls perfectly
over his forehead, I'm not sure that he should even be allowed to
be a practicing gynecologist, given that it's highly probable that
the bulk of his patients find him, just 35 years old, more arousing
than their husbands. And for those ten minutes on the phone
when he calls, it's like I'm a normal girl who might have a normal shot with a normal guy.*

*So between my pathetic ruminations on Jake—Where is he?
Is he banging groupies? Does he ever think of me? (and to answer some, if not all of these questions, I logged in nearly two
hours on Google last night)—and my realization that despite
my rising lust for my gynecologist, I cannot, nor will I ever, be
his, it's easy to see that I fell into a bit of a funk. All of which I
raised with Janice at our next session.*

*After assuring me that (a) I was still entirely sexually viable
to men (snort, as IF, Diary!) and (b) my topsy-turvy emotions
were perfectly normal, Janice did mention that she wasn't sure
about opening up the doors to my past via this very diary (remember, the hunt for my exes?) when I was already dealing with
so much change, but she wasn't there to judge. That's what she
said, "I'm not here to judge, Natalie, just to help." As if that
didn't make me think she was judging. It's like back in high
school, when my mom would purse her lips and say to me, "Well,
if you think it's the right decision," when clearly, she thought it
was entirely the wrong decision, and pretend that she wasn't dropping a passive-aggressive bomb. But I told Janice that I felt like*

sorting through my past might help me come to terms with the present, so she nodded and said, "Well, that's progress."

We spent the rest of the session talking about my theory that in every relationship—friendship, romantic, whatever—there is an alpha and a beta. Namely, one strong person, the rock, so to speak, and one weaker link, the one who does the leaning. By weaker link, I don't mean to imply that they're a less critical component: In fact, if you put two strong types together, they often combust, sort of like two opposing elements that explode in chemistry class.

I wasn't sure why my alpha dog theory had been weighing on me as of late, until Janice suggested that other than you, Diary, it would be nice for me to find someone on whom to lean. You know, so I didn't have to bear my burdens all alone. I told her that I liked living as a solitary being, and that really, at the end of the day, I was the only person I trusted enough to rely on. (No offense. I do find you to be a fantastic listener.) She nodded and said she understood, so she suggested taking baby steps, that I shouldn't be afraid to also look for small gifts, for people who outstretched their hands, even if they weren't offering a full shoulder. I remembered Sally running my errands for me last weekend when I couldn't find the energy to restock my toilet paper, and Lila blowing off her afternoon of work after our walk to sit in a tea shop and regale me with all the latest gossip from our group of friends. Still though, Diary, if I'm going to be honest— which is really the point of this whole thing, isn't it?—it all felt flat.

So anyway, Diary. I know that it's only my second entry and I've already lost track of the purpose of this damn thing in the first place, which namely was to provide a diversion from my wallowing and self-pity parties. So this week, honestly, I'm going to shovel myself out and stop Googling Jake and move on to Colin, from high school, and then to Brandon. That should be fun. (Note heavy sarcasm.)

I HEARD THE latch turn before I actually saw it. I was flattened on the couch, staring up at the ceiling and mentally calculating how many square feet someone could live in without officially going crazy. The 650 feet of my one-bedroom apartment had me choking with claustrophobia, my daily walks be damned. I remembered the room that I'd shared with Lila back in college—it couldn't have been more than thirteen by thirteen—and yet I never felt suffocated there. But inside my apartment, I truly felt as if I might crawl the walls. I was debating how the view might appear from a Spiderman-esque perch on the ceiling when I heard the *click-click* of the door, and I shot straight up, my butt sinking into the down pillows. I ran through a mental checklist of who had access to my keys. *Sally.* But she was working this morning; she'd already e-mailed me. *My parents.* But they were safe in Philly. *My doorman.* But he always called before he came up. And then my stomach dropped. *Ned. That rat-bastard, skunk-smelling, motherf—ing Ned.*

He poked his head through the door and muttered, "Shit," as he dropped his keys. I stared at him the way that a rabid dog might size up a postman's shin, and when he straightened up, I pelted him with the fluffy angora pillow that he'd insisted on buying because he'd seen something similar in *Metropolitan Home.*

"Holy shit," he yelped, as the pillow smacked him on the side of the head, and he jumped two feet in the air, coming dangerously close to the door frame. *Damn,* I thought. *Nearly fifty points for a concussion.* "What are you doing here?" he asked, cautiously taking a step in. "You're never home from work on a weekday."

I crossed my arms across my chest. "Need I remind you, oh valiant one? I'm in the middle of chemo. I'm working from home." I reached out my hand. "I guess it goes without saying that I want my keys back."

"Look, Nat, I'm sorry. I didn't think you'd be here." He squeezed the bridge of his nose like he was getting a migraine. "But I left . . . well, you didn't pack up . . . anyway, some of my work files are here. I just wanted to grab them."

"Get out," I said, raising another pillow as ammunition.

"C'mon, Nat. Be reasonable. I just need to find this stuff, and I'll be gone." He shuffled over and dropped the keys on my coffee table.

I reached for the remote and flicked on *All My Children,* increasing the volume until the entire block could surely catch wind of Erica Kane's latest romantic embroilment. Out of the corner of my eye, I watched Ned walk to my desk, open up the bottom drawer, and filter through the papers. He stuck two manila folders into his messenger bag and paused for a minute to read over a memo, which he then crumpled up into a ball and tossed in the trash can that sat at the foot of the desk. Then he kept digging.

"Do you need this?" He held up a business card. I squinted to make out the writing, so he flipped it over to read it himself. His voice grew soft. "It's for a wigmaker, Adina Seidel."

After I got home from my first appointment with Dr. Chin, I'd tossed it in my "junk" drawer. Surely, I'd thought, it will never come to that. Resorting to a wig was like relying on a wheelchair: It was a crutch, and I didn't need anyone—or anything—to hold me up. My mother's voice echoed through my mind. *"There's no 'we' in Natalie,"* she used to say with an overemphasis on the last syllable. *"Just an 'I' and almost a 'me.'"* She'd made up that little rhyme back when I was eight.

It was my first day at my new private school, and when she dropped me off at my homeroom, running late and jotting down to-dos on her notepad, I knew she had to leave. I knew that she *wanted* to leave, but that didn't mean that I couldn't try to stop her. So I clung to her side until her suit jacket became so twisted that the buttons faced the wrong way, and I sobbed hard enough that snot ran clear down to my neck. My mortified mother, my mother who labored with me for a mere thirty-five minutes and (she'd like you to note) drug-free, apologized to the teacher and walked me out of the room. I thought I'd been granted a reprieve, freedom from my new, marbled-hall school, but instead, she firmly grabbed me by the elbow and said with a just-kind-enough smile, *"There's no 'we' in Natalie. Just an 'I' and almost a 'me.'"*

I blinked at her, uncomprehending. So she sighed and said, "Natalie, I can't be here for you all of the time. You're a big girl now, and big girls do things on their own. I expect you to be a big girl. You need to rely on yourself now." I started to protest, but she cut me off, spun me around, and after planting a kiss on my head, left me to wipe the mucus off my own face and in the care of my new homeroom teacher.

"There's no 'we' in Natalie." And from the age of eight on, indeed, there hadn't been.

I glanced at the wigmaker's card, and unconsciously, I ran my fingers through my thinning hair. "Just put it on my keyboard," I said to Ned, and turned my attention back to *AMC* before my voice could break and belie the loneliness behind it. I heard him start to say something more, but he thought better of whatever it was and kept sorting through his files.

"Oh my God," he said, which I could make out over the announcer on the Swiffer commercial. "I totally forgot about this." I didn't turn to look, so he stood up and came over to the couch. He held out his hand, but I tucked mine farther into my armpits. In exasperation, he grabbed my arm. "I bought this for you," he said. "The day after we got back from the Vineyard."

I didn't bother looking at the baby blue Tiffany box he'd placed in my palm. "Why don't you give it to *Agnes*?" I spit out her name as if it were chewing tobacco. I'd tried it once in college and found the two things—Agnes and Skoal—equally revolting.

"Because it isn't for Agnes. It was for you." He shook his head. "I was so inspired when we got home from the trip. And I saw it in the window . . ." He paused, and I almost thought he was going to cry. "And so I bought it. Because it reminded me of us." He sighed. "It reminded me of what I hoped we would become as a couple." He shrugged. "But then I didn't see you for a week straight, and so I stuck it in the bottom drawer where you wouldn't find it. And obviously, I never gave it to you."

"Obviously," I said dryly, fingering the white satin bow, and then setting the box aside.

Ned shrugged and walked back to the desk to gather his files. "You should open it. Whether or not you hate me."

"I do," I interrupted. "For the record."

"Fine. Forget that I gave it to you. Whatever. I think you still might like it."

After Ned left, I placed the box on my glass coffee table next to his relinquished set of keys, leaned my elbows on my thighs and put my face into my hands, and stared at it. The box. I stared at it for so long that eventually my eyes crossed, and I saw double. Two boxes. Two reminders of what had left me behind. Two taunts, tempting me to open them. Finally, I blinked forcefully and snapped out of the trance, and then I reached over, and in one graceful tug, pulled off the white ribbon.

I placed the box in my lap and lifted the lid. There, tucked inside a tiny, soft fabric pouch, lay a gold necklace. I drew the chain out of the bag, careful to avoid knots or snarls, and when I'd nearly lifted it clear out of the pouch, I saw that a charm weighted down the end like an anchor.

On our second-to-last day in the Vineyard, Ned convinced me to explore a deserted lot far down the beach. We must have walked two miles before we stumbled upon it. He lifted me over the fraying picket fence, and we found ourselves atop a grassy knoll that reminded me of the pictures I'd seen of the hills of England. We hiked for about fifteen minutes before I begged Ned to give my blistered feet a break, so he plopped down, offered me a sip of lemonade from the cooler that we'd packed, and began plucking up grass. Not for any reason in particular, I think. But just as something to do to occupy his hands. He was about to toss another handful of blades into the wind when he noticed it.

"Nat, oh my God, check this out," he said, leaning closer to show me. "A four-leaf clover. That must be a sign."

I smiled and agreed with him that perhaps that was an omen, even though at that very moment, I'd been thinking of Jake.

As the charm now rested in my palm, I kind of understood what Ned meant. Why he'd rushed in and plunked down his Amex. Why he'd been certain I would like it. Because when you're on a sinking ship, you'll cling to just about anything to keep you afloat.

I held the gold chain up above me and saw the beams of light from the window bounce off the four-leaf-clover charm. And then I walked into the bedroom and tucked it in my dresser drawer, underneath my cashmere sweaters. True, it was from Ned, so maybe it was tainted. *But still,* I thought, *if anyone ever needed a harbinger of good luck, surely, right now, it is me.*

IT SEEMED AS if every morning, I awoke to more and worse news on the front page of the *Post*. In fact, the senator's tax returns had even made the front page of the *Times,* which meant that we truly were in deep shit. So I paced my living room, my slippers flopping on my floor and practically ingraining tread marks around my couch, and I tried to Jedi mind trick my e-mail. "Go off," I chanted and pressed my eyes closed, envisioning a new e-mail from Kyle in my in-box. "Go off," I repeated as I looped the couch once again. I actually jumped when I heard the *ping* in my in-box not thirty seconds later. *Maybe I do have ESP powers after all?* I mused as I darted over to my computer.

From: Richardson, Kyle
To: Miller, Natalie
Re: The increasing problem of the returns

Hey Natalie,

Hope you're feeling okay. Your constant e-mailing really isn't helping: do keep in mind that I'm juggling your work load too, so despite my highly adept skills, I'm a little over-loaded and replying to you 24/7 isn't doable. Are we clear?

Anyway, I know that you're concerned about the head-lines, and so am I. In fact, word is that it's only going to get worse—Blair got a call this morning from the *Post* asking for a response to some very damaging shit. And word is that Taylor's people are the ones doing this. Wanted to gauge

your response. (Which must make you spectacularly happy.)
While I hate to admit it when I need your help, I know that
you've played this game many times before. So how should
we move forward? Should we leak something back? Let's
ruin him.

KR

I felt my blood rush through me like a tidal wave. Though Kyle
and I didn't always agree on everything, when it came to feasting
on our prey, we had no problem working in harmony. I grabbed a
stress ball from my desk and picked up the speed of my pacing.
Circling, circling, circling, until I knew exactly how to proceed. I
sank into my lumbar-supporting chair—the one that Ned had insisted on paying far too much for, but that I did admit provided
quite the cozy feel—and typed frantically, occasionally madly hitting the delete button to correct the typos that came with such
frenzied keyboard pounding.

From: Miller, Natalie
To: Richardson, Kyle
Re: Let's Play Ball

K—

Feeling okay. Thanks for asking. Been better, but what am
I going to do?

First off, have you actually gotten your hands on her tax
returns yourself? Before we say anything to the press, it'd
probably be smart to do so. (Obviously, right?) I think you
might have mentioned it awhile ago, but yeah, I suspect that
some gifts from dignitaries might not have been appropriate/
legal/totally up-and-up. But we always accept them—no one

cares. Call Gene Weinstock, Dupris's accountant, and ask
him directly.

Yes, let's screw with this bastard. He's a sinking ship, so
he's doing anything he can to torpedo Dup. F-it. Call Larry
Davis, 212-872-0419. He's the guy I hired to get back-up dirt.
I know, don't get pissy—you were kept out of the loop so
you could deny any accountability in case Taylor found out.
Turns out that Taylor likes hookers. Think his wife will care?
—Nat

"Take that, you little shit Taylor," I actually shouted out loud,
as I spun my chair in a circle and let out a whoop of victory. Jake
used to tell me that he'd never seen someone sent so high from a
win at work; that he thought that at least half the time, the only
reason I drove myself at 160 miles an hour was to beat everyone
else at the race.

"Will you be satisfied once you're elected president?" he asked
one night when I was paged back into the office at 11 o'clock at
night to oversee a Middle East policy crisis.

"Only if I've stomped on the little people on my way up," I replied, leaning down to kiss his forehead while he sat propped up
reading in bed. I walked toward the door and turned back to see
him shaking his head. "Kidding, Jake. I'm kidding." But I could
tell that he wasn't so sure.

The microwave timer dinged, and I bolted up to take my medicine. As I pried open my orange prescription container, the rush
slowly wore off, the way that a tide might when it begins to ebb.
I needed another hit, so after gagging on my pill and eventually
swallowing it, I moved back to my computer screen and leaned
over on my elbows and stared. Stared for a good twenty minutes
until my sight grew fuzzy and the muscles between my shoulder

blades ached. I straightened up and ran my fingers through my hair. Clumps. For the first time, it wasn't strands, five here, twenty there. It was a massive, heart-sinking, spine-chilling clump. Whether or not I had evidence that Taylor was screwing hookers had no effect on my cancer or my impending baldness. Nothing it seemed, not even the fleeting rush of victory, would slow that down.

· FIVE ·

I'd gotten into the habit of not setting my alarm—a far cry from my prior 5:45 A.M. daily wake-ups to NPR, but now I didn't see much of a point. It wasn't as if I had anywhere to be. So when I heard the phone ringing early the next morning, I at first assumed that it was part of a dream. In fact, it was part of a dream. It was only when my semicognizant self realized that there were no phones on the desert island on which I was presently stranded in my dream that I shook myself awake and grabbed my cordless from my nightstand.

"Natalie dear? I'm sorry, did I wake you? I only have a minute— I'm about to take off to head to Nashville for the day for a meeting, but I understand that you've spoken with Kyle."

I rubbed my eyes and swiped the sleep off my face. "No, Senator, I'm awake. And yes, I did speak with Kyle. I'm handling things."

"Very good. But I want to make something clear, which is why I'm calling. Whatever you do—should you choose to do something—I want to be kept out of the loop. Do not 'CC' Blair, do not address me about the situation. Understood?" I pictured her waving her hand in front of her face as she locked her seat belt on the office's private plane. Deniability: It's more critical than ethics in our line of work.

She cleared her throat. "However, do what is necessary." She paused. "And by that, I mean *anything* necessary. We're in it to win it."

"I understand, Senator." I stood up and reached for my robe. "As I said, I'll handle it."

"Do you feel up to it?"

"I'd feel up for anything these days, I'm so bored." I paused. "Forgive me for asking, but can the IRS really nail you for accepting those gifts?"

"I'm not worried." She went silent. "We really do seem to have this election locked up, anyway."

I realized that she didn't answer my question but figured that she more than earned those gifts: the intricately carved desk, the gold elephant planters, the porcelain eggs.

"Fair enough, Senator. Consider it taken care of. Oh, I'd also like to talk to you about your support on the birth control initiative."

"Natalie, I'm losing you, and we're taking off. Thanks for the help." She clicked off.

Typical, I thought, and then frowned because I wasn't at all sure where that thought came from. I hung up the phone and checked the time. 9:15. Kyle would have been in the office for two hours by now, and I had an hour-and-forty-five-minute window before *The Price Is Right*. I logged on to my e-mail. Bingo.

From: Richardson, Kyle

To: Miller, Natalie

Re: Taylor is getting dirty, response2

Nat,

   Holy shit. Smoking gun. Hookers? I'll give Larry a call. I didn't know that we had the resources for a private investigator. You sly little bitch! I always knew you were, actually.

   But doesn't Taylor's wife have ovarian cancer? Shouldn't we give him a chance to recant before we ruin the marriage and/or kill her?

KR

Recant, my ass, and then I thought of Jake and his stupid theory of my love of the win. *Screw you, too,* I muttered, as if Jake were in the room, as if we hadn't broken up two and a half years earlier, and as if he were still judging me. But Kyle did have a point, albeit one that I was readily willing to overlook. It was true: Susanna Taylor had very publicly and very bravely been battling ovarian cancer, and it wasn't the kindest move to out her husband's sexual proclivities while in the midst of such a battle. I tapped my fingers together, weighing my next move. On one hand, my logic argued, I should be sympathetic, given my own situation and all. On the other hand, I'd been told to do what it took. I bit my upper lip and ran my fingers over the keyboard, mulling over my reply.

From: Miller, Natalie
To: Richardson, Kyle
Re: Taylor is getting dirty—response

K—

   Yes, I know that you think I'm a bitch. Turns out, you might
not always be wrong. Go figure.

   Since when have you grown a conscience? We're in it to
win it. Call Larry.

—Nat

THE NEWS BROKE the next day. Dr. Chin had called just as I
was reaching for the morning papers to tell me that he was very
pleased with my initial progress. At each checkup, he monitored
my cell count, and the very preliminary reports pointed to signs
that the chemo—despite its horrid side effects, despite the jack-
hammer headaches that came in the late evenings and the occasional loss of feeling in my hands—was indeed frying these fuckers.
I thanked him for the call, clicked good-bye, and frantically ran
my eyes over the headlines.

   The *New York Post* ran dueling captions: "Taylor Hooked!"
read the top half of the page, while the bottom read, "Dupris Duplicitous!" "At least we're at the bottom," I muttered to my empty
apartment.

   I plodded over to the couch, dropped the *Post* beside me, and
tore through the *Times*. Okay, not bad: Our escalating scandal
was older news so it landed on page sixteen. No one, except for political junkies like myself, has the time to read to page sixteen,
anyway. Regular people scan the headlines, ensure themselves that
their world isn't coming to an immediate end, then flip to the sports

section or the gossip tidbits. Taylor made the front page of the Metro section, which wasn't quite as prestigious as the front section, but was certainly more visible. I nodded my head—one point to us.

I put my bare feet up on the coffee table and began to read. The good news was that Taylor came off like a philandering scumbag. "What sort of husband does this when his wife is sick?" a woman on the street was quoted as saying. The bad news was that the senator still wasn't coming off much better. "The rich keep getting richer," read the *Post*'s lead to the story.

Picking up the phone, I called Kyle but was shot straight to voice mail, so I made my way to the kitchen to pour a glass of water, then tried him again. And then again, and then again. The embarrassing truth was that nearly two hours later, by not even 11 o'clock, I had desperately and frantically and shamelessly called him over twenty times. Not even *The Price Is Right* proved to be much of a distraction. I could feel my shoulders tightening up and my core temperature rising; I pictured Kyle and his smarmy, weasely smile basking in the glory of my work, *my due,* and I simply couldn't stand it one second longer.

I suddenly felt compelled to drop my robe on my taupe Pottery Barn rug, grab the stand-by tweed suit off the lid to my hamper, and hail a taxi, despite an increasingly dizzy feeling. For my second trip into the office in less than a week, I wasn't quite as presentable. I'd pulled my hair back into a pseudobun, but my nonwashed, ratty ends poked out of it like chopsticks. And let's not even talk about my face: I'd tried to apply some under-eye concealer and mascara in the cab, but my driver appeared to be auditioning for the Indy 500; thus, with every lurch or sudden break, the wand painted black stripes all over my eyelid. I spit on my finger and tried to rub it off, but really, that just sort of grayed it and left bruiselike splotches just below my eyebrow.

The cab screeched to the curb at Fifty-fifth Street. I staggered through the revolving glass door, and the security guard asked me if I was okay when I flashed him my ID, but I waved him off with an "I'm fine."

"Holy crap, Natalie, should you be here?" Blair asked me when I got off the elevator. "You look paler than a ghost." Evidently, my decision to forgo any blush was a mistake.

"Fine. I'm fine. Where's Kyle? Where's Dupris? Is she back from Nashville yet?" I cocked my head looking around for them. *He better not be stealing my damn glory.*

Blair nodded toward the senator's office. "Yep, she's back, and he's in there." She lowered her eyes. "I'm not sure if you want to go in."

Ignoring her, I spun on my black pumps and opened the door just in time to catch the senator mid-diatribe.

"We are getting annihilated from this, goddamn it! His wife is a sympathetic figure, and people know that it came from us!" She stopped, startled when I joined them. "Natalie, what are you doing here? This isn't the best time. Too much going on right now. I assume that you saw the papers?"

My mouth dropped, and I looked over at Kyle, but he was strangely fascinated with his hands in his lap. He glanced over at me and mouthed, "Nice work," then continued staring at the floor.

"I saw the papers, yes, which is why I came in. No one would return my calls." I suddenly felt much dizzier and more nauseated than just a moment before, so I steadied myself on the empty chair beside Kyle.

"I think you should go home," Dupris said tersely, folding her arms across her chest. She couldn't have stood more than five foot three, but she made so much of those sixty-three inches that she towered as if she were eight feet tall. Even from behind her desk, Dupris conveyed the sense of power. Of drive. Of being someone whom you could only aspire to be because her aura made you well-aware that you weren't quite there yet. She was arguably the prettiest of the female senators: She was meticulous about her blond highlights at the salon, and in six years, I'd only seen her twice without makeup. Even so, she'd been blessed with sharp bone structure, so she didn't need the spatulaed layers to begin with.

"What's the problem?" I asked, befuddled. "This is a good news day. The tide is turning in our direction."

"Did you leak this? The stuff about Taylor? Because the phones have not stopped ringing, and frankly, I'm furious. You should have informed me." She paced back and forth behind the very hand-carved desk that had gotten her in trouble.

"You said you didn't want to know. And you told me to do what I needed to." I paused to let that sink in. "And besides, I still don't see the problem! We needed to make Taylor look like the bad guy. We did. End of story. We win."

"No, Natalie, we don't win," Dupris snapped back and pointed to a chair, which I immediately sank into. "This? Is a major fuckup. This? I would have wanted to know. Totally unacceptable. True, I don't give a flying fuck that Taylor's favorite pastime is sleeping with prostitutes, but I *do* care about the fact that his wife is one of the leading faces of cancer right now and people want to champion her. Do you know how many calls I've had this morning from people who now think that if Taylor loses, Susanna will lose the will to live? Because *she has nothing else to live for.* That's actually what three of them said."

My glory, I thought. *There it goes. Right down the shitter.*

"That didn't occur to me," I said with less assurance than

I'd have liked to. I felt my stomach rise up into my throat. I hadn't eaten breakfast, so I wasn't sure what, if anything, I had in me to throw up. A cool layer of sweat began to form on my neck, and my fingers felt tingly, as if they were about to detach themselves from my hands.

"Damn right, it didn't!" The senator tossed her arms up in the air and stopped pacing. She pointed at us. "Kyle, I want you to clean this up. Natalie, I want you to go home. Kyle will call you if he needs you, but for now, I suggest that you stay out of it. Enough damage has been done." I saw Kyle shake his head and watched his hands clench into fists of rage.

"No," I said firmly and stood up. "This is my doing, this is my idea, I'm going to get us out of it. I started it, and I want to be the one to finish it."

"Absolutely not," Dupris seethed. *"Go home. Now. Stay. Out. Of it."* As if I were ten, and she was sending me to my room for bad behavior.

I started to protest, to tell her that I'd finessed her out of larger jams in the past, and that we were still seventeen percentage points ahead, and that when the dust settles, frequenting hookers really can sink a political career, but before I could say any of that, I went to move toward her desk, and, instead, made a mad reach for her bamboo wastebasket. But I didn't make it in time. So I lurched over and vomited on my too-pricey Joan and David pumps.

"I couldn't have said it any better myself," Kyle said, and he went to get paper towels from the kitchen.

I sat on the senator's creamy white rug, the outline from my puke sinking deeper and deeper into the strands of the carpet, and peered up at her.

"Go home, Natalie," she repeated firmly. "Take care of yourself. I think you've done enough."

"I suppose this is a bad time to discuss the birth control bill?" I looked up at her and closed my eyes.

"That discussion is over. There is no discussion, in fact," she said, as she walked out of the room.

By the time I had the stomach (literally) to turn on the TV that night, Taylor had eaten five percentage points into our lead.

· SIX ·

*D*ear Diary,

 This is shit, Diary. My life is shit. I know that I should feel guilty over outing Taylor, but guess·what? I don't. In this job, anything goes. Kyle knows that. Dupris certainly knows it. And how am I repaid? By being cast off and ignored. So you know what, Diary? F-them.

 So it looks like it's just the two of us, Diary. Ready to make a run for it? Well, maybe not just the two of us. Sally showed up last night to listen to me bitch, even though it was pretty clear that she didn't agree with my tactics. I guess she'd interviewed Susanna Taylor once last year and thought she was a pretty okay broad. That's what she said, "She's an okay broad. She cares about making a difference. I think she's helped a lot of women in her . . ." and then she paused and looked at me, "well, in your position." Truth be told, Diary, I felt a pang of irritation because I hardly wanted to be compared to other cancer victims, but still, for the most part Sally listened, and I don't even think she judged me too much. So I guess it's just the three of us, Diary. Maybe that's not so bad.

Anyway, the fact that work won't call me back is actually working out just fine because I finally got this little endeavor of mine off the ground. I know that you'll find this surprising, but my first manhunt went off without a hitch. Ha! See, now I told you not to worry!

I called up Colin the other day to get some answers. And, in fact, I plan on calling them all—no need for jokes, my list is not so long that I'll be two breasts smaller by the time I'm done—until I've successfully come out on the other side.

Colin was, understandably, surprised to hear from me. We broke up just after graduation, our senior year in high school. Five months before that, he'd robbed me of my virginity, though, if I'm being totally honest and I guess I should be since I'm the only one reading this, I'd given it up pretty easily. He still lived in Bryn Mawr; actually, his wife answered the phone. God, I hope she didn't get suspicious that some strange woman was calling their house around dinnertime. Colin was never the type to cheat; in fact he might have been the most loyal of the lot of them. He set the bar high and all of that.

When he asked why I was calling, I explained that I was trying to work some things out with myself, and I thought maybe he could provide one sliver of the answer. I didn't mention the cancer, but I think he already knew—heard it in the hometown gossip cycle. So when Colin paused and asked, "How are you?"

with the overemphasis on the "are," I knew that he knew. I got that sort of emphasis all the time now . . . it was as if people thought that by stressing the "are" and casting their eyes downward and shaking their head, they were asking enough about my health without actually having to broach the subject. I know, I know, both Janice and Sally have told me that cancer makes people uncomfortable. So does death. But would it actually kill people (pardon the term) to address the overriding theme in my life now? For the first time, in like, ever, it's surprisingly not work—the senator has ignored my calls and I haven't heard from Kyle in two days—it's cancer, and no one seems to want to acknowledge, other than with the use of overexaggerated "ares," that anything's changed.

But I've digressed. Colin knew, but we didn't speak of it. Instead, when I asked him why we didn't stay together forever, as you think you might be able to do back in high school, back when you dry-humped in the back of your forest-green Volvo station wagon and believed that your SAT scores defined the rest of your life, he just said, "Natalie, we never planned to. I mean, I thought that we both understood that you were going off to Dartmouth, to the big time, and I was staying behind, doing my best to get decent grades at Penn State and then come back to join my dad's business."

"But weren't we in love?" I pressed. "I remember loving you. Feeling like you would have done anything for me."

"We were," he answered. "But you were bigger than me, bigger than what I wanted. And I was smaller than what you dreamed. And besides, high school relationships never last. They're all about idealism: no screaming babies, no bills to pay, no jobs to get in the way. So we just enjoyed ourselves and let it run its

course." He paused. "Natalie, really, there's no dark secret here. Sometimes, the relationship is just supposed to be a stop along the way, not the one you end up with."

This was true, I thought. And then I remembered that he left out some of the details: that our last summer together, he tried to preserve our bond, stoke our love, as if to reassure himself that I wouldn't forget him as soon as I hit Hanover. Truth is, the more he pushed, the more I pulled. We danced like magnets around each other. By August, when we snuck into my parents' swimming pool well past midnight to burn off the oppressive humidity and make out under the iridescent glow of the patio lights, I was already thinking, I don't feel a thing. I didn't have to go to Hanover to stop loving Colin. I was already gone. Bigger than him, he said now. Maybe I thought that I was.

So when his two-year-old started crying, and I heard his wife calling for him, I thanked him for his honesty, and he told me to take care of myself, and that was all of Colin that I got.

◆ ◆ ◆

From: Miller, Natalie
To: Richardson, Kyle
Re: What's going on?

K—

I haven't heard back from you. Left you four messages in the past two days. I've been watching the polls—Taylor is only 8 points back. Why haven't you done any damage control? This is fixable, but you're letting it sink us.
—Nat

From: Miller, Natalie

To: Richardson, Kyle

Re: Please call me

K—

   Still no word from you. Please don't make me come down there again—I don't think anyone wants that. We're ten days out—why the hell aren't you guys being more pro-active? I'll tell you what needs to be done: You need to promote Dupris's generous donations to cancer charities. She made some, right? If not, pretend that she did. On this short notice, the press won't be able to dig up any records anyway. Compared to Susanna Taylor, she's coming off like Satan.

—Nat

From: Miller, Natalie

To: Richardson, Kyle

Re: I'm coming into the office

K—

   At the risk of sounding condescending, you still work for me. Why the hell am I being ignored? We have just over a week left, and something has to be done. Fine. If you don't want to fabricate cancer donations, you need to launch a full-scale attack on Taylor's record. Call Larry Davis: Get anything you can (other than the hooker stuff) and put it out there to demonstrate that he's a shit decision maker. Once people see that the hookers are just one of his many bad choices, the polls will swing back in our favor. If I don't

hear back from you by this afternoon, I'll be in the office tomorrow. Don't make me come down there.
—Nat

From: Richardson, Kyle
To: Miller, Natalie
Re: I heard you the first time

Natalie,
    Chill out. Your incessant messages and e-mails aren't help-
ing. I'm under a bit of pressure here, you know. The senator
told me directly not to retaliate to Taylor, despite his increasing numbers. She thinks that we botched the hooker
thing so badly—and thanks so much, it's been a lovely few
weeks here dealing with the fallout—that she doesn't want
to touch another thing.
    Btw, I don't know if I ever told you this, but I'm truly sorry
to hear about your diagnosis. So really, shouldn't you be focused on something other than this right now?
    KR

I sat at my desk, struck by his comment. I remembered that
Janice had not so subtly intimated something similar to Kyle's re-
marks at our last session.

"Being kind to yourself and taking time to enjoy that kindness
is very important right now," she said, lacing her hands in front of
her and leaning forward toward me as if to make her point.

I rubbed my temples and told her that I wasn't sure if I were cut
out for this therapy thing; that the only reason I was there to begin
with was that I'd checked the "counseling" box on my forms (when

I was clearly not in my right mind), then answered her introductory phone call at the precise moment when I felt like throwing myself out the window, not because I really gave any thought to the counseling or even believed in it much.

She nodded the way that I assume all therapists do—it must be something they teach them when they get their degree—and told me that anything I chose to do with myself during this ailing time was acceptable. "As long as it's done out of a kind place," she added. And then she urged me once again to find someone else to be kind to me: a survivor's group (as if), a website (I'd rather watch TV), my mom (ha!).

I reclined in my desk chair and closed my eyes to try and ward off the oncoming chemo headache that I felt leaking into my cranium. *Kind.* I snorted out loud. *Clearly Janice didn't understand my line of work. Or what sort of armor you had to build to succeed in it.* I mulled over what to say back to Kyle, whether or not to make the *kind* choice, the one over which Janice would award me a figurative gold star, much like the literal gold stars my mom tacked on the fridge when I'd bring home an A in elementary school. And then I decided, much like I suspected back when I was seven, gold stars are overrated.

From: Miller, Natalie

To: Richardson, Kyle

Re: Big mistake

K—

  I appreciate your concern, but I'm doing just fine. With all due respect to Dupris, she's acting like an idiot. What's the first thing we learned on this job? Protect yourself above

everything else. And what's she doing? Leaving herself open to be shot. Taylor is within nipping range of the polling margin of error. Do something. Now.
—Nat

From: Richardson, Kyle
To: Miller, Natalie
Re: No go

Nat,

I agree. But this is the senator's choice and I'm not going above her. Maybe you would: I wouldn't put anything by you (no offense . . . okay, maybe a little). But I won't on something as important as this.

Just go vote, isn't that the mantra—"use your voice to be heard at the polls" (or something ridiculous like that), and hopefully, we'll all still be employed at this time next week.
KR

KYLE WAS RIGHT, of course. They were *all* right. Given my floundering health, I damn sure should have directed my energies elsewhere. So I tried to. At least for a day. Rather than harass him, I committed to an afternoon of pampering. I knew that there wasn't much of a point of getting a haircut, but I booked one anyway. Along with a manicure, a pedicure, and a shiatsu massage.

I hadn't seen Paul, my stylist, since my diagnosis, and when I walked through the glass doors and inhaled the peachy scent of shampoo and candles, I saw his eyes widen in the way that one's might at the climax of a horror movie.

"Darling!" he said and gave me a hug. "Are we okay?"

I swallowed the lump in my throat, and said, "Cancer. I have breast cancer." I looked down. "I know, I know. I'm going to lose my hair, but I'd like to do something with it, anyway. Even if it's just for a few weeks."

He waved his hands with a flourish. "Done! Consider it done! Can we finally make you the redhead I've always wanted to?"

I paused and thought of the reaction on the Hill. Flaming red was hardly professional: considered more stripper than senator, really. And I know that Dupris most certainly would not have approved. "It's all in the presentation," she once told me when I was just starting out. Still though, the tug of something fresh, of something new, of something that was entirely not me, pulled at me.

I opened my arms widely and smiled. "Do with me what you will."

Paul led me over to the sink, and I arched my back, leaning my neck on the cool porcelain and closing my eyes as he massaged my scalp. Neither one of us commented on what I knew to be true: that as he ran his hands over my head, more strands of hair were coming undone than should have. And that when he was done with shampooing, surely, his fingers would be tangled with knotted, dying reminders of my ordeal.

He ushered me to his station and went to the back to mix up the perfect blend of color: less Little Orphan Annie, more Julianne Moore by way of Nicole Kidman. I was listlessly flipping through an old issue of *Vogue* when I noticed the background music. *Of course.* I thought.

Jake's voice hummed out from the speakers that were built into the walls of my all-too-hip salon. I stared into the mirror, my limp and thinning hair strewn over my shoulders, and wondered how you ever escape someone who never left you in the first place.

Paul emerged from the back, and ninety minutes later, my hair, that which I would surely lose anyway, no longer looked like my own. I was gleaming, glamorous, and for a minute, underneath the flattering lights of my chichi salon, I didn't look like who I was: namely, a cancer patient who wanted to pretend that she wasn't. Paul kissed both of my cheeks good-bye, and I pulled my coat tight as I walked three blocks south to the nail salon. I should have felt relieved, reborn almost, even though I knew that it was fleeting. But the only thing I felt was heavy. Lonely, really, and achingly hungry for alpha dog. I stared down at my feet as I walked, unable to shake Jake's latest song from my head, replaying it in beat with my steps.

> *Dangerously close. Dangerously close to the ledge.*
> *Take a step further, and we're off the edge.*
> *Take a step back, and we don't know where we'll be.*
> *But maybe we'll find we'll set each other free.*

I looped my scarf around my neck and kept moving. And as I always do when I hear one of his songs, I wondered if he wrote it about us.

THE DAY OF beauty worked well enough as a distraction. At least for twenty-four hours. Still though, six days before election day, I was pacing even more frantically around my couch, and neither my newfound discovery of the Game Show Network, nor my scary knowledge of the intricacies of the *Passions* plotline could distract me. Taylor's steam train was moving full speed ahead, and thus my pulse was increasing at approximately the same rate. So you'll understand why I woke up the Wednesday before election day, and before I even brushed my teeth, clicked away on my BlackBerry until I found what I needed.

I wasn't surprised to catch her at her desk, even if it was 7:30 in the morning.

"Jodi. Natalie Miller, how are you?"

"Natalie! I was wondering when I'd hear from you. This call's about two weeks later than I thought it would be."

Jodi Baylor was one year ahead of me at Dartmouth and currently one of the top scoop-getters at the *New York Post*. The beauty about having a friend in the media was that while the media was almost never to be trusted, I trusted her about 7 percent more than other reporters. Not to mention that she prided herself on never revealing her sources, which was critical when you were said source. And when your boss had explicitly asked you not to be.

"I know. Things are in the crapper, right?" I sat down in my desk chair and looked out the window to the dim late-October skies.

"Well, you're still up 6 percent. But you guys really screwed the pooch with the hooker debacle."

Pretending I didn't hear her, I picked up the card of the wig-maker, Mrs. Seidel, which was tucked next to my pen holder, and flicked it with my fingers. "So here's the deal. And you didn't hear this from me. But honestly, the senator is getting an incredibly unfair rap here. She's donated over twenty-five thousand dollars to cancer research this year. Why isn't anyone printing that? I mean, I know that Susanna Taylor is suffering through it herself, but it's not as if Dupris has turned a cold shoulder to the cause." I got up to make some chamomile tea in the kitchen, but found no clean mugs, so started scrubbing a dirty one from the sink.

"I hear you, Nat. But Susanna comes off like a martyr. She gives the campaign a sympathetic face. Dupris needs to muster up some sympathy of her own."

Distracted, I turned the water up too hot and dropped the mug into the sink.

"Ow, fuck! Sorry. Okay, well, I can inject a bit of sympathy to the story. But this didn't come from me, you got it?"

"Got it."

"You want sympathy to match Susanna Taylor? One of Dupris's top aides may or may not be dying of cancer herself. And Dupris is so sympathetic that she's doing everything she can to help out." Not quite true, but the senator had vaguely mentioned a connection at the NIH if I needed it, and she certainly was paying me for my time off. Oh, and let's not forget those orchids that she sent over, which now, unfortunately, were doing about as well as the limp hair strands on my head. I filled my semiclean cup with fresh water and plopped in a tea bag.

"So, what you're saying is that you want to play up this aide's cancer so that you guys can garner some votes?" Jodi asked, as she typed in the background.

"Whatever works. And reminder: This is *off* the record," I replied and popped my mug into the microwave. "And don't forget her donations."

"Will do." She paused. "Do you mind me asking who it is? Who's the one with the cancer?"

"Sure," I said. "It's me. I'm the one with the fucking disease."

•   •   •

From: Richardson, Kyle
To: Miller, Natalie
Re: I'm going to give you the benefit of the doubt

Nat,

I'm sure that you saw today's paper. You're mentioned in the leading story. I know that we discussed that the senator didn't want any PR, so I'm going to assume that you didn't plant this. I CAN assume that, correct? Because I'm hoping that you didn't go public with your disease just to turn public sympathy.

KR

From: Miller, Natalie
To: Richardson, Kyle
Re: Never

K—

Not only did I not go public, I'm terribly upset that someone did. I feel like a pawn. Truly. But I bet it helps us at the polls.

—Nat

ROUND THREE

· · ·

November

· SEVEN ·

The first Tuesday in November, just as I had on every other election year, I made my way to the voting booth. The only difference was that today, I couldn't make it there myself. I'd had my third chemo infusion the Friday before, and this time, it knocked me on my ass.

By Monday, I was still in bed, burning through nearly eighteen hours of the day asleep. Sally was back in Puerto Rico doing some wedding planning. ("I swear," she said, "I sent in my absentee ballot," just before I was about to launch into my "it's your citizen's duty" speech.)

Back in August, Sally's boyfriend, Drew, got on bended knee and asked her to take him for life. That he surprised her proved to me just how right they were for each other: The girl was a journalist, which essentially made her a hired snoop. She could sniff out clues to a story like a bloodhound to a juicy steak ten miles away. Hell, I always said they should have hired her, not Ken Starr, to get to the bottom of Monica-gate. So that Drew, an advertising exec, was able to dupe her—(and trust me, she tried valiantly not to be duped: hacking into his e-mail, checking his Palm Pilot, filtering through receipts)—and propose one lazy morning when they'd just gotten back from a jog in Central Park, well, it was enough for me to turn in my key as her best friend and keeper and hand it trustingly over to him.

Still though, I missed her, not least because on days like today, days when I begrudgingly admitted that I *needed* someone, days when every other person I knew was gainfully employed, I would have liked to have her to lean on. So when Dr. Zach called to check in on me, I took him up on his offer to accompany me to the polls.

I didn't have the stamina for a shower that morning, but clearly was in need of a hygiene fix (night sweats will do that to you), so instead, I sat at the base of my porcelain tub, and let the scalding water pour down over me, head bent over, breasts in hand. Just before buzzing Zach up, I'd also managed to brush my fabulous newly hued hair and noticed an alarming number of strands making suicide leaps from my scalp. I stared into the mirror, trying to ignore the purple circles underneath my eyes—they sat like bruises on my pallid skin—and willed myself not to cry at the prospect of going bald. As soon as Sally got back, I resolved, we were shaving it off, even though it now gleamed like a movie star's. I sniffed in any leaking emotion.

After complimenting me on my new color, Zach placed one arm firmly around my waist and with the other, he grasped my elbow as we shuffled along the five blocks to the Gothic-style church on Seventy-third Street where we were to cast our votes. Most nights, you'd find homeless men hovering under the scaffolding that had stood there for nearly a year, but today, it was solely plugged full with dutiful voters.

"Are you all right?" Zach asked, just before letting go of me at the entry to the voting booth. I caught my breath for a second when I was certain that I was going to collapse right on top of the table that held pamphlets for various causes, the kind of causes that the Upper West Side demographic held dear. A light blue flyer called for a nurse-in, so breast-feeding moms could gain the right to openly feed their babies in local restaurants. A pink Xerox sheet asked neighbors to join them in a rally for gay marriage rights.

But I managed to steady myself before I gave in to the gravitational pull, even though I felt like melting into a rumpled heap on the tiled floor.

"I can hardly allow these horrid little cells to rob me of my God-granted right," I replied and managed a wan smile, as I pulled the booth's curtain closed triumphantly. After I performed my citizen's duty by tugging the lever, I pushed back the curtain and reached for Zach's arm before my legs defied my will and gave way.

"You need to eat something," he said, as we made our way back to my apartment.

"I can't. I throw it all back up. Even with the antinausea pills that Dr. Chin prescribed."

"Have you tried ice cream? A lot of my patients can hold that down. Besides, it gives them an excuse to eat ice cream. I think most of them swore off it after the age of twelve."

"Me included." I smirked wistfully.

"Come on, let's go for a cone." Zach tugged my elbow to cross the street.

"It's freezing out," I said, as I saw puffs of air from my breath explode around me. "We can't eat ice cream now."

"No one ever told you that eating cold foods in the winter will warm you up?" he said, as I looked at him warily. "Nope, seriously. My grandmother swore by it. And eating hot foods in the summer will cool you down. She used to make us sip hot cocoa whenever we visited her in Florida."

"I suspect that your grandmother might have been prematurely senile."

"Oh." He nodded and laughed. "She definitely was. But that doesn't mean that we shouldn't eat some ice cream."

And this is how I found myself in a diner on Seventy-seventh Street sitting across from my gynecologist and my close friend's ex-boyfriend, devouring a cup of mint chocolate chip on a blustery day in November while everyone else scurried around outside wrapped in wool scarves and Nordic-styled hats.

"God, I'd forgotten what real ice cream tasted like," I said, as I spooned down toward the second scoop, gorging like a rescued castaway. "Actually, I'd forgotten what food tasted like." I paused and looked over at him. "So, are you going to ask me about her?" Even from my first appointment two months back, Zach had never broached the subject of Lila.

"Nah, it was a while ago. I'm moving forward." He bit his lower lip and thought it over. "It took me a few months, but I think I get it now. I don't bear any ill will."

"I'm impressed," I said, as I scarfed down another bite. "I thought that I'd made my peace with Ned, but the truth is that I'm living in a constant state of alternatively wanting to bash his head into a wall and wishing that he would beg to come back to me."

"It gets easier. Eventually you figure out what went wrong and you sort of breathe a sigh of relief that you didn't make a more permanent mistake. And then you just hope that you find someone who won't end up being another misstep."

I shook my head and pointed my spoon at him. "See, it's your perspective that amazes me. I mean, how did you reach that point—the one where you felt like you really knew what went wrong?" I stopped and took a bite. "Take Ned and me. Yeah, I worked a lot, and, true, I was a little self-absorbed, but how did we go from conceivably having small problems that could have been talked out to him banging some work associate in Chicago and dumping me when things got rough?" I licked the back of my spoon and thought of the charm necklace he'd bought me. A sign of hope that never blossomed. My tone softened. "Anyway, that's sort of what I'm trying to figure out right now. How I can be thirty, and be just as pathetically single as I was a decade ago."

"You were pathetic a decade ago?" Zach smiled and looked over his cocoa at me. "I can't really see that."

I started to tell him about how back in college, I'd sit on the bench of our main walkway underneath the imposing trees, feet folded up below me on the wooden slats, and just take people in. Envision where they were rushing off to. Mull over how they'd spent their previous evening. Wonder if their hearts had been broken or if they were in the thralls of heady love or if, as was often the case both at that time and beyond, they were lonely like me. Not that I had reason to be lonely: I had Brandon (the next ex on my list to call); I had friends; I had, from the outside, a very vibrant life, but I was lonely all the same. I thought about telling him my alpha dog theory, and that now, with no one to cling to, with no one to prop me up, I felt like an anchor that was sinking even further into loneliness, and that I couldn't help but wonder if I would literally die alone. True, I had Sally, but now Sally had Drew; I couldn't expect her to rescue me the way she had when I brushed up against anorexia or to remain connected in the way that friends pledge themselves to always do but then occasionally falter in doing because life gets in the way.

Instead, I waved my hand and said to Zach, "Well, you know, in the figurative sense of the word 'pathetic.' I mean, really, over the course of ten years, not much has changed, even when it seems like it should have."

"You know, Nat," he said, leaning back in the booth and looking at the ceiling, "I'm not sure where the perspective comes from. But they teach you in medical school and in your residency to be analytical. When a patient dies, you can't just pull off your scrubs and say, 'I fucked up,' and go have a beer. Your attending forces you to address what went wrong because if you didn't, all of your patients might wind up dead." He paused and took a sip. "So I guess I sort of treat everything in my life that way: Even when I'd rather have a beer, I better first make sure that someone isn't dying."

I dissolved another bite of the ice cream in my mouth and bit into a rich dark chocolate chip. Suddenly, I wasn't sure who I was: the one who would rather have a beer or the one who was actually dying.

• • •

Dear Diary:
Don't have much time to talk because I'm trying to reach

Kyle, but I promised Janice that I'd try to write something every week, so here I am. The good news: Dupris won the campaign! The more good news: No one at the office seems to have picked up on my tip off to the Post. *The even better news: The senator called the day after the election and told me that although she's sorry that we won't be following up on the birth control agenda that I wanted to pursue, she is prepared to go guns a-blazing on stem cell research. So she asked me to start tackling the project . . . which at least gives me something to do on top of hunting down my exes.*

But I'm leaving the greatest news of all for last: I got a dog! Yes, that's right. A pooch. A hound. A canine. A four-legged friend. I know, everyone thinks I'm nuts, so don't get all judge-y on me, too. My mom was especially annoyed—she didn't think I should be around the germs, but I asked Dr. Chin, and he said no problem, and besides, I've never felt so in love with anything in my life. Manny. That's his name.

Anyway, after Zach and I got some ice cream, I got to thinking about my loneliness, how I probably chased it as much as it chased me. Sitting on benches staring at strangers, pulling down my blinds at work so I didn't have to see the world around me. You know, all of those "isolating techniques" (as Janice likes to call them) that I tend to fall into out of habit. It probably stems from being an only child, but both Janice and I agreed that passing the buck and pointing the finger at my childhood, much of which I spent reading in my room with my door closed, was probably counterproductive.

Anyhoo, this deep philosophizing explains how I found myself at the ASPCA after my last appointment with Janice. I didn't even mean to end up there, but I'd gotten a flyer from them the

day before in the mail, and so I guess I took this as a sign. Huh.
Go figure. Maybe I do believe in God, after all?

Okay. Gotta run. I think Kyle could use my help at the office.
More later.

PS—Yippee! I love Manny.

· EIGHT ·

I cannot believe that you got a dog," Sally said, as she stared down at the big-eyed mutt that ran to the door to greet her. "I mean, he's adorable, but Nat, it's a huge responsibility. Did you even consider that?"

"I saw him, and I wanted him." I shrugged and waved her in. "Besides, Janice said that pets can be healing. Can't you quote some study on that? Anyway, he's already house-trained."

I dropped to the floor to nuzzle him. Part black lab, part they-weren't-sure-what, Manny had been found rooting around a trash bin in the Bronx before a Good Samaritan dropped him off at the shelter. They figured he was about eight months old, so right now, he was all paws. Well, paws and eyes, which belied his mutt roots:

He looked exactly like a lab except that his eyes drooped like a bloodhound.

I'd cased the rows of cages at the ASPCA, holding my breath to avoid the pervasive urine scent that clung to the air and peered in to see who might be mine, and the force was magnetic. I was looking up and down and up again, and suddenly, I just stopped. He stared out from behind the stainless-steel bars and pressed his nose up as if to say hello. When the volunteer opened the door for me, he practically leapt into my arms, smothering my face with slobbery puppy breath and a moist, wet tongue. Today, he lapped my face up all over again, and I pulled Sally down on her knees for a similar tongue bath until she agreed that having Manny around wasn't the *worst* idea ever conceived.

After wiping ourselves down, Sally asked if I wanted to get started. She'd had come over to do it—to shave my head until I looked like a cue ball. Every morning after I showered, I'd have to unclog the drain; my hair would create such a backup that I'd practically be taking a bath by the time I was done. So this morning, I called Sally and told her that I was ready, ready to face what I might have dreaded most about this ordeal. Losing a breast seemed scary, but losing my hair was horrifying. Sally dutifully showed up with Drew's electric razor and a pair of scissors that she used to cut the tips off artichokes when she felt like cooking.

I poured some kibble into Manny's bowl and offered a squeaky toy to occupy him. And then she and I moved into the bathroom. I ran my fingers through my red locks, red like fire, red like blood, ignoring the strands in my hands as I went.

"Funny," I muttered to Sally. "I feel like I have no idea who I'll be when we're done with this."

I saw a perplexed look wash across her face in the mirror.

"What do you mean? You'll be Natalie. Just without hair." She put her hands on my shoulders. "Nat, nothing's changing."

"No, what I mean is, it's funny how much of our identity is wrapped up in our hair. I mean, think about it: Remember that haircut you got right out of college? The one that was sort of lop-sided, and shorter in the back than in the front?" Sally groaned and stuck out her tongue. "Right, so what I'm saying is, it's funny how your hair can make you feel uglier than Chewbacca." I paused. "God, I remember when I showed up at the salon with a picture of 'The Rachel.' And, even though Paul cut my hair to perfection, I still wasn't as glamorous or as skinny or as whatever as Jennifer Aniston." I laughed at the irony. "But I thought the perfect haircut might somehow lead to the perfect life."

"And sister, you definitely weren't dating Brad Pitt." Sally smiled.

"True that." I sighed. "Anyway, all I'm trying to say is that I wonder who I'll be once this is all gone."

Sally thought for a minute and then plugged the razor into the outlet by the sink. "I guess you can be anyone you want to be." Then she laughed. "I think I wrote something similar for *Cosmo* last year. Change Your Hair! Change Your Life!" She snorted. I knew that Sally loved her job as a writer, but these days, she was increasingly bored by it all. Last week, she vented that she wanted to cover something that mattered—*hard news*—she said, but I told her not to underestimate the powers of *Cosmo* on the masses. She sighed and said that there's only so many times you can write about the anatomy of an orgasm without wondering if you're fak-ing it yourself.

In my bathroom, I poked my head through a garbage bag and stared myself down in the mirror. As a kid, my hair was always flying in my face. My mother would push it away or clip it back with barrettes. "You look so unkempt," she would say, over and over again, as if tangled hair led to vagabond ways, but within minutes, it was in my eyes again, offering a safe layer between me and the world. Now, I wondered, what was left to protect me?

I took a deep breath and told Sally that I was ready. She started in the back, where I couldn't see the damage. I felt the vibration of the razor and heard the hum of its motor, but for those first few minutes, it didn't seem so bad. And once you've shaved the back of your head, you really don't have much of a choice but to continue. Even if you wanted to stop, which I did when I saw the horsetail-like chunks falling to the ground, you realize that you'll look too much like a freak to not press on. I mean, you simply can't get by with a half-shaved head. Even in New York, where trust me, just about anything goes, including a man who wears only skintight polka-dotted spandex and bright green Converse high-tops just about every day of the year. I walk past him most mornings, and no one even turns to notice.

Sally moved on to the sides, and we both agreed that if I'd sported said mohawk while Ned was still around, he wouldn't have had the balls to leave. I considered stopping there—I'd never have had the guts to pull off a mohawk in my former life, and I reveled in the fact that I looked like an ultimate badass—but I knew that the look was only temporary. Within weeks, those strands, too, would be clogging the drain, serving as a reminder of how much I'd already lost. So I told her to keep going, and not ten minutes later, it was gone.

Sally and I sat silently for five minutes and just stared into the mirror. And then she wrapped her arms around me and held me until I stopped crying.

"I think you're very brave, you know," she said.

"I don't feel like I am. I'd like to be, but I don't feel that way at all."

"You are. Without even knowing it."

I thought about what she said long after she left. Manny curled up in bed with me, and I watched his breathing grow heavy and his eyes flicker from his deep doggie sleep. I'd read once that brave men aren't those who never sense fear. The brave men are the ones who sense fear and keep walking toward it. I wondered if it counted if you didn't have a choice in the first place.

A WEEK LATER, on an overcast Saturday that had me staring out the window watching the planes soar past on their way to JFK, Dr. Zach called. I'd been contemplating how to move forward when the only place I felt like moving was into a burrowed hole in the ground. So when he offered to help me run errands or come over to keep me company, I declined, sticking my feet on top of the radiator and wiggling my toes. The solitude of myself would be just fine for today, thanks very much.

But when Manny went to the door and whined, I realized that an errand boy might come in handy. *Look for small gifts,* I heard Janice's voice in my ear. Zach was at my place in fifteen minutes.

"Are you planning on leaving the apartment at all today?" he asked, as he latched Manny's leash to his collar.

"Not if I can help it." I pulled my red chenille blanket over my chest and reached for the remote. "You know, moping and all. Good for the soul. Everyone needs a good mope now and then." I curled my legs under me on the couch. "Besides, I have studies to read." I waved to the pile of papers on my desk. "We're working on a stem cell push for next year."

"Sounds important," he said, then paused. "Actually, I believe the saying is that fresh air is good for the soul." He got a puzzled look on his face. "Or something like that. So why don't you take off your slippers, put on your shoes, brush your teeth, and join us." He paused and smiled. "I like your new 'do." Then his face fell. "Are you okay with it?"

I shrugged and steadied my voice, trying not to betray the enormity of the loss I felt. "I didn't have much of a choice."

"Well then." He clapped his hands together. "Hop to it. Let's get this show on the road."

I sighed and gingerly lowered my feet to the floor. "Christ, if I'd wanted a drill sergeant, I would have asked my mother to come over. Fine. Give me a minute." I went into the bedroom and self-consciously ran my hand over the rose-colored silk scarf on my head. I pulled on my now too-baggy jeans, a ratty Dartmouth sweatshirt, and my sheepskin winter boots. Then I reached for the babushka-like hat that Lila had bought for me on her recent work trip to Prague—as a consultant, she spent half of her life around the world—and surveyed myself in the mirror. With the hat, you could barely tell that I was bald, which I supposed was the sole perk of shaving your head in the winter. I grabbed my North Face jacket and a ball for Manny and rejoined Zach in the living room, where he was crouched over Manny, tousling the hair behind his ears.

"Let's do this. Get this show on the road," I said unenthusiastically.

"With that kind of attitude, I think maybe Manny and I could make do without you."

"Is that a promise or a threat?" I said, opening the door and locked up, trudging through my overly lit apartment hall to the elevator.

"What's with the dreariness?" Zach asked, as we stepped in and I pressed the lobby button.

"What's not with it? I think I'm entitled to a little self-pity." I caught myself. "I know, I know, statistically, a positive attitude helps beat cancer. I swear, if Sally tells me that one more time, I'm going to punch her lights out."

"Well, that certainly wouldn't be constructive. Though perhaps therapeutic." He laughed. "I'm not telling you that you can't feel sorry for yourself. You'll never hear me say that. It's just . . ." He paused and looked at me. "It's just when your face is clouded over like that, it disguises how beautiful you really are."

Before I could reply, the elevator opened, and Manny hurled himself out the door to the waiting street, pulling Zach in his wake. I stood behind them and watched them go, astonished, confused, and a little bit flattered. Not that I thought that I was beautiful. Because right now, I assuredly wasn't. But the way that Zach said it—the look on his face when he took me in and I saw him consider whether or not to put it out there—well, I knew that whether or not I believed that I was beautiful, he most definitely did.

I caught up to them outside, and we walked the five blocks to the dog run in silence, the tension-filled bubble floating between us. Finally, because I felt weird and then felt weird about feeling weird, I broke the silence with some small talk, misconstrued as it might have been.

"Lila asked about you the other night." I regretted it as soon as I blurted it out, since this seemed to be perhaps the only thing I could have said to exacerbate the already blooming awkwardness.

"Oh. Okay. Should I ask what she said? Or just leave it at that?" Zach kicked at the gravel.

"Just passing it along." I shrugged and got up off the bench to throw Manny the ball. But Lila had asked about him when she called to check in on me. She'd been single since they'd broken up, and I think she was starting to see that the greener grass—you

know, the perfect open field that you think exists in your neigh-
bor's backyard—turned out to already be in her own backyard.
She'd also made a passing reference of her rediscovered lust to
Sally, who told her to stop waxing nostalgic, that nothing good
ever comes from going back to a broken relationship, but Lila
didn't seem to listen. She was too busy looking back at Zach with
rose-colored glasses.

"I think I'll just tuck that away into my folder called 'useless
information,' and let it go at that," Zach replied when I sat back
down. "Besides, I'm not a big fan of revisiting the past. There's too
much else to look forward to."

• • •

Dear Diary,

*Well, I'm back at it! Finally, right? I know, I know, I've
veered wildly off course with this diary-writing exercise, but this
time, I'm not writing to bitch and moan or otherwise philosophize.
No, the reason I'm writing is because I tracked down Brandon.
He was a little harder to find than Colin. Yahoo didn't work, and
Google gave me hundreds of matches—I guess that there's a
Brandon Fletcher who also plays for the Florida Marlins—but
I diligently searched through each one as if I were conducting
background research for the senator until I found him. Turns out
that he's landed in San Francisco and is running the trading
floor for a private equity fund. That sort of suits him. He was
always looking to trade up anyway.*

*It was weird. He picked up the phone, and it was almost as if
ten years hadn't passed. He voice was so etched into me that even
if I hadn't known whom I was calling, I'd have known it was
him. He, of course, had heard about my diagnosis, so he apolo-*

gized for not being in touch. He should have been, he said. He just didn't know what to say.

I asked him about Darcy, and he cleared his throat and told me that they were divorcing, and because he had said the right thing about him not calling me, I said the right thing about his divorce. I said that I was sorry. But, of course, dear Diary, as you must know, I wasn't really sorry. I was vindicated. You see, I knew that I'd win!

I told him that I was calling with some odd questions, and if he didn't mind, he should try to give me as honest answers as possible. He said he'd try, and so I opened with the only one that I could think of, perhaps because it was the only one that mattered. I asked him why he cheated on me.

Oh, Diary, before I go any further, I suppose that you need some background. Brandon and I met our freshman year at Dartmouth. I saw him on the lacrosse field one afternoon while I was running on the track, and he literally took my breath away. I mean it; I had to stop and remind myself to inhale. We circled each other until sophomore year just before the Christmas holidays. We were in the basement of his fraternity house, dancing to the pulsing music of Marky Mark, and suddenly were both too drunk to keep up the farce. He pushed me back into the wall and kissed me. I slept with him that same night. The first and only time I'd done that. I hated the loss of control, but I gave into it anyway. With Brandon, the air of intoxication just sucked me in. It was like that from the first night and all the nights after.

What I didn't realize and actually wouldn't realize until we broke for summer vacation was that Brandon was still promised to his girlfriend back home. She was happily tucked away at Michigan State, doing things like knitting him freaking socks

*and naming their firstborn, and when he went home that sum-
mer, it was as if I never existed. He only mentioned her in passing, as we kissed good-bye in the van to the airport. "I might be
sort of busy this summer," he said. "In case you call. There's,
uh, someone back home who I need to sort things out with." The
first time it happened, I literally had no clue. Our flights were
being called, and he offered a halfhearted explanation, and then
we split up toward our respective gates.*

*But this pattern replayed itself each passing year. Each fall
or each return after Christmas break, I'd pretend that Brandon
hadn't returned home to Darcy and he'd pretend that he didn't
love her. Until my senior year. I was sick of it, so I told him to
choose. And because he was there in the moment with me, I won.
He chose me. But what he really did was tell me that he chose me
while he kept on talking to her. And because these things do
eventually find their way to the surface, I ended it. But only after I felt humiliated.*

*Of course, this didn't stop me from sleeping with him again
for the last few weeks of our senior spring. We hadn't spoken
since.*

*So a decade later, when I asked him why he'd cheated on me,
I honestly didn't think that he'd come clean, be straight with me.
Being straight wasn't exactly his thing, which I probably don't
need to point out at this moment but feel compelled to do so anyway. When I asked him, he cleared his throat and said he'd call
me back. Said he'd never really thought about it, but that he
wanted to do the right thing and give me a real answer. He said
that he thought he owed me that, but he needed a little time to
sort it through. I passed him my number and figured it was a
dead end. Manny and I were twenty-five minutes deep into a*

Press Your Luck *rerun on the Game Show Network when the phone rang.*

"It's because you let me," he said.

Before I could launch a series of protests, all of which would suggest that his misogynistic reasoning pointed the finger firmly at me when he was the one who refused to be pinned down, he elaborated. "You didn't give me permission, that's not what I mean. But I never got the sense that you'd fight for me, that you loved me enough to go to the mats. Darcy did, so I was too scared to let her go and risk that I'd gambled it all for someone who was in it to win it." When I pointed out that I had, actually, laid down the ultimatum, he made an excellent point. "That was just because you didn't want me to be with her, not because you necessarily wanted me to be with you."

When I replay his words, Diary, they sound shallower than they were. Because the truth of the matter is, he was probably right. I only raised the stakes because someone else threatened to steal the pot.

Before Brandon and I said good-bye and swapped e-mail addresses he said, "You know, Natalie, I read about you in the papers, I've followed your career. And if you'd fought for me the way that you do for so much else in your life, I think I would have married you." I smiled and told him that, despite the cancer, it's blessings like these that make me believe in God.

· NINE ·

The next weekend, Sally, Lila, and I set off for bridesmaid dress fittings. I was feeling moderately decent, so when Sally asked if I felt strong enough to join them, I managed a glass of milk and an apple, and slowly made my way to the subway.

The 1/3 train cruised us down to the meatpacking district, and we were buzzed up to the too-chic boutique where Sally had commissioned our dresses. I'd ordered mine in August, back in my halcyon days before the current pulled me out like a tidal wave. The boutique's size charts were beyond skewed to begin with. As anyone who has ever been a bridesmaid surely knows (and that includes just about every unfortunate woman on the planet), bridesmaid dresses fall into the Twilight Zone of sizing. If you order a four, the dress will actually fit someone who is the equivalent of a size ten, except perhaps in the breast area, where it will actually fit someone who is concave or prepubescent. Should you actually be a size ten, you will most definitely be handed a dress that will have the specifications to fit a five-year-old. It's as if there is a conspiracy against bridesmaids—maybe the tailors are in on it, too, because by the time you're done, you've shelled out the equivalent of the price of the damn dress just to get it to somewhat adhere to your proportions, much less not humiliate you as you saunter down the aisle with a groomsman whom you may or may not be making out with at some point in the future.

Tess, the perfectly blond, perfectly perfect designer who ran the salon, offered us tea and did a double take at the beaded navy scarf wrapped around my head. I saw her trying not to look, her smile freezing one second too long as we locked eyes, and she attempted to determine whether I was or was not bald, and if so, why that might be.

"It's okay," I said to her. "Breast cancer."

Her face flushed. "Oh. I'm sorry."

I waved her off. "Don't worry. Everyone wonders." She nodded as she disappeared into the back, and Sally moved over to hug me.

"Here we are," Tess said, as she emerged toting our light-blue, tea-length dresses. I held mine up: I didn't even need to try it on to see that what I had guesstimated would fit me three months back would now drape over me like a curtain after a dip in the ocean.

I shuffled into the dressing room and slowly unzipped my wool cardigan, folding it neatly on the velvet bench that sat beside the full-length mirror. I tugged my turtleneck over my head and dropped my jeans to the floor in one smooth motion: All I had to do was unbuckle my chunky brown belt and they fell to the ground.

There was nothing there to hold them up—no hips, no waist, no thighs, which just last summer I'd willed to be two inches smaller in circumference.

The light in the dressing room was designed to make you look good from any angle. No fluorescent bulbs to illuminate under-eye circles that turn you into an eerie incarnation of a character from *Dawn of the Dead* or to spotlight the backs of your legs in such a way that they resemble your grandmother's Jell-O mold. So because I was given an early advantage, you'd have thought that I would have looked better.

I'd stopped examining myself in the mirror about two months back, just after my second chemo treatment. I found it too depressing to stare at my dollhouse-size waist and make bargains with God to do something, anything to get my old body—really, my old life—back. So I stopped looking. When I stepped out of the shower, I'd avert my eyes. When I'd disrobe for bed, I'd simply drop my clothes by my nightstand and crawl under the covers.

"Can we peek?" Sally asked and pulled the curtain back. Before I had time to stop her, she and Lila stepped into the room. I watched them try to hold their faces steady, but Sally's eyes popped unintentionally and the corners of Lila's mouth twitched the way that they always did whenever she was upset.

"Oh sweetie," Sally said and moved toward me, resting her hands on my shoulders, then running them down my arms until she interlocked her fingers in mine.

"It's okay." I shrugged, before my eyes filled with tears.

I stood there, nearly naked, and exposed the skeleton of my former self. I turned toward the mirror and ran my fingers over my ribs and moved my hands lower where they rounded over my protruding hip bones. My legs looked like kindling, like the twigs you'd toss into a fire to stoke the ambers that weren't hearty enough to get the fire started in the first place. I turned to the side and felt paper thin. From the rear view, I craned my neck and could see that my back dove into my upper thighs; it no longer bothered to stop at the curve of my butt.

"Stop," Lila said, waving her hand in front of her. "Enough. Enough of examining yourself and of us gaping and making this much more horrible than it has to be." I turned to look at her. "I'm serious," she said. "This is all too heavy. Too melodramatic. There have to be some positives here." She pleadingly looked at Sally for help.

"True," Sally agreed, picking up on her lead. "Let's see. You are as thin as the tiniest of supermodels. Heidi Klum best watch her back." I tried to force a smile, but my face refused.

"Oh, okay," Lila continued. "And you never have to worry about going to the gym anymore!"

"Good one," Sally said, raising her finger in the air. "And if you so choose, you can live on bonbons and éclairs for the rest of your chemo and not gain a dime."

"Lucky bitch," Lila grunted with a smile, at which I had to laugh.

"Fair enough," I said. "Now get out so I can finish getting dressed. I thought we were pressed for time." Lila had to be back uptown in order to make a 6:00 train to Delaware for her father's sixtieth birthday party.

They shuffled out into the showroom, and I felt my smile falter. I turned again and faced forward, staring myself down, willing myself to look away yet remaining paralyzed in the horror of it all. I was a ghost of my old self. A ghost with a fabulous bridesmaid dress but a ghost, nevertheless.

✦ ✦ ✦

"I NEED SOME pot," I announced to Sally on the subway ride home.

She did a double take at Lila and practically spit out her Diet Coke.

"You need some what? Did I hear you correctly?"

"I need some pot," I repeated. At my last appointment, Dr. Chin had casually mentioned, in a I'm-not-recommending-this-because-it's-illegal-but-should-you-choose-to-do-this-it-might-be-a-wise-thing sort of way, that many cancer patients find that smoking marijuana helps both their pain and their appetite.

You should know that in college, pot was not my thing. In college, everyone has their "thing." For me, that was white wine. Brandon preferred rum and Coke. Lila was a fan of vodka shots. Sally? She knew where to score a bong hit without having to actually pay for the pot itself. Sally wasn't the only one. In fact, an entire posse of our friends would disappear to the "flight deck" (where, ahem, one might take flight) of Brandon's fraternity house and emerge forty minutes later enshrouded by a plume of smoke and with a somewhat glassier look in their eyes. I didn't judge. It just wasn't for me. I worried it would put me too far out of my control. Chardonnay I could monitor—I knew exactly how much I could handle before the blurry line between tipsy and so-drunk-the-paper-gossip-column-might-write-you-up crept its way into my impaired cerebrum.

So understandably, today on the subway, Sally was caught off guard.

"Nat, I stopped smoking after college, you know that," she said, and I raised my eyebrows. "Okay, but really, I totally quit when Drew and I started dating. You know he can't stand it. Besides, don't you get tested for work? Couldn't this go on your permanent record or whatever you politicians have?"

"Work's sort of a nonissue right now." I sighed. "The senator bailed on the birth control bill I was pushing, so now she has me researching some stem cell stuff from home. Other than that, I'm just treading water." I shrugged. I didn't want to admit that the senator had demoted me due to the hooker debacle. "It's a slow time until the start of the term and all. Anyway, back to the issue at hand," I continued. "I'm quite certain that you have to still know someone," I said, as the subway operator overshot our station, sending our balances out of whack and propelling us into one another. Lila grabbed my arm and steadied me. "I'm okay," I said, as the car finally lumbered to a stop.

"Let me make some calls," Sally said. "I might know someone who might know someone."

"That's what I thought." I reached for the handrail on the stairway and forced myself up toward daylight.

IN A STRANGE turn of fate, we ran into Dr. Zach on the walk home. In the largest city in the world, chock-full of, oh, I don't know, a gazillion nameless faces, it figured, given the strange karma that had blown my way in recent months, that while standing in front of Gristides, mulling over whether to stop for a cup of tea, Zach would walk out of the revolving door and practically trip on our huddle.

"Ladies!" he said, and he leaned over to kiss me hello on the cheek. "Lila." He nodded in her direction and forced a dimpled smile. They hadn't seen each other since she split from him, though I'm pretty sure that he called her twice in the weeks right after, but she didn't bother phoning back.

"Just doing my Saturday grocery shopping. I have quite the whirlwind life! Big-time doctor plus milk and cereal purchases equals Hollywood movie." He laughed, trying to shed the tension. He looked at me. "How are you feeling? I planned to call today."

Lila cast her eyes toward me, and I felt my ears redden beneath my scarf. "I'm hanging in there."

"She's toying with the dark side," Sally interjected with a laugh. "Looking to score some pot. Did you ever think? I mean, our Natalie, part of the stand-up citizens' brigade for Senator Dupris. Ready to get stoned out of her mind."

I shook my head and looked at my feet, mortified that my gynecologist might catch wind of my new toking habit.

"Still nauseated?" he asked. "I'll tell you what. Let's just say that, hypothetically, I know how to get you some of what you need." He dropped his bags and put his fingers into air quotes, emphasizing "you need." "How would you girls like to join me for a home-cooked meal tonight? Natalie, I promise, we'll get you high enough to scarf down an entire cow."

I looked at Lila to take my cue. Zach picked up on it, so he nodded in her direction and said, "Lila, you're more than welcome to come. All four of us. Helping Natalie put some meat on her bones." But I knew that Lila was off to Delaware, and I knew that it killed her that she was.

"I can't make it," she said, waving her hand in the air and putting on a stoic face. "But you two. Must go. No doubt about it."

She said it with such gusto that we didn't even have to formally accept. Zach just said, "Great, I'll see you at 7:30. I'll take care of everything. Seventy-eighth and Columbus."

All three of us turned and watched him saunter north, a grocery bag on each arm, and I'm fairly certain that if a bubble were to inflate over each of our heads, you know, in the way that they do in cartoons, the only thing that each of us would have shown was a big fat question mark.

I'D NEVER ACTUALLY been inside of Zach's apartment. When he and Lila were dating, we always met out—that is, when I could actually get out.

"Do you think this is weird?" Sally asked, when we met up outside of his building.

"Uh-hum," I said, nodding in agreement.

"Oh man, though, you look fab," she said and made me turn around for her. Sally had forced me into a shopping excursion the weekend before for a few wardrobe pick-me-ups. My old jeans had grown so baggy that when I held out the waist, I looked like I belonged in one of those cheap weight-loss ads. (You know the ones: These are my old jeans, and thanks to this super-duper little pill, I'm now thirty-seven sizes smaller!) We headed to Bergdorfs, and when Sally saw me in the pair of deep-hued low-riders she had nabbed for me, she deemed me reborn.

"You look like a freaking model with that body," she said. I reminded her that my noncurves were hardly something I desired.

"True," she agreed. "But since you have it right now, why not make the most of it?" I looked in the mirror (I was dressed, it was acceptable) and agreed in spite of myself that skinny did look pretty okay. Tonight, I paired those low-riders with a black cashmere crewneck, and as I was pulling on my Via Spiga boots, I realized that I might have been nervous.

"I hope he realizes that I'm engaged," Sally said, as his doorman waved us in.

"Stop being such a twit," I said. "I'm sure that he does."

I didn't mention that somewhere in the back of my heart, I might have had a teensy-tiny-eeny-weeny crush on him, but that I stomped out that minuscule feeling I heard in the distance because (a) he'd dated my second-best friend, (b) my second-best friend may or may not still pine for him, and (c) (and this was the one that really mattered) I had cancer. Certainly, no one could be attracted to the bald, spindly version of me, and even further, I don't even think that you can have sex when you have cancer, even though Janice had assured me that I could. I made a mental note to ask Dr. Chin. Not that I had a sex drive. The chemo sapped that one, too.

"Fear not," I told her after I pressed the elevator button. "I'm fairly certain that he won't put the moves on you."

"Then why the invite?" I saw a flicker of realization in her eyes. "Oh my God, he totally likes you!"

"Okay, first of all, we're not ten. Second of all, no, he doesn't. He's just been a good friend. Walking Manny, bringing me ice cream. I'm hardly going to turn away the help these days."

"Fine," she said. "I just can't wait to say 'I told you so.'"

Zach's apartment was perfect. And by that I mean that most New York apartments feel like a thousand square feet of leased space that the renter never truly inhabits. The living room might be half done, or the closet in the bedroom overflowing into the sleeping area, or the bathroom so minuscule that your knees touch the sink when you pee. There's a tangible sense of movement in New York: People are always moving up, moving on, moving toward something bigger, richer, better. So we never stop to fully embrace where we live because we know that circumstances might arise that call us onward. A two-year lease feels like handcuffs; actual ownership is a prison sentence.

I ran my fingers over the cool granite countertops in his kitchen, which wasn't one of those miniature kitchens designed for the Keebler elves, but a quintessential gourmet kitchen, complete with stainless-steel appliances and a small wine refrigerator. I stared out at the view of the Hudson, lost in thought, so I didn't hear him come up behind me.

"This is why I bought the place," he said. "For this room. And for this view." We both looked out over the lights for a minute before he broke our silence.

"So, I got the pot."

"Zach, you're a doctor." I turned to face him and tried not to gasp. He was in perfectly rinsed jeans and a green checkered button-down that brought out the hazel specks in his eyes. I looked at him and wondered if a speculum could be considered a sex toy. I shook my head as if to snap out of it. "Really, should you be giving your patients drugs? I mean, can't you get your license suspended?"

"Nah, I've actually recommended this to patients myself." He reached for the bottle of wine on the counter. "So I know a guy . . . I mean, I haven't done it since, God, like before med school, but if it gets you eating, light me a fat one."

I laughed. "Well, I've never done it, period. You and Sally will have to show me the way."

He pointed toward the Ziploc bag on the coffee table and ushered me to the faded chocolate leather couch in the living room. "Your tutorial awaits, my dear."

Sally sat cross-legged on the Persian rug, and Zach and I plopped down on the couch.

"Okay, so you've smoked a cigarette before, right?" he asked. I shook my head no, and he dropped his jaw in mock horror.

"I know, I'd be, like, the very picture of health if it weren't for this fucking cancer." I laughed dryly at the irony.

"Well, then, this is probably going to burn a bit. Go slowly. Don't overshoot what you can handle." He and Sally had me practice first. I took deep, deep breaths, then held the air in for ten seconds. When I'd mastered that, Zach grabbed a joint from the baggie, flicked a lighter until the flame caught hold, and inhaled languidly, blowing smoke out the side of his mouth so it didn't float my direction. I watched him and wondered why he'd do this, why he'd sit around getting high with a friend of a former girlfriend, a patient who conceivably could be just another chart. He saw me looking and gave me a grin. I was pretty sure that he wasn't stoned yet, so I smiled back.

After Sally took a hit, she passed it to me. I held the joint awkwardly between my thumb and pointer finger and brought it up to my lips, peering down on it the way that a dog examines a new toy.

"Just inhale slowly, not too much," Zach reminded me, and before I could think otherwise, I did. I felt a burning in the back of my throat, and I fought the urge to cough as Sally counted in the background, telling me when to push the smoke out.

"You're a pro!" Zach declared. "Are you sure you aren't a closet pothead? Because with that lung capacity, you should be."

We passed around the joint until it was finished. At one point, Zach got up to put Duke Ellington on the stereo and pour me a glass of water. I hadn't even asked, he just did it because he suspected I needed it. He was right.

When the stub grew too small to salvage, Zach declared that dinner would be served in fifteen minutes and to make ourselves comfortable in the meantime. My head was lighter than it had ever been, and my eyelids felt as if they'd been weighted down, but I followed him into the kitchen, offering to help.

"So what's on the menu?" I opened and closed the refrigerator door, just because it seemed like a fun thing to do.

"Roasted chicken, salad, a side of risotto, and some homemade rolls," he said, as he took plates down from the glass-door cabinets.

"God, that all sounds fantastic. Wait, you make your own bread? Seriously? Are you from, like, the 1800s?" I shut the Sub-Zero door and let it stick.

"Nope, I just love to cook. I know, go figure. A heterosexual man in Manhattan who doesn't have Empire Szechwan on speed dial." It was true. Ned was on a first-name basis with the delivery guy.

"Where'd you learn?"

"My girlfriend in med school," he said, as he lifted the lid on the pot to check on the risotto. "Come taste this. Will you be able to stomach it?"

I slid between him and the stove and dipped in the spoon.

"Perfect," I declared, rolling the pesto-flavored granules over my tongue. "I swear, I've never been so famished in my life." From behind me, he put his hands on my shoulders, and quietly said, "I'm glad," as he let his palms slide down my arms until they dropped away. I felt as if I'd stuck my fingers in a light socket, but I tried to suppress the tingle. Sally yelled in from the living room, looking for the remote control, so Zach excused himself and returned a minute later.

"So. This girlfriend. What happened to her?" I leaned back against the kitchen island.

"She wasn't the one," he said simply, moving toward the oven. "Although she could whip up a mean batch of pasta Bolognese."

"Come on, it's never that simple. Really, what happened?"

He stopped stirring the risotto and looked out the window. "Well, I guess the people who we were when we met—which was just out of college—and who we ended up being by the time we split—we just weren't the same. She wanted me to be something I wasn't, and I wanted the same of her." He shrugged. "Sometimes the math just doesn't work out, even if you think it will."

It must have been the pot talking because I pressed him for more. "So how'd you know? I mean, you loved her, right?"

"Oh, I really loved her. Natasha. That was her name. She's a pediatrician in Ann Arbor now. How did I know that we weren't going to live happily ever after? I don't know. She knew before me. I had a position lined up in Michigan; I was going to follow her there. But right as I was making my final decision, she asked me not to come. Over a bowl of pasta on a Thursday night. She just said, 'I think you should take the residency in New York,' and kept eating." He started stirring again.

"I'm sorry."

"No, it was years ago, and besides, she was right. I would have stuck around, I would have moved for her, but it was more because of inertia." He stopped to take a sip of his wine. "I was touch and go for a while, but when I got to New York, everything was much clearer. And that's when I realized that she wasn't the one. I managed to recover, and I don't think about her much. And those two things reassure me that there's someone else who is." I thought about Jake, how I thought I'd never get over him. How, even when I was with Ned, I still dreamt of him, I still tasted his presence like he never left.

"Did you fight? I mean, why did she end it?"

"Well, yeah, we fought like anyone fights. But it wasn't anything big. I mean, it wasn't like we had different views of the world or that she wanted kids and I didn't or anything like that. But our last year together, we just sort of drifted. And when we did, I think we both saw that we could build lives, happy lives, outside of each other. And that was all Natasha needed to know. She figured if she didn't miss me when I'd be pulling a double shift at the hospital, then maybe she wouldn't miss me if I weren't around at all."

I flashed back to Jake, to his seemingly unending road trips, to his nights out with the band. And how, though I ached for him during his time away, he reveled in his freedom. I could see it in his eyes right before he took off for a tour: the lust for independence that he lost whenever he was attached to me.

"God." I sighed. "You have, like, the most insightful perspective on relationships, like, ever."

He laughed. "You, my dear, should sit down before you fall over. What can I say? Both of my parents are psychiatrists."

"Maybe I can get their number if I survive all of this."

He froze and looked over at me. "Don't talk like that. Telling yourself all of the things that you can't do. Don't you think of giving up. You don't know what you're capable of surviving until you're forced to survive it."

I felt tears rise out of nowhere; I waved them off and blamed the pot. So Zach tugged off his oven mitts and set down the wooden spoon and came over and pulled me tight. And true, I was stoned, and more true, I wanted comfort, but I wasn't too intoxicated to hear him say, "Lean on me." And when I did, the most beautiful part of it all was that he held me up.

AFTER DINNER AND when we had burned through another joint, I wobbled up, stood on top of the couch, and made my announcement.

"I would like to officially . . ." I stopped and stuck my hands out like a surfer might to keep my balance. "Whoa. Okay. Let me start over. I would like to officially, here in the safety of my friends, and perhaps with the help of a slight touch of pot, declare that Bob Barker has been added to my list." I nodded authoritatively and jumped off the couch.

"Your list?" Zach asked with a puzzled look on his face.

"Yeah, my list." I looked over at Sally to explain, but she was curled up in a fetal position, shoulders shaking with laughter, tears streaming down her face. "You know: the five people you could sleep with, even if you're married, and face no consequences." I paused and cocked my head. "Although I guess now, since I'm single, I could sleep with Bob and no one would give a shit. Huh. All right. I guess the list is moot."

Sally sat up and fought back her giggles. "Bob Barker? Nat. I mean, isn't he, like, 947 years old?"

"Mmmm, yes," I said, wrapping my arms around myself. "But there's a reason that they call them 'Barker's Beauties.' I think he's done them all. And a man of his age? Well, let's just say that he probably knows his way around a woman's anatomy." I nodded. "Yes indeed."

"A man his age," said Zach. "You'd be lucky if he could *find* your anatomy without the help of bifocals." Sally fell over again in a heap of laughter. "Okay, so geezers aside, who else is on your list."

"Well," I said quite seriously. "I've given this some thought. Because Bob had to bump someone off, and whenever someone gets bumped off, you have to do a bit of mental math. And prioritizing, of course."

"Of course," Zach said solemnly.

"So obviously, there's Scott Speedman," I said, holding my thumb up to count as number one.

"Obviously?" Zach asked.

"Because he reminds her of her old boyfriend, Jake," Sally said from the floor.

"Right, there's that. And he's just fucking hot," I added and took a deep breath. "Okay, so the next, in no particular order, are: well, Bob. And I'd have to go with Hugh Grant."

"Ooh, Hugh Grant. He's on my list, too," Sally agreed, still from the floor. "I almost interviewed him once, and Drew got very nervous. Knowing that he was on my list."

I held three fingers in the air. "So two left. And here's where it gets tricky. I'd like to throw Michael Vartan into the mix because that boy looks like he can do it up. But Kyle's friend, Jackie, knows someone who slept with him, and I don't know, that somehow muddles it, you know?" Zach looked at me like he didn't know, didn't know at all, but I just ignored him. "Eh, but we'll say Michael Vartan because he makes me drool. And lastly?" I sighed. "Oh, I'm not sure. Patrick Dempsey?" I felt myself blush, knowing that Zach looked like his doppelgänger.

"Ronnie Miller?" Sally said, finally sitting up. "Come on, you can land one better than that." Zach looked even more confused. "Can't Buy Me Love," Sally said in his direction. "All aboard the Ronnie Miller express!"

"Okay, if big fish is what you want, big fish it is: I'll go with . . ." I stared up at the tract lighting and curled my lips into an O. "I'll go with . . ."

"Pat Sajak?" Zach offered helpfully, and I threw a pillow at him.

"No. I'll go with Dennis Quaid." I nodded my head conclusively. "And now it's your turn." I pointed at Zach in the way that a hunter might target a deer.

"Okay." He laughed. "I'm game. But keep in mind that I've never done this before."

"Pul-ease," Sally said, placing a pillow underneath her ass. "Like every guy doesn't have a fantasy list at his mental fingertips. Christ, if I find one more porno site on Drew's computer, I'm going to throw it out the window."

"Hmmm, okay." Zach rubbed his hands together. "Well, to start, and in homage of Bob Barker, I'll go with Diane Keaton. Sexy, sure of herself. And older women are great in bed." I felt myself go slack-jawed. *And you would know that how?* I physically bit my tongue. "Angelina Jolie. Yeah, definitely. God, that body alone. And you just get the sense that she's an animal. Oh, and Carmen Electra for the same reasons. I imagine there's nothing that girl won't do." Suddenly, this was decidedly less fun than I'd pictured it. I got up to light another joint, leaving Zach weighing his options underneath his breath. I plopped back down on the couch in an effort to let him know that I was completely and entirely disinterested in whomever else he added to his list.

"You're right," he said, reaching for the joint. "This is much harder than you'd think." I clamped my mouth shut. "Okay, for the last two, I'll go with Halle Berry again, that body, and Pamela Anderson. Just because you have to go with Pamela Anderson or else no guy will ever speak to you again."

Sally flopped back down on the floor and groaned. "Oh God, could you be any more obvious? I mean, clearly, it's all about the bodies on all of them."

"No, clearly," I interjected, "it's all about the breasts. Zach, it seems, is a breast man." There was more than a trace of bitterness in my voice.

"Not fair," he protested, handing the joint to Sally, who waved him off. "I couldn't even tell you the size of Diane Keaton's breasts. Besides, isn't that the whole point of this list: to fantasize about your ideal?"

"Aha!" I clapped triumphantly. "So they *are* your ideal."

"I'm not dignifying this discussion any longer." Zach laughed. "Who wants dessert?" He stood up and headed to the kitchen.

"Men," Sally grunted, before she pulled a pillow over her face. "Tits, tits, tits, tits, tits, tits, tits. God, you'd think they were the eighth wonder of the world."

I didn't answer her. Instead, I looked down at my stricken chest and wondered who would want me at all when this fucking cancer had taken them from me.

· T E N ·

*D*ear Diary,
   I know, I know, I've been slacking. Dylan is next on my list to call, but I haven't had the time yet to hunt him down. And Janice has been urging me to keep up the writing, so I'm logging in an entry that has nothing to do with Dylan, but it sort of does have to do with men, so I figured that you wouldn't mind.

   I'm happy to report, well, happy might not be the right word but I'm using it regardless, that I have officially smoked my first joint. I know, like, fifteen years too late, right? Well, better late than never because I was finally able to eat a full meal afterward. But I've already gotten ahead of myself.

   Sally and I went to Zach's for dinner, as well as for some pot-smoking lessons. Weird, right? But it gets weirder: I woke up there the next morning. Now Diary, don't go jumping to conclusions! Though trust me, it's easy to because I did the same thing—I practically broke out in a sweat from my panic when I jumped to conclusions.

So what happened was this. Zach, Sally, and I got very, very stoned. At some point late in the evening, right when we were winding up a heated game of Trivial Pursuit, Sally looked at the time and realized that Drew would be livid if she didn't bolt pronto, so she grabbed her coat, gave us both kisses, and left us with our pies half full of tiny wedges. Despite my impaired judgment, I do recall whipping Zach's ass in the end. And as we know, I like to win, so I got up and did some little hoochie dance or something, but then I suddenly felt very, very dizzy. Like I do when the chemo is still running rampant through my system.

So Zach walked me over to his couch, and I put my head on a cashmere pillow, and Diary, that's all I remember until I woke up at 7:17 alone in his bed. I wasn't even sure where I was at first. I looked out of the twenty-second-floor window and ran my hands over the maroon sheets and tried to jumble together the preceding twelve hours. I was fully dressed, so at least that was a relief.

In the living room, Zach had left me a note next to the bag of remaining joints. "Got paged and had to run. Take the rest of this. Will call you soon."

See, Diary? This? Is why I didn't smoke pot in college. Bad things happen when I let myself slip just a tiny bit out of control. Sigh. Note to self: From now on, get high alone. (Don't worry, Diary, since it's for medicinal purposes, I'm pretty sure that Narcotics Anonymous wouldn't consider this a warning sign.)

So, Diary, this is the pickle I now find myself in. Did I or did I not engage in some sort of entirely inappropriate behavior with my gynecologist who seems to have a strong D-cup fetish, and for whom one of my best friends still may harbor a bit of love and, oh, this part matters, who I would most definitely have jumped like a monkey by now if it weren't for this fucking disease.

You can't hear me, Diary, but I'm sighing right now. There's really nothing much else to do.

◆　◆　◆

From: Foley, Blair
To: Miller, Natalie
Re: The holiday party

Hi Natalie!!

I hope that you're doing great! We all just got back from our little vacations after the election madness! I went to Florida with my boyfriend. It felt soooooooooo good to take a few days off and recover. I can't believe that the time has gone so quickly, and we're already gearing up for next year's congressional session. Weird! Right?

Anyway, I'm writing because the senator is so glad that you can make it to the Christmas party!! We all are: It feels like forever ago since we've seen you!

But she did want me to alert you to the fact that Councilman Taylor and his wife are attending. The senator felt like inviting them was the nice thing to do—I'm sure you understand!! But the bad news of this is that she told me, well, there's really no easy way to say this, but the senator told me to tell you that when you show up, she'd like you to issue a formal apology to Mrs. Taylor. You know, for the hooker thing and all.

Sorry. ☹ But I'm sure that it will go great!
Best,
Blair

From: Miller, Natalie
To: Foley, Blair
Re: Apology

Dear Blair,

Please inform the senator that if I apologize to Susanna Taylor, it will be a direct admission of our role in the dirty press game that we played. I can't see how this benefits anyone.

Please further inform her that with all due respect, I really don't feel like looking like an a-hole.

Thanks for the well wishes. I'm glad to hear that Florida was fun.
—Natalie

From: Foley, Blair
To: Miller, Natalie
Re: Spoke with the Senator

Natalie,

I mentioned your feelings to Dupris, and well, unfortunately, she feels VERY strongly about this. I don't want to get into the ultimatums that she might have mentioned, but if it were me, I'd apologize. My mom used to tell me that saying you're sorry couldn't undo your actions, but it could make you look like a decent person in spite of them.

Sorry again. But see you at the party!!!! Should be fun!!!!

Best,

Blair

I rolled my eyes at the computer screen. So now I was taking moral advice from a girl whose favorite thing in life appeared to be the use of the SHIFT + 1 button. I sank my face into my hands and considered calling Dupris directly, telling her all the things that were running through my head, things like, *I am not your scapegoat, you slippery little politician.* Or *I distinctly recall you giving me tacit permission to sink Taylor with whatever means necessary.* Instead, I pushed my chair away from my desk until I rolled back and hit the couch. *Shit,* I thought next. *How long have I been someone else's lackey?*

ZACH CALLED LATE on Monday while I was in a mid cleaning binge. Now that Manny was in the mix, it seemed virtually impossible to keep my apartment clean: The minute I got done vacuuming, he seemed to shed an entire coat all over again. I was just about to start scrubbing the toilet when the phone rang.

"Uh, hey, hold on, I'm on top of my toilet," I blurted out, then realized exactly how that sounded when he didn't respond. "Um, no, I mean, I'm cleaning my toilet and was leaning on it to reach in the back and get the nasty grime." *Holy Christ. Shut up!* My bumbling mind was too busy frantically trying to recapture what, if anything, had transpired over the weekend to pull out a coherent sentence. So after he asked how I was feeling, and after I thanked him for the home-cooked meal, I just put it out there and asked.

"Did anything happen between us on Saturday night?" I paused, trying to possibly maintain even a shred of dignity while admitting to a blackout. Then I realized this was an oxymoron, and I felt my pulse quicken and continued. "Um, because I woke up in your bed, and I really don't remember much." I stuck the phone between my ear and my neck and peeled off my rubber gloves.

"High-class marijuana can do that to you." He laughed. "Relax, Natalie, no. Nothing happened. I figured that you could use a good night's sleep, so when you passed out on the couch, I took you into my room and left you there. No peeking, no nothing. I slept in the living room."

"Oh. Okay. I wasn't sure," I said, as I washed my hands in my bathroom sink.

"Would it have been so awful if something had?"

I saw my cheeks flame in the mirror and worried that he could see them through the telephone line.

"I have cancer."

"I know."

"I'm not available. I have cancer."

"I don't see what one has to do with the other."

"Cancer makes me unavailable, Zach. I'm not sure what you don't get." I plunked the lid closed on the toilet and sat down.

"Okay," he said slowly. "Well, if that's your reasoning."

"And I think Lila wants you back."

My stomach plunged with both relief and regret: relief because it changed the subject, regret because it wasn't a subject that I wanted to illuminate. Zach went silent, and I heard Manny whimpering from a bad dream in my bedroom.

"What makes you say that?" he finally said.

"She called earlier. Wanted to know about Saturday night. She pressed me for details—how you looked, what you made, how you acted." I started scraping my thumbnail over a hard water stain on my shower door.

"I hope you told her that the company was second only to the fine food," he said.

I ignored him. "But I'd say the real tip-off was when she said, 'I think I want him back.'" I heard him sigh, and an awkward silence filled the line again. I slipped off the toilet onto the cold white tiles on the floor. "So you wouldn't take her back?"

"No," he said quietly.

"I don't think that will stop her from trying." And it was true.

His cell phone rang in the background, and he asked me to hold on. I heard him muttering into his phone but couldn't make out the details.

"Natalie. I'm sorry. I have to take this; it's work. Listen, have a great time at your holiday party, and a good holiday if I don't speak with you. Go easy on yourself. Remember that next year can't be worse than this one. And I'll talk to you soon."

We clicked good-bye, and I leaned back onto the porcelain tub. *This is going to be complicated,* I thought. *And maybe complicated isn't what I need.* Then I thought, *Maybe I won't know what I need until I can't live without it.*

ROUND FOUR

. . .

December

· ELEVEN ·

Nobody particularly enjoyed the annual office holiday Christmas party, but Dupris threw it each year regardless. Initially, I figured that I finally had a slam-dunk excuse not to go: my bald head and ailing condition and all of that. But after Blair's e-mails, Dupris had called me personally and told me how much she'd like to see me there. Since my job made me a professional ass-kisser who wasn't used to telling her boss no, I found myself agreeing to her invitation over the phone, all the while willing myself to make up a reason that I couldn't. That the senator's true intentions shined through—namely, for me to hang my tail between my legs with Susanna Taylor, not bestow my fabulous personality on the crowd—was not lost on me.

The best thing about this party was always the food. The company? Well, these were people with whom I spent eighty hours a week already; honestly, was it any surprise that we all had to be sloshed to endure the night? True, there were often various dignitaries and fairly high and mighty government officials in attendance too, but still, it was the buffet that beckoned—thus my rationale when, just before I left for the affair, I sat on my couch, with the lights dimmed and Van Morrison playing on my stereo, and smoked through nearly two joints by myself. When I felt sufficiently high, and by that I mean high enough that even the buffet at the Olive Garden would have looked five star, I opened my windows to air out my living room, grabbed my black cashmere overcoat and leather gloves, and left Manny in a plume of smoke. No need for a hat: My embroidered black scarf already kept my head warm enough.

As it always was, the party was held at the Rainbow Room, perched on the top floor of Rockefeller Center. When the elevator landed on the nearly sky-high floor, just for a second I felt a flash of vertigo—like the car was going to plummet as quickly as it rose. But then we settled to a stop, and it let me off with nothing more than a pleasant *ding*. I followed the holiday music around the corner to the ballroom.

Each year, the senator hired one of the city's top party planners ("I pay for it myself," she said, in case anyone worried that this was on the taxpayers' dime), and this year, Parker Hewitt had outdone himself. The theme was White Christmas, and everywhere you turned, there were glowing white lights; blossoming, fragrant gardenias; and stark, towering candelabras. Cascades of white rose petals hung from the ceiling, so that it literally looked like it was snowing. In each corner, Parker had erected regal Christmas trees, replete with glimmering, silver ornaments and topped with perfect, radiant angels. Maybe it was the two joints or maybe it was simply that it really was magical, but either way, when I stepped into the room and inhaled the scent from the rose petals, spiced cider, and glorious buffet, I felt like I might faint. My eyes saw double, and my head started to spin, and when I looked down at my silver Stuart Weitzmans, they barely seemed connected to my feet. I was contemplating my ethereal, world-spinning existence when Senator Dupris came up behind me.

"Natalie, so glad you could make it," she said, as she air-kissed both cheeks. Then she caught a look in my nearly glazed-over eyes. "Is everything okay?"

Nodding yes, I forced myself to breathe in through my nose and out through my mouth and tried desperately to focus. I grabbed a glass of sparkling water from a passing waiter and felt my pulse slow down.

"Good, dear, because as Blair might have mentioned, I'd like you to compose yourself and go speak to Susanna Taylor." Dupris cocked her perfectly bobbed head and peered around. "Oh, there she is. By the piano in the blue dress. Please take care of this before anything else, dear. Oh, and Merry Christmas, Natalie. Good things are in store for you next year, I'm sure of it." She leaned in to give me another air kiss, and before I could wrap my brain around her missive, she flitted off.

Fuck. I clenched my jaw and heaved my feet forward. *What the hell do I say to a woman whose life I torpedoed like a submarine?* I still didn't have an opening line by the time I reached the baby grand. So instead, I stuck out my hand.

"Susanna, I'm Natalie Miller, Senator Dupris's senior aide."

She offered a thin smile. "Yes, I know who you are. I'm sorry to hear about your ordeal. I certainly know how it feels to be struck with something so debilitating." I met her eyes and took her in. Her hair was already growing back—longer than a crew cut but shorter than a pixie, the style reminded me of the hip late nineties androgynous model look. She was thin, but not emaciated like me, and underneath her silk shawl on her shoulders, I could make out the shadows of growing muscle tone. She was a veteran of war, rehabilitated, sent home from the front lines. I was the reinforcement.

"Yes, well . . ." I stopped, unsure of how to fill the dead air. "Look, I just want to cut to why I came over here." I paused, slowing down so that the room wouldn't spin. "And that was to say that I'm sorry that the campaign got so nasty. Some of the things that we did, well, we shouldn't have, and for that, I'm truly regretful." I looked at her as I spoke. What I didn't see when I first took her in was that a darkness had been cast over her eyes, a weariness had washed across her face, even though her makeup was immaculate and her diamond earrings sparkling. And I realized that though I was just recognizing it for the first time, I *was* truly sorry. Not even for what I did, but for the wreckage it could have caused. I reached out for her arm. "Honestly, Susanna, I wouldn't do it over again."

She looked down at her feet and sighed. And then she shook her head and said, "People have certainly made worse decisions in their lives. And it's not as if my husband didn't give you ammunition." She smiled.

"So you knew about it?" My eyes widened.

"You know, Natalie, if there's one thing I've learned through this whole horrific mess, it's that the world isn't necessarily black and white. I'm a good person, and yet . . . and yet this." She gestured down at her body. "I love my husband, and yet, he does what he does. People do the wrong things and people certainly say the wrong things—I'm sure you've gotten some outstandingly inappropriate comments since your diagnosis—and then you have a choice: to either stew in it or to move past it." She shrugged. "I moved past my husband's 'problem' because for me, right now, there is no other way."

I nodded and pressed my lips together as if to say that I understood. "Well, anyway, I just wanted to come and say that our office regretted it. It was nice meeting you." I smiled and turned to go.

"Natalie, listen." She touched my shoulder. "I run a support group for women who are dealing with cancer: breast, ovarian, uterine, you name it. If you'd like to come to a meeting, I'd love to have you there."

"Oh, well, I'm not sure if that's really my thing," I said, as I looked at my feet. *There's no 'we' in Natalie.*

"It tends not to be anyone's thing until they discover that they have cancer." Susanna laughed. "Look, it's not touchy-feely, and we usually don't even discuss our illnesses, but it's nice to know that we can if we want. Sometimes we'll go shopping and sometimes we'll sit around and cry, but I think that most of the women have found it very therapeutic." I thought of a group of sorry sobbing thirtysomethings sitting around in a circle, and my nonexistent hair stood on end.

Look for small gifts, I heard Janice's voice, and quickly pushed it away. "Yeah, I'm not sure."

"Well, just in case you change your mind." She reached for her purse and pulled out a card, pressing it into my palm. "Call me. It would be nice."

I assured her that I would, though I had no intention of ever, ever engaging in public displays of grief with various other cancer victims, but I lost track of that thought because suddenly I was ravenous. Rabid, fervently hungry. I pushed past a swarm of VIPs to the buffet table. A mountain of hors d'oeuvres awaited. A virtual volcano of dips, vegetables, fruits, cheeses, crackers, quiches, crab cakes, skewers, samosas, spanakopita, and sushi. And this didn't even include dessert. I reached for a plate just before a congressman and squeezed past him. I had tunnel vision and no one—not a congressman, not his wife, not even the senator herself—was getting in my way. I was eating before things even touched my plate. I'd put one quiche in my mouth, then grab two more and move on. I'd stuff fried shrimp in with the quiche and barely wait to swallow before inhaling another. By the time I made my way down the buffet and stacked my plate so full that not even a speck of white showed through, I'd practically eaten an entire meal already. But, you see, when you're a novice toker and still gauging the impact of marijuana on your system, and when you've recently smoked two joints by yourself, that was neither here nor there.

I was standing near a small, round cocktail table, halfway through my second serving, and licking my fingers when suddenly, just as I had when I entered the ballroom, I felt a rush of blood to my head. I twirled around, hands outstretched, looking for a chair, a windowsill, anything to sink into until the floor stopped moving like I was on a cruise ship. And in the absence of these stabilizers and with the ever-increasing spinning of my brain, coupled with an extreme drowsiness that almost instantly walloped my system, I half-leaned, half-sat on the cocktail table, pushing aside the partly drunk plastic cups and balled-up, dirty napkins. Feeling perhaps overconfident by the relief this half-lean brought, I scooted my butt nearly completely on top of the table, and for a second, heaved a sigh: The twinkling white world high atop Manhattan had stopped rotating. I nodded my head. *This, ladies and gentlemen, was good living.*

I heard the crunch before I felt it. Rented cocktail tables—and let me be the first to tell you this, in case you are unaware and should find yourself in similar such circumstances—are not made to support the weight of a grown woman, even if said grown woman has recently lost a healthy portion of her body fat. Because as soon as I heard the metal legs collapsing, I felt them, too: I was sucked to the floor as the table folded nearly on top of me.

The impact of my crash landing was so loud that the band stopped playing, and the guests literally spun around and jumped, as if a bomb had exploded. I might have died of embarrassment underneath the mound of broken plates, half-eaten appetizers, and splashes of white wine and vodka if I hadn't found it so damn funny. By the time Kyle made his way over and managed to unwrap me from the previously lustrous white tablecloth and pull me to my feet, I'd nearly cried off all of my makeup, I was laughing so hard.

"Are you okay?" he asked, with a sympathy not normally heard in his voice. "Let's get you home."

"That would probably be best," I responded, mocking his solemnity and brushing off tiny bites of pigs-in-a-blanket from my black A-line dress.

"I suspect you may hate yourself in the morning," he said, as he handed the coat checker my ticket.

"That probably won't be hard," I replied, as we got in the elevator and I pressed the button to take me down.

ON A BLUSTERY day in mid-December, my mom cashed in some personal time from work, took the train up from Philly, and embarked on an adventure that most mothers would consider themselves lucky not to endure. Wig shopping.

"This should be fun," my mom said in a halfhearted tone that I recognized from high school, back when, in an effort to add some extracurricular activities to my resume, I'd signed up to be in charge of the costumes for the drama department's production of *Fiddler on the Roof.* My mother, who left the house at exactly 8:15 every morning, silver coffee cup in hand, Ferragamo pumps clicking on our marble foyer floor, had been taught to sew by my grandmother. You wouldn't think it, not with her couture-filled closet that was steadfastly organized by color, but when my parents first married, long before she became the first woman partner at her law firm, long before my father became a preeminent engineer who helped construct Philadelphia's largest buildings, she whipped up her own outfits and living room drapes. So I figured, when I announced my new costumer position just as she arrived home at 7:15 sharp—this was every night for as long as I could remember—that she would be thrilled. Instead, she pressed her lips together and said, "This should be fun." Thus, for the next few weeks, after some initial instruction, she left me on my own, and I spent the bulk of my free hours huddled over an old sewing machine in the garage, shoulder blades aching, neck in knots, kept company by nothing more than the smell of oil cans, Y100 radio, and our golden retriever, Curly.

And although wig shopping was not exactly the *wedding-dress-must-have-Mom-there* experience, I wanted my mother there all the same. Because now that I had adjusted to the cycle of chemo—exhausted, then somewhat delirious, then a-okay—I wanted to go back to work. True, I was mortified, almost wary to the point of paralysis, to show my face at the office, but it was a risk I had to take. As Janice predicted, my journal did indeed point my thoughts elsewhere, but it wasn't enough. I could watch only so much daytime television and hunt down old boyfriends without turning into my own personal soap opera. So I put my pride on hold and called the senator.

"Are you sure that you're ready?" she asked, politely overstepping the elephant in the room; namely, my performance at the Christmas party.

My impulse was to jump in with an overly confident yes, but I held it back for a second, because the truth of the matter was that I had no idea if I were ready or not. So instead, I answered, "The thing is, Senator, I know that I can make a difference. And I'd really like to this term. Remember how inspired we were when you first won your seat?" She murmured that she did. "Well, that's how I feel now. Inspired. Like I've been given a new shot. And I'd like to make something of that."

And it was true. The more information I garnered about stem cell research, the more I felt the fire rise up inside of me. At first, after the senator asked me to start digging on the subject, I'd logged on to the Internet whenever I had a free moment from my time spent watching game shows on the couch or Googling my exes. But as I dove further and further into the research, and uncovered the potential miracles that it held, it snowballed on me: I began to tear into the task like Cujo does to his next victim. Namely, rabidly. And my ferocity arose because I had a genuine interest in advancing a bill that would allow for public funding of stem cell research. Not just a genuine interest, but a personal one. I knew that if my cancer chose to launch a new attack on me or if the doctors hadn't found it in time or Ned hadn't rubbed up against my breast that morning, the insidious disease might have made its way into my bones, and that one day, whether in the near or distant future, stem cells might save my life. Or the life of someone just like me.

"Fair enough, Natalie. We'll see you when Congress resumes session in a few weeks," Dupris said, and I heard Blair enter her office in the background. The senator paused. "Are you feeling better? No more 'incidents' like at the party?"

And there it was. My cheeks burned as if on fire. "No. No. Definitely not." I paced up and down my living room. "That was, uh, a weird response to my medication. It won't happen again."

"Very good. I'll see you then. Looking forward to having you back on the team." Before I could say good-bye, she'd clicked off.

Now, I know that it would be wonderful and heartwarming and *terribly brave* of me to tackle the Senate or even just the subway with my cue-balled head. And I know you'd be reading this and thinking, Hurrah! Go her! She's triumphant: staring down cancer and defying it to rob her of her pride. She's a Lifetime television movie and a feminist icon all rolled into one. And I know that I might have mentioned that getting a wig was maybe not my thing, that I took it as a sign of weakness, that I saw it as a crutch.

But the truth of the matter was that over these months, cancer had robbed me of enough. It stole my health, along with my confidence, my sense of self, and my understanding of how life evolved. And yes, it also stole my pride. So I figured that if donning someone else's hair that had been fashioned into something that I could pass off as my own somehow gave me just a small sliver of my dignity back, so help me, I was reaching for it. And besides, really, look around. How many bald women do you really, truly see on the streets of New York City? Don't get me wrong: I have total respect for them. They are, indeed, *terribly brave*. But I figured that brave was all subjective. The mere fact that I was still alive in light of what I was facing made me brave enough to live with myself. And that's all that mattered to me.

So I ignored that tiny voice in my head that still softly reminded me that *"There's no 'we' in Natalie,"* and I called my mother and asked her to join me for my appointment to one Mrs. Adina Seidel, wigmaker to the stars (or New York's upper-crust Orthodox set, at the very least).

"This is just the pick-me-up you need," Mom said, reaching for my hand as the subway rattled and clanked and hurled us to the outer stretches of Brooklyn to pay a visit to the infamous Mrs. Seidel. I was too self-conscious of our hand-holding to answer her back. Never in my thirty years had my mother ever reached for my hand. Not when Jake left me, not when I got wait-listed at Harvard, not even when she sat with me through my first round of chemo.

The train lurched to a stop, and I wearily climbed the two flights of stairs, leaning on my mother's arm with each step. Though it was December, the sun shone brightly, so I squinted my eyes and peered around. Brooklyn. Tiny storefronts cluttered every last open space on the street. Electronics. Shoe stores. Family-run grocers. The din of voices rose above the honking of taxis, and I noticed an overweight man with a bloodied apron tied around his waist shouting and raising his arms at another man just to my right. The sidewalks milled like ant farms with bearded men in long, dark coats and high hats who took pains to walk around my mother and me, casting their eyes downward, touching their tzitzit as they passed. Sometimes, they strolled with gaggles of children, one on each hand, along with a woman, I'd assume the wife, who would try in vain to discipline them. My mother and I pushed off from our perch on the subway, wordlessly taking it all in. It felt like a foreign country, this little outpost of Manhattan, as if their little community was protected from the thriving metropolis that pulsed to their north. Here was what mattered. Here, they had everything they needed.

You wouldn't notice the wig shop unless you were looking for it. In fact, we *were* looking and walked right by two times. Crammed between a kosher bakery and a tailor was a window full of bodiless mannequins topped off with more hairstyles than an '80s band. A bell rang as we opened the door, and an enormously bosomed, apron-clad woman with graying hair that was pulled back into a tightly wound bun emerged from behind a sea of manes.

"Ah, you must be Ms. Miller." Both my mother and I nodded our heads. "Oh my darling," she said in a heavy Yiddish accent and beckoned us with her arms. "Come, come. Let's give you back a head of hair today."

She pulled me over to a swivel chair in front of a mirror and clapped her hands.

"So! Let us begin. What are you looking for? Something to match your old hair?"

I thought of my chestnut locks, strands that I'd always wished would be more interesting, straighter, shinier. Now, I just wished that I had them back.

"I'm really not sure what I want," I demurred.

"Okay, well, let's take a look at your face." She stood behind me and ran her fingers over my skin and cupped my cheeks in her hands. "So beautiful, you are. Cancer has not changed that. High cheekbones, wide eyes. Perfect." She looked over to my mother and smiled. "You did a nice job, you know." She clapped her hands again. "Okay! We will start with a few options, and you can narrow as you go."

She ran into the back, behind a curtain, to grab some choices that conceivably could redefine me. While she was gone, I looked around the shop. It was immaculate. Literally, not a hair out of place. On the counter, near the front, was a desk calendar in Hebrew that sat next to a beige phone that you might have seen in 1987. And beside the phone was a box for *tzedakah*: where patrons could donate money for the less well-off. I glanced out the window and watched passersby scurry past on the sidewalk, all of the women in matching bobbed wigs, long skirts to cover their skin. I wondered if their faith in God would be enough for them to get through an ordeal like mine. If they would read the Torah and sing at synagogue and trust in Him enough to pull them through. Or if He didn't pull them through, if they would accept their fates as acts of His will, quietly resigned to the fact that God dictated this path, even if it was not one they would have chosen for themselves.

Mrs. Seidel emerged from the back with a flourish. "My darling, here are your first few choices. We will narrow from here until we find just the right match."

The first one I tried was too ordinary: It looked just like the molded hair I'd seen on the sidewalk minutes before. The next was too red: My pale skin looked even more wan next to it, and for a second, I was reminded not just of the fact that I was buying a wig, but the reasons for it in the first place. I waved off the third before even trying it on; a brunette version of Little Orphan Annie, I was not. With a quick turn of her heels, Mrs. Seidel was off again to the back, returning with more bounty.

We got it right on the seventh try. In my past life, I was an ordinary brunette, my quick flirtation with fiery red aside. My hair fell squarely on my shoulders, and Paul dutifully trimmed the ends every six weeks so it neither wandered too long nor grew too unwieldy. It was, in essence, the perfect haircut for politics: It was there because it had to be, neither offending nor impressing, flying under the radar, and getting the job done. So when Mrs. Seidel adjusted the seventh wig, muttering in Yiddish under her breath as she pinned it on and brushed it out, even I was surprised to discover that I had to have it. The rich chocolate, nearly black, locks cascaded down my back, landing just below the bra strap that crossed under my shoulder blades. When I turned my head side to side, the layers flowed effortlessly over one another, the light from the ceiling bouncing off them as if in an Herbal Essences commercial.

"This is it," I said. "This is the one."

"Natalie," my mom said. "It's so different from before. So . . . I don't know. Showy." She paused, and I searched her voice for criticism, but found none. "Not that anything's wrong with that. But are you sure? For your line of work?"

Mrs. Seidel fluffed out the hair in her hands, and I swear, it felt as if she were combing out my own. I stared through the mirror and wondered if, in just a moment, you could reinvent yourself.

AS WE WERE leaving, after she'd shown me how to maintain the wig and after she'd run my mother's credit card through, Mrs. Seidel grasped my hand.

"You are Jewish, no?" she asked.

"Yes, well, partly." I gestured to my mom. "She is, so I am, too."

"I thought so. This is good." She paused, holding her finger to her chin. "I look at you, and you are so beautiful. Too young for this disease, it is true, but still beautiful. But you do not seem to have much faith."

I wanted to run. It was like my bat mitzvah lessons all over again. My tutor, Ms. Goodstein, called my parents in for a meeting six weeks before I was due on the bimah.

"She is a good learner," she explained to my parents, while I hung my head and folded my hands in front of me. "She has memorized her parts, she can sing clearly and even beautifully." She stopped. "But she has no passion. She doesn't seem to even want to learn. She has no connection to what she is supposed to be telling the congregation."

My parents looked at me, and I shrugged. I'd only agreed to go along with the bat mitzvah thing because it hadn't been phrased to me as a question. When I was twelve, my mother announced that I'd start my lessons in a few months, and before I had a chance to explain that I wasn't sure about my faith, her office called, and she stepped out of my bedroom as quickly as she stepped into it.

"Is this true?" my mom asked, as she unconsciously cracked the knuckles on her fingers. "Are your lessons boring you? Would you rather not be a Jew?"

I shook my head and pressed back the rising tears. What could I say? That I memorized my Torah portion because I was told to? That I learned the melodies of the haftarah as if they were an algebra lesson? That God was as unclear to me as my new and muddled feelings for boys, and that even though I knew I should revere Him, all I really did was question? No. Instead, I murmured that I would try harder, and six weeks later, I was showered in presents after delivering the most passionless haftarah portion my synagogue had ever sat through.

I stared at my wig, held captive on the other side of the Formica counter, and realized with a wave of nausea that Mrs. Seidel was Ms. Goodstein déjà vu.

"It's hard to have faith right now . . . with all this," I answered, and waved my hands in front of my body. And then, as they always do when I think about my destiny, my eyes filled with tears.

"But that is when you need to have faith the most, my dear." Mrs. Seidel placed her hands on my shoulders and looked into my welling eyes. "That is when our forefathers believed more than anything: when they were oppressed and when life seemed too terrible to even fathom and when there was no light for them to cling to. That is when they most believed."

"Maybe they were better people than I am."

"No," she said, dropping her arms. "Maybe it's just because they didn't think that there was any other way."

I shrugged. "I'm not sure if God can be my way. I've tried to believe in Him several times in the past few months, and it seems each time I do, more crap flares up, and I get angry all over again." I paused, not wanting to offend her. "I'm just being honest."

"Oh, you can be angry," Mrs. Seidel said, as she retreated behind the counter to retrieve my bag. "There were many times when our people were angry. But they didn't stop believing, no matter how often they threw their hands up and raged. They had faith that this was part of His plan."

"I guess I don't have that sort of faith," I said. "I guess none of this seems fair. I guess God hasn't quite clearly explained to me why the hell this happened, and each time I think, okay, I might just make it, I get slapped down with something else."

Mrs. Seidel clasped my hand in her chubby, wrinkled fingers, so even if I wanted to bolt, I couldn't. I was her captive. "If you choose not to believe, that is okay." She smiled. "So the question becomes, not why hasn't God brought you good fortune, but how can you bring good fortune upon yourself?"

◆　◆　◆

Dear Diary,

I haven't spoken to Zach since I last wrote, nearly two weeks ago. He e-mailed me a few days ago to make sure that I was doing okay and to see if I needed more "stuff," that's how he put it because I suppose that he couldn't very well write "pot" in his work e-mail, but I wrote him back and told him that I was okay. I've figured out how many hits I need to stimulate my appetite without getting ridiculously high, so I haven't burned through (literally! ha!) the whole bag yet.

Even though he didn't mention it, I know that Lila called him. As soon as she got back into town after New Year's. (Which,

Diary, I should note, I spent curled up with Manny on the couch watching Ryan Seacrest host numerous lip-synching tweeny pop stars. It wasn't a personal best.) I don't think she really suspected that anything happened between Zach and me, but I guess seeing him happy and normal and well-adjusted with other women sent her into a spiral, so I think she's presently in the midst of concocting a plan to win him back. I know that he told me that he wouldn't take her, but Sally mentioned that he and Lila were getting drinks last weekend, so I don't know. Maybe I misinterpreted that whole thing between us.

So, Diary, after having brought you up to speed on that situation, I guess the reason that I'm writing is because I did manage to catch up with Dylan. You know: law school assistant professor who went totally amuck? Yeah, well, who knew that he was right here in the city? It's a small miracle that in day-to-day life, I haven't run into him because he's actually working at Cravath right around the corner from the senator's office. I know that I'm questioning my faith in God right now, but I would like to say a short prayer of thanks for steering me in the opposite direction of Dylan in the city. It's almost fate that our paths haven't yet crossed. Or was almost fate, I should say, since I took it upon myself—you know, in my efforts to retrace the past—to pretty much change all of that.

I found him in Yale's alumni directory, and when I called him up, his secretary asked me to repeat my name three times, then unceremoniously put me on hold for six minutes. "He's in a meeting," she said, when she came back on the line. "In a real meeting meeting?" I asked. "Or a fake meeting because he doesn't want to talk to me?" "A real meeting," she responded curtly and asked if I wanted to be put into his voice mail. Before I had a chance to reply, she dumped me in.

I left a fairly idiotic message, stumbling, stuttering, repeating my phone number twice, which in hindsight might have made me sound a little desperate. As if, just in case he missed it the first time, here it is again! Call me. Call me! Oh well. I'd done it, and I really didn't expect him to call anyway. Dylan really was the type who faked meetings and illnesses and all sorts of things just to get out of whatever he didn't want to do. I saw him master his skills when he was in the midst of a divorce (he married young) at Yale and screwing around with me.

But I digress. I was just about to take Manny out for a walk when the phone rang. Frankly, I figured it was Kyle. He and I had been e-mailing about how to appease the senator's constituents who felt like she might back off some of her tax reduction promises, and it was getting a little too complicated to keep writing. He wanted PR spin; I thought, and this was a new tactic for me, that we should just tell them the truth: that in order to fund Homeland Security measures and keep the garbagemen happy with their pay, tax cuts simply weren't on the agenda for the year.

Anyway, so when the phone rang, I answered it with a run-on sentence, something about coming clean with the voters because ultimately, they had to trust the senator's overall vision. When he cleared his throat, I immediately recognized the deep baritone—think Barry White, but on a handsome yet pale blond guy—and knew that it wasn't Kyle.

"Miller," he said, calling me by my last name like he always did. "I never expected to hear from you again. What gives? Does your senator need someone to bail her out of hot water?" I felt dirty, and sort of like I wanted to vomit, but I resisted the urge and didn't take his taunting bait. That was our thing, or at

least it used to be. Our banter was never playful: It was pushy, it was in-your-face, it was borderline hostile but not enough so that we ever stepped back to question what the hell we were doing. Dylan, in essence, was the quintessential alpha dog, really, Diary, perhaps the male version of me, and during my second year in law school, when he led a lecture in Professor Randolph's absence, I was mesmerized, no, maybe infatuated is a better word, with the way that he took command of the class. Yale students were notoriously diligent; we paid attention to most lectures regardless. But when Dylan spoke it was different—he wasn't the teacher and we weren't his students. Rather, he was the star and we were his mere audience. He posted office hours at the end of class, and I went. I had to have him.

Now, when I heard his voice, my mind flashed with tumult. And I instantly felt foolish for calling. I didn't need to pick apart why this relationship dissolved. I already knew: We were too similar—in our quest for the top, in our desire for control, in pushing someone away when they'd rather move closer. But I asked him anyway, Diary. I figured, why not? And besides, he'd definitely think I was a huge ass for calling with nothing to say.

So I said to him, "Why were we so combustible? Why did we settle for a half-warm relationship when I think we both knew that it would never get hotter?" And he said, "Miller, is that really how you see it? Six years later, that's what you think? Because I thought we had a pretty damn good time." Fair enough, I agreed. We certainly didn't have a bad time. In fact, the sex might have been the best ever (needless to say, Diary, I did not tell him that), but still, wasn't there something that was lacking? I mean, together for two years, we were. And never once did we say, "I love you." Never once did we talk about our future. I graduated and moved on. Left him in New Haven. And he never tried to stop me, so I assumed that he never wanted to.

"You're missing the point, Miller," he said. "You're analyzing this like a lawyer would, not like someone who was in our position at the time would. At the time, we held our own pretty well—it wasn't a fairy tale, but it was great for what it was. And I was just coming out of a divorce; I didn't want to fall in love. And you? You were tough as nails, so you weren't looking to be loved in the first place."

I held the phone to my ear and stared at the picture frames that littered my desk. A college formal, law school graduation, my folks and me in Philly on our back deck. Who ever said anything about not being loved? I finally caught my breath and asked him why he thought that, why he thought that anyone would possibly choose not to be loved, because certainly, that wasn't my intention.

He thought about it. I heard him crushing some ice in his teeth and realized he was really thinking about it. And then he said, "I don't know, Miller. I always had the impression that for you, other things came first, mattered more. I was just someone who was a warm body for you to mark time with, nothing more, nothing less. And I thought that's all we wanted from each other, even while we were having a grand go of it." He grew quiet before something else came to mind. "I guess I always figured that you were a hard enough nut that you didn't want to be cracked. And that somewhere along the line, you figured that love came second. The rest of your life came first."

I stood for a long time after talking to Dylan, staring out my living room window. My apartment was quiet; I couldn't even hear the street noise below. All I could hear was Mrs. Seidel's gentle but firm voice as she handed me my wig. "So the question becomes, not why hasn't God brought you good fortune, but how can you bring good fortune upon yourself?" How can I indeed?

· TWELVE ·

W e're going to run some tests," Dr. Chin said. "Similar to what you first got when we diagnosed you. We'd like to see how well you're responding to the chemo."

I nodded and tried to go numb. I knew that this was coming; they'd warned me at my last appointment. After the fourth round of chemo, they like to gauge how well it's working, whether or not the chemicals they shoot into me every three weeks are killing more than just my hair follicles and my spirit. If the tumors are reduced, they continue. Or they might even operate. If the tumors are still thriving, we'd need to rethink our efforts. Effectively, these were the tests that would tell me which side of the 50/50 odds of beating Stage III I'd fall into.

It was hard to believe that I was halfway done. Time does a funny thing to you. Sometimes, it goes so slowly, like in your senior year in high school when all you want to do is press the fast-forward button and get out, that it's almost excruciating. And sometimes, like when Jake and I were resting in bed, listening to each other's heartbeats, it was as if gravity had taken hold and no matter how hard you tried to hang on, it roared past; you'd do anything to get it back.

Sally had come with me. My father was receiving an award in Australia for a bridge his company designed and my mother was with him. The plans had been made long before my diagnosis, so Sally was my next best option.

"This is such a big honor," Mom had explained on the phone when I mentioned that Australia seemed like an awfully long way away from Sloan-Kettering. "You dad would be terribly disappointed."

I snorted and wondered if my dad had any say in the matter to begin with. "Mom, I just . . . what if something goes wrong? You'll be halfway around the world." I paused. "I'd like to know that you're here if I need you."

"Oh honey." She sighed. "We're always here if you need us. We'll just be a bit farther away."

Today, while I sat in my flimsy flowered paper robe in the stark examination room, waiting for the nurse to wheel in the ultrasound machine, Sally casually brought up Lila. And Zach.

"Do you want to know what's going on?" she asked, as she pressed her palms into her thighs.

"Why wouldn't I?" I asked.

"Because every time his name comes up, you get this sour look on your face, so I'm pretty sure that you either want to know so badly that it's eating you up inside or else you truly don't want to know, and thus, I won't tell you."

"Unfortunately, no, that's not what's eating me up inside. If that were the only thing that was eating me up inside, I certainly wouldn't need an ultrasound to tell me how to treat it." I sighed. "Fine. Yes, tell me what's going on."

"Did something happen with you two? That night at his apartment? Because why all the bitterness?"

"No, Sally, nothing happened. Need I remind you? I have cancer." I focused on the pale green wallpaper and tried to avoid meeting her eyes.

"Yes, that's clear," she said. "But I'm not sure why it's relevant."

"Because I have cancer."

"Uh-huh. Again, clear."

"How can I possibly be attractive to someone right now?"

Sally let out a long breath. "Okay then. If that's how you're going to play it. Here's the lowdown. From what Lila has told me, they met for drinks twice. Both times she initiated. And after the second time, she kissed him."

I felt myself blanch and didn't respond. Finally, I said, "Did they go home together?"

"No." Sally shook her head. "Lila tried to work it, you know how she does. But they left it at that. I think she's going to call him for dinner this week."

"Figures," I muttered, and stared at my toes.

"What? What figures?"

"Just that he told me that he wouldn't take her back." I picked imaginary lint off the sterile hospital gown.

"Well, maybe he wasn't sure. Or maybe whatever Lila said

made him change his mind." She paused and put down the dog-eared copy of *Glamour* she'd been flipping through. "Sweetie, if you want to be with him, why not just tell him when he expressed it to you?" I glared at her. "I know. I know. You have cancer." She looked a bit too harshly back at me. "Nat, Zach knows that, too."

I wiggled my toes and then stared up at the rectangular fluorescent light on the ceiling.

"I was trying to protect him, Sally. Why should he be with a damaged set of goods like me? I don't know if I'll ever be able to have kids. Hell, I don't know if I'll be alive next fall. It's just so much better for him not to get dragged in. Besides, how can my body possibly be attractive to anyone at this point?"

She looked at me, her harsh gaze growing soft, and for a quick millisecond I thought I saw pity. In that moment, I relented: Maybe she was right. She took a breath and responded.

"It seems to me that *he's* not the one you're trying to protect."

THE NEWS COULD not have been better. Dr. Chin actually said this. "The news could not be better."

The tests indicated that the chemo was having the desired, even better than desired, effect. My tumor had markedly declined in size, and my lymph nodes were virtually cancer-free.

"Your progress is remarkable," Dr. Chin told me, after I'd gotten dressed and was seated in his office, clenching Sally's hand and trying with every healthy cell in my body not to explode into a waterfall of tears. He flipped through some pages in my chart. "Better than we could have hoped for. So what I'd like to propose is that we do the mastectomy sooner rather than later. The tumor is of operable size, and I think the earlier we get it out of you, the better."

I inhaled sharply and squeezed Sally's hand tighter. I knew from the original diagnosis that there was little choice, that this moment was coming, and that hacking off one part of me to save the rest seemed like a reasonable compromise. Still though, when he said it, when the time crept up on me before I'd really given myself a chance to say good-bye to my breasts, I felt my heart break in the same way that it had that morning when it all started, the morning that Ned discovered the lump. But I didn't tell Dr. Chin any of this. Instead, I nodded and told him that was fine— that he could take my breasts whenever he felt necessary.

"You need to consider whether to have a single or double," he said, clearing his throat. "Obviously, there are pros and cons to each. Because you have a family history of breast cancer, there is a greater chance that it could reoccur in the left breast. Of course, you have to weigh the odds of this against how much you'd like to keep a part of yourself intact." He fell silent. "Many women opt for reconstructive surgery at the same time that they get the mastectomy. I suspect that it helps to get something back when we've just taken something else away. If you'd like, we can certainly schedule that as well."

I nodded again and didn't speak.

"I'll give you some time to think about this. If possible, we'd like to get you in next week. Why don't you take the night to consider your options and call me tomorrow."

I stared out the window the entire cab ride home and wondered whose life I was in, how it was possible that Natalie Miller, the supposed future American president and current feared and revered aide to a powerful senator, had been demolished into this.

How an otherwise healthy thirty-year-old found herself in the position of choosing how many breasts to surrender.

"What would you do?" I asked Sally when she dropped me off at my building. She was already distracted by an e-mail on her Palm from an editor she was trying to impress.

"Oh sweetie," she said. "I can't make this sort of monumental decision for you. I can't pretend to know how it feels."

"But what would you do?" I pressed, and my eyes welled with tears. "My parents are away, and I don't know who else to talk to. I'll make my own decision. But if you were me, what would you do?"

She took a deep breath and hugged me. "I would tell them to take them both. And then, I'd tell this cancer to fuck off and get back to living my life."

MY APARTMENT FELT claustrophobic, so despite the nearly freezing temperatures, Manny and I went out for a walk. *Fresh air is good for the soul,* Zach had said.

Manny and I cut over to Central Park West to head into the park. He stopped to sniff a street lamp, then tugged me harder and harder until we were in a near sprint. Then he stopped abruptly, tangling his leash under his front paws. When I looked down to unknot him, I saw the object of his overly zealous olfactory system: a lifeless squirrel, curled up on top of a patch of dried, skeletal leaves. On instinct, I tugged Manny back, pulling him up in the air, until he was far enough away that he couldn't take the squirrel in his teeth. We started to walk away, but I looked back: The squirrel looked perfect, alive almost, like it went to sleep on a bed of leaves and happened not to wake up in the morning. It was only when you peered closer that you noticed that its abdomen didn't rise and fall, and that there was a thin layer of white, crusty foam around its mouth. Dead. It was for sure.

My cell phone vibrated in my pocket, so I shifted Manny's leash to my left hand and flipped it open.

"Dr. Chin told me," I heard Janice say into my right ear. "And I wanted to make sure you were okay with things. This can be a very hard step."

I kept walking and watched the cold air billow out from Manny's snout. Rather than respond, I asked her the question that had been weighing on my mind.

"Do you think anything happens to us, Janice? You know . . . after we die?" She went silent, and I knew she wouldn't answer, that it was up to me to come to peace with the issues I wrestled with. "I mean, I'd always believed before my diagnosis, this time around was simply your one shot: that you better make the most of it now because once this opportunity passed you by, there were no second chances." I shrugged and pulled Manny across the park drive. "But now." My voice faltered. "I don't know."

"How does it make you feel?" she asked, and I heard her take a sip of what I imagined to be her green herbal tea.

"How is it supposed to make me feel?" I said and kicked the dead leaves in my path. "Terrified. Totally fucking pissed off." I paused. "Curious, I guess, too. I mean, what if there are just, like, millions and millions of people up there waiting for us, having, like, an incredible party and wondering why we're all so scared to die."

"So you believe that there's something more than this?" Janice asked.

"Honestly, who the hell knows?" I sighed. "I mean, up until a few months ago, no. We were worm food. But now . . ." I faltered again and bit my nearly frozen lip. "I guess that when you're staring down the barrel of your own mortality, it's awfully difficult to accept that this is all there is."

"You realize this is normal," Janice said when there was nothing else to say.

"And to think that most of our lives, all we want to be is 'normal.'" I laughed. "If people only knew how damn hard it really was." I exhaled. "Thanks for the call, Janice. To answer your original question, I'm okay. I'm fine. I'll deal."

She chuckled into the receiver before hanging up. "You know, Natalie, sometimes, it's okay to admit that you can't."

I dropped the phone back into my pocket, tugged at Manny's leash, and heard the frozen leaves crunch under my boots as we circled the park. I expected it to be deserted given the frigid air, but up in front of us, an elderly couple held hands and slowly strolled down the tree-covered sidewalk. We grew nearer, and I could hear her singing to him, though I couldn't quite make out the tune. He threw back his head and laughed, and moved his arm around her shoulder to kiss the top of her head. We passed them, and I turned to smile. They nodded back, and she kept singing. I thought of my grandmother who had faced this same disease with so much dignity, even when she didn't have a chance, and I imagined that if given that chance, she'd still be singing to my own grandfather.

No, I decided. These thirty years, they simply can't be it. There must be more than this. Or at least there had to be more for me. I didn't know if that meant that I'd come back as a squirrel or a dog or a man, or even if it meant that I'd just hover around up above, looking out for those who I might have been too busy for in the first thirty years, but as I watched Manny run his tongue along the three-day-old snow and dig in his nose, I knew that I wasn't ready to find out. At least not yet.

"I'M HAVING THEM take both. Lopping them both off," I said into the phone. "I wanted you to be the first to know." I stood in the kitchen and boiled water for my tea.

"Okay," he said. "Are you comfortable with the decision? Do you want to talk about it?"

"Not really." I shrugged. "It seems like the obvious choice: Why would I even risk the chance that I'd go through this again? Why even test it? I know that my grandmother would have happily given up her left breast in exchange for the chance to meet me."

"Seems reasonable," Zach said. And then we fell silent.

"I could use some more pot. It's really helping my eating, and I'm almost done with the original bag." I leaned back on the fridge and felt its cool exterior against my shoulder blades.

"No problem. Should I bring it over to you? I guess leaving it with your doorman could make him complicit in a crime. No need to drag him down into your sordid lifestyle, right?"

"Sure," I said. "That would be great. Tell me when, and I'll try to be here." And then I frantically grasped for some other reason for my call: The flimsy excuses that I'd already offered up were waving like pitiful white flags that the opposition was choosing to ignore.

"I'll bring it by this weekend." Zach paused. "Is that it?"

"I hear you're back with Lila," I said before I could think to stop myself.

"You might want to check your sources," he said. " 'Back with' connotes that it is something that it is not."

"So what is it?"

"Nothing. It's nothing. It was a few drinks and two dinners, and the sum of it is nothing."

"She doesn't think so. Which makes me not think so." I'd forgotten all about my water, which I just noticed had boiled itself into a fever pitch and was cascading over the sides of the pot. Frantically, I flipped off the burner and grabbed a dish towel from the hook on the cabinet.

"Why are you asking, Natalie? It seems that it's really not your place. You're close with Lila, so why don't you take it up with her?" His voice stirred with irritation. "If I recall, you suggested that we should stick it out as friends."

"You just said that you wouldn't take her back. So I wanted to know if you knew what you were getting into."

He sighed. "Natalie, I'm thirty-five. I'm pretty well aware of what I'm getting into. You don't have to warn me. Not with her and not with you." He paused, and I heard him tapping a pencil in the background. "Do you have some sort of problem with Lila and me, should there actually *be* a Lila and me?"

My ears flamed. "Of course not!" I replied, even though given the venom of my response, it was painfully clear that I had a terrible, terrible problem with it. I grabbed a tea bag from the cabinet and dropped it into my mug.

"It seems to me that you don't want me and yet you don't want me to be with anyone else."

"Don't be twelve," I said condescendingly. "I was just trying to be helpful."

"It seems to me," he said, just before we hung up, "that you should spend more time helping yourself and less time worrying about me. Maybe then, you'd let *me* help *you*."

. . .

I SIPPED THE tea and stared at the phone. I should have called him back. I should have told him I'm sorry. But I didn't. Instead, I curled my hands around my mug and felt its warmth seep into my palms, hoping that it might penetrate all the way to my core. *Maybe then, you'd let me help you.* I replayed his words over again in my mind, pushing my mother's age-old mantra, *there's no "we" in Natalie,* out of my head as it echoed just as loudly. I nodded to myself and walked into the living room to curl up on the couch. *Maybe then, I should.*

· THIRTEEN ·

I am woman, hear me roar," I thought to myself when I first opted for the double surgery. By the time it was here, I no longer had it in me. I was losing my breasts. And though there were a few things worse in the world—truly, I knew that there were—right now, with no one to talk to and not much to do, it didn't feel that way. Sally was busy with her deadlines: She'd just landed her first cover story for the *New York Times Magazine,* and though it wasn't due until after her wedding, she dove in headfirst out of sheer excitement. Quite coincidentally, the piece was on stem cell research, my pet project. I told her that I might have some information to help guide her, but she waved me off. "I'm still figuring out the angle," she said. "So I want to work independently until I see how best to tackle it." As a newly fledgling couple (or so Sally told me), Lila and Zach weren't options to keep me company, and my parents were in fucking Australia. I considered hitting the self-help section at Barnes and Noble or surfing the Web for some rabbinical spiritual enlightenment, but the thought just depressed me more. So instead I pressed the "on" button and heard my computer whirl its motors alive. I needed to write my mother.

I plunked down in my chair and ran my fingers over the keyboard. Surprisingly, it had been over forty-eight hours since I'd stared at the screen, which had to be some sort of record since high school. My monitor flashed on, and I ran my mouse over the icons that hovered over the backdrop of a photo of Dupris and me, just after we'd pushed a social security bill through Congress. I craned my neck forward to examine the picture on the screen a bit closer: Neither of our smiles quite met our eyes—hers almost always looked that way, but I suspect that my frozen facade had more to do with the fact that I was certain this bill would do nothing to actually improve the lives of senior citizens and less with the fact that I should have gotten used to hollow victories by then. Most of them were, it seemed. I pressed my index finger down on my mouse. Click. And pulled open my e-mail.

> From: Miller, Natalie
> To: Mom
> Re: Surgery
>
> Dear Mom and Dad—
>   I hope you're having fun on your trip. I had my checkup and things look so good that Dr. Chin is performing the mastectomy in two days. Mom—it looks like you don't know

everything after all because it turns out that it would have been nice for you to have been here. Maybe you should consider marking this day in history.

I guess it's too much for me to ask for you to come back, but since I am losing my breasts and all, I'll ask anyway. As I said, it would be nice to have you here.

Natalie

I reread the note. I tried not to make it sound too angry, too spiteful, because the truth of the matter was that though I *was* angry and I *was* spiteful and part of me just wanted to shout, "I fucking told you so," at my always-right, always-stoic mother, the other part of me knew that it wasn't worth it. That I could choose to rise above it and accept that my mother was who she was, and that no matter how angry I was, how fucking furious I was, and, ultimately, how betrayed I was that they could fly ten thousand miles away while I was in the midst of a literal life or death battle, at a certain point, you make a choice. And I'm not talking about the choice to accept my mother as is, which, I suppose, is also a very valiant, noble choice. No, the choice I'm talking about is whether to ask for help, whether to let someone in and say, "You know, you fucked up, and I'm hurting, but I still need you to come stand beside me, despite all of that." *There is no "we" in Natalie.* Maybe there wasn't, and maybe there still isn't, but that didn't mean that I couldn't ask. That I couldn't make the *choice* to put aside my ire and ask my parents to come join me as I faced down the most horrifying moment of my life.

I pressed Send and went into my in-box. There was only one new lonesome message, and given the address, I might rather that there had been none.

From: Taylor, Susanna

To: Miller, Natalie

Re: Meeting next week

Hi Natalie—

    I hope you don't mind that I got your e-mail from Blair. It was nice meeting you a few weeks back…obviously, the circumstances could have been better, but it was nice all the same.

    I hope that your treatments are going well, and that you're finding the energy to fight a good fight while still taking some time to pamper yourself. That was the hardest part for me, I think—remembering to be gentle both to and for myself.

    I'm writing because I wanted to let you know that the support group is meeting tomorrow, and I'd hoped that you might have changed your mind and would want to join. Don't worry—we don't sit around and sing "Kumbaya." In fact, I think we might go see a movie. Not sure yet.

    I do hope you'll come.

All my best,

Susanna

Well, I thought, rubbing my foot over Manny's stomach, at least I have a good excuse. I mean, losing your breasts had to be a "get out of jail free" card for at least a month or so. True, I was trying to be more open, but this I wasn't yet ready for. I hit Reply and kindly declined her offer.

TUESDAY NIGHT, THE night before they stole both of my breasts, I sunk into the bathtub and tried not to drown in my own fear. First, I called the senator to tell her that I wouldn't be back in the office by the fifth of January as planned. That I needed a few more weeks, but that I was well briefed in everything I needed to be on the stem cell situation, and that she could count on me for whatever she required. As soon as I hung up, the phone rang again. It was my parents from Australia: They'd changed their flight, but given the time it takes to fly back from halfway around the world, they wouldn't be back by tomorrow morning. They'd see me in recovery on Thursday. My mom hung on the line and told me not to worry, and she said that just because they were slicing away *part* of me didn't mean that they, in fact, were slicing away *all* of me. Because I detected more than just regret in her voice, because I detected love and fear and genuine compassion, I chose to believe her. That cutting off your breasts doesn't cut out your soul, but certainly, it cut deeply somewhere.

I sat up in the soapy waters of my tub and held them both, my breasts. I wanted to mourn them, to kiss them good-bye and say that I'd miss them, but really, I was too angry. Take them off, I'd practically spat at Dr. Chin when I called to tell him my decision. Take them off before they do any more damage. These *things,* these symbols of my womanhood, these swollen mounds that were supposed to feed my children and display my ripeness to the world had done just the opposite. They'd sucked me dry. And as I looked down at them that night, covered in frothy bubbles and hot water, I despised both them and what they'd done to me.

After drying my tears, I climbed out, dropped my towel, and crawled naked into bed. My last night when I was still whole. "It's just you and me, Manny," I whispered after he hopped into bed with me and as I ran my fingers behind his ears. Ned was gone. Jake was gone. My parents were literally gone. Zach, well, I'm not sure if I ever had him to begin with. If Sally hadn't been able to put aside her story and come with me tomorrow, I probably would have checked myself into the hospital by myself. I curled up against Manny and wondered if there was anything more depressing than that.

I'D OPTED FOR B-cups, same as before. Dr. Chin created a graphics program on his computer to show me what I would have looked like with Cs, but it was all a little too porn star. They'd never take me seriously in Washington if my breasts entered the room before the rest of me.

I don't remember the surgery. Of course, I shouldn't. They give you enough drugs to knock you out like a rock star in need of rehab. I'm sure it's to dull the pain, but I also figured it was because if you were awake and in your right mind, they'd have to forcibly put you in restraints when they began to lop off your chest.

I woke up in a beige room with a view of the East River. It had started to snow, and the water was blanketed in a sheet of white. A TV hovered on the wall in front of me, and a crimson armchair from the '80s sat to my left. I tried to move, to reach for my bag on the faux-wood table next to my bed, but was met with excruciating pain. I looked down under my gown and saw my upper body taped down with a compression belt of sorts: a girdle for my breasts. Before I could press for the aid button, a heavy-bottomed, blond-bobbed nurse ushered in.

"Natalie. I'm Carol. I'll be looking after you during the day shifts. How are you feeling?" She said it in a warm tone that would work small wonders on kindergartners and felt pretty all right to me, too.

"Okay, I guess. Sore. Sad. But okay." I tried not to look down at my chest.

"All of this is normal, my dear. I need to check your fluids and take a few vitals. Don't mind me." She scampered around the room, talking quietly to herself, making notes in her chart, moving around me as if she'd done this a thousand times. Which she probably had.

"Do you see a lot of patients my age?" I asked her, though I wasn't sure why.

"I do," she said, then reconsidered. "Well, not a lot. Not the norm. But certainly enough. Young women are always the toughest to watch, but they're also the most inspiring. You guys are almost always the fighters, the ones who won't let cancer get the best of them."

I nodded. "That's nice to hear. I hope I have it in me to be like that. I'm trying, I mean, God knows I am. But half of me is just so tired." My voice faltered. "Everyone tells you to keep your head up, but they don't even realize that you're just trying to stay afloat."

"The worst part of it is over, darling. From here, it's only sunny skies." She dropped my chart into the slot at the front of my bed, handed me my bag when I asked for it, and gently closed the door.

I had three missed calls, but my phone wasn't what I searched for like a prize at the bottom of a Cracker Jack box. I gently dug past my toiletries and the magazines Sally had dumped in, swearing that they'd ward off the boredom, until my fingers caught hold. My wig. I know, it seemed silly that after all this, I'd brought my wig with me. After all, I'd barely had time to break it in: I'd shown it off only to myself in front of my mirror. Well, and to Manny, but he didn't care if I were bald or looked like Carrot Top, as long as I fed him and scratched his tummy before he went to sleep.

When my mom and I bought it from Mrs. Seidel, I was instantly in love: like the "Rachel" I once aspired to, hoping it would give me something, anything, just more of a good thing. This time, it actually did: It armed me with confidence, made me feel (relatively) beautiful, and, for a second, allowed me to forget that I had Stage III breast cancer.

I pulled the wig out of my bag and gingerly glided it onto my scalp. I wasn't sure if it was on straight or if the locks fell exactly as they should, but there, in the motorized hospital bed, robbed of my breasts and swaddled like an Egyptian mummy, it made me feel almost complete.

SALLY WAS MY first visitor. She and Drew, who pledged to look after Manny until I got home, stopped by in the late afternoon. I'd fallen asleep with the wig still on and was just waking up for an early dinner (in the hospital, everyone gets the early bird special, even if you're thirty, even if you're not interested in the daily meatloaf—they bring it anyway), when they popped in.

"Darling!" she screeched and leaned in to give me a kiss. "You look fabulous! I don't know what they did to you in there, but if possible, can I get it done myself?"

"You like?" I said with a smile as I pushed up the ends of my hair like a '40s pinup.

"Divine. Simply divine. Honestly, it's like Demi Moore and Angelina Jolie all rolled into one. That wig-making gal is a genius. Maybe I can pitch a story on it."

"Yeah, how cancer made me beautiful. I'm sure it will be the new rage out in Hollywood."

Sally struck a serious pose. "Don't joke. You know those actresses will do anything to lose a few pounds. *Allure* just might go for it."

"So, how'd it go? What did the doctors say?" Drew interrupted.

"Well, I guess— I mean, I'm waiting on tests to see if they got most of it out, but Dr. Chin said that they were very pleased. We'll know more tomorrow."

"Has Zach stopped in yet?" Sally asked.

"Kick me while I'm down, why don't you." I grinned. "No. I'm not so sure he will. I called him the other night in a slightly pot-induced haze, but really, in more of a jealous one. He didn't seem so happy to hear from me. He said he'd drop off more pot at my apartment and that he didn't want to leave it with my doorman, but he left it with him anyway." I sighed. "I guess me calling up and acting like a twelve-year-old to see if he was sleeping with Lila again wasn't as genius as it sounded like after the joint."

"Sweetie, no worries. I'm sure it wasn't so bad. And I'm sure he'll stop by tomorrow."

"It was that bad," I said. "And I should have called him back to apologize."

"I thought apologies weren't your thing. Haven't you told me that about ten dozen times over the years?" Sally laughed. "Looks like Zach has penetrated the formidable armor." I just shrugged and wondered how many other people like Susanna Taylor, like Zach, I'd mowed down in my wake. "What's that?" Sally asked, pointing to my neck.

Instinctively, I reached up and felt the gold weight against my collarbone. The doctors had let me wear it during surgery, just turning the charm over so it hung down the nape of my neck, rather than down the front.

"It's silly, actually," I said, feeling self-conscious. "It's just a stupid necklace that Ned gave me." I shrugged, as Sally's eyes widened at the mention of his name. "Don't worry. It has nothing to do with Ned. It's just . . ." I paused and thought about it, about why I'd clasped it on after I uncovered it in my drawer while packing for the hospital. "It's just that when he bought it, he did it because it gave him hope. Because it reminded him of better days. And I thought that maybe I could use a bit of that now, too."

"Makes sense to me," Sally said, reaching over and squeezing my hand. "You have to find hope wherever you can."

Twenty minutes later, my head was throbbing and I needed another hit of Vicodin, so when Carol brought me my meds, Sally and Drew kissed me good-bye and promised to stop in the next day and to take good care of Manny. I'd drifted off to sleep before they even made it to the elevator.

I woke up to a light knock on my door.

"Carol, come in," I muttered under my breath. But the knocking continued. I mustered some more strength and reached for the pack of gum on my nightstand to beat back my dry mouth. "It's *open*. I'm *awake*. Come in."

I heard the hinges on the door creak, and without looking up, held out my arm for her to take my blood pressure and draw whatever blood she felt like drawing this time. I was practically a human pincushion, why stop now?

"Natalie," a voice said, a voice that shot my nerves clear to the sky.

I looked up, and it wasn't Carol at all.

It was Jake. And he was back.

ROUND FIVE

· · ·

January

· FOURTEEN ·

Dear Diary,

D   *I'm so glad that I threw you into my bag at the last minute when packing for surgery. Who'd have known that a stupid diary—and I mean no disrespect by that, but really, when I started out with this writing project, I sort of figured that diaries are for eight-year-olds and women who watch too much* Oprah*—but who'd have thought that a diary would become such a security blanket?*

It turns out that I didn't have to track down Jake, the next one on my list. Maybe the only one who mattered. He found me.

You know how it's every girl's nightmare to run into an ex when she's just heading back from kickboxing class or on her way home from a facial when her face resembles the pepperoni pizza from Famous Ray's? Well, clearly, I can one-up them. Imagine running into your ex—and clearly, that's a very loose phrase, since I was quite obviously running nowhere—after just having lost both breasts and enduring surgery that left you with breath no better than a fish's and skin as pasty as raw dough. Except that I didn't have to imagine it because that's exactly what happened.

Diary, I don't have much energy to write—in fact, things that have never throbbed before in my life are presently throbbing as if they're dancing to an electronic orchestra—but just wanted to update you.

So I'll just say this: I hoped and I wished and I would have done just about anything to bring Jake back to me. Funny that I had to go and get cancer to bring him home.

THANK GOD I'M *wearing my wig.* That was literally my first thought. Thank God I'm wearing my wig because if Jake saw me bald, I don't know what the hell I would do. When you've just undergone surgery, surgery that both saved your life and took something from it, and your ex-boyfriend, feasibly the only man you've ever truly, organically loved, walks back into the room, into your life, one would think that your first thought would not be about your hair covering. And yet, there it was.

"Natalie," he had said, and I looked up, expecting Carol with her various needles and gauze.

"Jake," I said back, my hand instinctively rising to my hair, as if I were holding it in place. I opened my mouth to speak again but found myself entirely out of words.

"Oh my God," he said, moving toward my bed. "Why didn't you call me?"

I looked away. "How did you find out?"

"Your mom. She e-mailed me from Australia. She found an Internet café and wrote with the news. I think she didn't want you to be alone."

Figures, I thought. There goes my mom again, alpha dog to the rescue. My parents, needless to say (and I say that this is needless because when you're diagnosed with Stage III breast cancer and your mother takes the time to track down your ex, it's pretty obvious how she feels about him), adored Jake. He was, as my mother once put it after he and I had spent a weekend in Bryn Mawr, "the perfect antidote to you." I sulked for an hour after her comment, but when I told her I was more than a bit insulted, she just shushed me and said that I misunderstood. "What I mean, darling, is that you are each other's perfect complements. He knows how to handle you. No one else has ever done that," and then she breezed into the dining room to offer him a scotch.

"I came straight from the airport," Jake said, as he hovered near the wall and stared at me in the hospital bed. Then I noticed his suitcase by the small foyer that led to the door.

"You shouldn't have. I certainly didn't mean to inconvenience you." After all this time, it was still the same thing: Jake's life was always in flight; I needed him on the ground.

He shook his head. "Don't be ridiculous. It worked out well: We'd just finished opening for Dave Matthews, and I'd planned to head back anyway." He paused and his voice grew soft. "But I would have come here regardless, whenever, if you'd just called me. I would have left the tour, done whatever you needed. But I didn't know."

"I didn't expect you to know," I said flatly.

"But I would have liked to." He dug his hands into the pockets of his perfectly worn jeans.

"That stopped being your concern approximately two years ago."

After we'd been together for seven months, the Misbees got their big break. He called me at the office on a Tuesday, his voice at a near fever pitch. "They're gonna sign us!" he screamed. "They're fucking going to sign us!"

The "they" in question was Sony records. Their scouts had been following the band for a few months, and that weekend, when Jake crawled into bed with me, waking me up after he got home from a Saturday late show, he told me, "I think we nailed it. I think that this is it." I had rubbed the sleep from my eyes and gotten up to crack open a bottle of champagne.

And it *was* it. But nothing was ever the same. Now, before you start judging me, telling me that I wasn't supportive of my boy-friend's career or didn't cheerlead his fame, let me clarify. There was no one, I repeat, no one, who was more proud of him. From our first date, Jake inhabited me. He swept me up so completely that there were days when it ached just to be apart. When I'd find myself staring into my computer monitor and wish that time would speed up so that I'd be back home with him. I coveted him more than anything else that had ever come into my life. So before you suspect that I didn't wish him raging success and multiple Grammy nominations, know that. Know that of everything I'd seen and felt and breathed in my twenty-five years, Jake was what I loved most.

And now, he was back.

"How did this happen?" he asked, as he pulled a chair over to my bedside. Its legs squeaked against the linoleum floor like chalk on a blackboard. "I don't understand. How can you—I mean, you were so healthy—how do you go from that to this?"

I told him about how Ned found a lump. And I reminded him

about my grandmother. "Bad luck." I shrugged. "You can't outrun bad luck."

"So where is he? Ned? Why wasn't your mom e-mailing him, not me?"

"He dumped me," I said matter-of-factly. "Just when I found out about the cancer. Dumped me for some bitch he met in his office in Chicago." I reached up for the four-leaf clover that lay around my neck and caught myself, so I tried not to sound so bitter.

"And to think," Jake said with a smile. "I was always the one who you hated going out on the road."

"Yeah." I sighed. "Go figure. I'd never pegged Ned for that . . . he was just so . . ." I paused, choosing my words carefully. "Different from you."

I looked right at him. The same floppy blond hair that would curl into ringlets if he didn't get it cut in time. The same penetrating blue eyes. The same desire rising inside of me.

"Sometimes, it was easier," I continued. "To not have to struggle, not have to feel like it was a fight to tie him down. Ned was happy to be tied. He was my beta," I explained. "And it worked."

"Until it didn't."

"Funny how that happens," I said.

Jake and I started to become unhinged after about a year. It took nearly two more years for us to fully break, but the year mark is around when I saw the first clear signs. Before Sony made the Misbees into superstars in the United States, they decided to sell them abroad. Jake packed up his duffel bag, made love to me twice the night before, and let himself out to catch an early flight at dawn the next morning. I heard him whisper "I love you," before he left, but I think I was too tired to manage one in return. He was gone for nearly six weeks.

The first time he left it didn't bother me so much. The next time, later that fall, it wasn't as seamless. My grandfather had died; I wanted Jake home. But we both knew that he couldn't be— Prague was too far gone to fly back for a day—so I didn't place blame. But it's hard to keep building a life together when "together" isn't really part of the equation.

Every time that he'd come home, I'd fall in love with him all over again. His returns were like my drug: I fantasized about them, fed off them, and ultimately told myself that they were enough to keep us alive. He'd bring me chocolates from Switzerland or roses from Austin, and he'd swear to me that he couldn't bear to be without me for another day. He'd pour salve on both of our wounds and at least for that hour, it would be enough. As we neared our three-year anniversary, his road trips grew more frequent and our silences grew longer. The distance he put between us was more than literal: It penetrated every layer of our love.

When I sat down on our couch and told him that I was broken, he tried to talk me out of it. But I shook my head no, and instead, on the day before our third anniversary, I helped him pack up his things, the things that collect over time in a relationship and become so much a part of your living space, it's hard to imagine that there was a point when they weren't there, and then we said goodbye. Before he left, he asked me again to take it back. I started crying and told him that I couldn't.

"I love you, Natalie," he said, right before he closed my front door.

"That's not enough," I answered, and watched him drag his suitcase down the hall.

Two years later, I lay in my hospital bed with my chest wrapped in bandages and drugs running through my body to numb the pain. Only now, as I stared at Jake underneath the jarring lights of Sloan-Kettering, it felt as if the wounds that lay below my chest, the ones that had been carved around my heart, were the only ones that were beginning to heal.

"HE'S STAYING IN town," I said to Sally, who had taken my 911 call and immediately rushed to my bedside. I'd decided that if my physical exhaustion from the surgery didn't kill me, perhaps my emotional exhaustion would.

"He is NOT! Oh my God, what did he say?"

"That he wasn't going anywhere this time. That it was his turn to choose to stay instead of having me ask him." I tried to fight back a smile.

"But you *didn't* ask him, did you? I mean, wait, how has this happened so fast?"

"No." I shook my head. "I didn't. In fact, I very firmly told him that I was *fine*. That showing up here two years later acting like my knight in shining armor was a fine costume for him to slip into, but that the act would get old after a while."

"And what did he say?" She leaned in toward my bed.

"He told me that it wasn't an act. That he'd been thinking of me these past few months and that he was doing everything he could not to call me. And that when my mother e-mailed him, he took it to be a sign."

When Jake left after we split up, I asked him not to be in touch. He ignored me initially, still calling once a week or so, breaking up my thoughts on the tail end of a meeting or as I was unwinding from a draining day at work. He'd call but have nothing really to say. The first few times, he'd try to convince me to undo what I'd done. By the fourth or fifth time he called, he stopped asking, but I'd feel just as empty, just as scattered when we hung up as I did when he was still here. Every time we spoke, he drew me back into his web again. If he did it often enough, I'd never be able to untangle myself. Finally, I told him to stop calling at all.

"Do you believe him?" Sally asked, as she got up to change the water in the flowers that the senator had sent over. "That he was thinking of you before this happened?"

"Sure. Why not? I was dreaming about him—literally having dreams, so why shouldn't I believe that he was doing the same?" It was true. I was having that dream again: the amusement park one where I was nearly suffocated with clowns and sand and claustrophobia. Only last week, when I looked up to see who saved me, who outstretched his hand to pull me out, it wasn't a faceless blur, it was Jake.

"So now what?" She plunked down on the foot of my bed.

"Now he stays." I looked at her and felt my nose tingle and my chin quiver. "Maybe it took cancer to bring him back to me."

"And you're okay with that? That after two years, he's sliding back in?" She put her hand on top of mine.

"He's not sliding. There's no sliding. He loves me. And I could use someone in my corner right now."

"I'm in your corner. And besides, didn't he love you back then?" she pointed out.

"He did," I conceded. "But maybe this time, it will be enough."

· FIFTEEN ·

I don't know how I didn't see it, but I guess when you're doped up on Vicodin and confined to an adjustable bed (which I actually sort of enjoyed: with the press of a button, you're in any position desired! Just like they say in the commercials!), things can get overlooked. So it wasn't until my mom was doing a last-minute check to ensure that I hadn't forgotten anything in the hospital room that she found it. It had fallen underneath my bed; it must have floated off the swivel tray where Carol placed my food and Sally stacked sundry magazines.

"Do you need this?" My mom waved the sheet of paper in the air while still crouched down. I'd never actually seen her do anything even remotely like housework, so I just sat in my wheelchair and stared, mouth agape.

"What is it?" I asked.

She stood upright. "It looks like a note. From Zach." Her eyebrows rose higher. In a momentary lapse of weakness (which were steadily increasing these days), I'd confided in my mom about the debacle of my stoned phone call. She handed it over to me.

Natalie,

I stopped by but you looked so peaceful sleeping that I didn't want to wake you. Figured you could use the rest. Dr. Chin has kept me updated, and it sounds like we're in the home stretch. I couldn't be happier for you.

If you need anything, please call. Really. Please do. Whatever weirdness came between us certainly isn't worth you not allowing me to help.

I know that you'll be back on your feet and running the world in no time.

Love,
Zach

I tucked it into my purse that was wedged beneath my arm in the wheelchair, then told my mom that I was ready. I surveyed the room: its view of the river, a crumpled gown near my desk, empty water bottles that never seemed to quench my thirst. And I decided I'd never be back.

"Let's go, Mom. Please take me home."

JAKE KISSED MY parents hello like he'd never been gone. Like two years hadn't passed, and like, until three months ago, another man hadn't taken his place in my bed. He supported my weight as I slowly rose from the wheelchair and hobbled into bed.

"Dr. Chin told me that I should feel better by Monday," I said, already offering up excuses for my own flimsiness.

"I'm in no rush," he replied while pulling back the covers. "And I dig your new method of transport. Can you do wheelies yet?" He smiled.

I groaned and leaned into my pillows. I hated the damn wheelchair, what it stood for, how it made me feel. "Don't get used to it. I'm ditching it after the weekend."

I closed my eyes and overheard him talking to my mom in the living room. My parents were staying at a hotel in midtown, but he assured her that he'd look after me. I listened to him and wondered if he'd really do that this time: give me what I needed, even when I hadn't asked. I saw that my closet door was open and noticed that he'd already hung up some of his shirts. I check into the hospital and two days later, my ex-boyfriend has slid back, not just into my closet, but into my life as well. Who's in need of a doctor now? Jake still had a studio apartment in the East Village where he'd crash when he was in town, but I'd agreed to let him stay with me so that someone would be there in case I literally fell.

My dad came into the bedroom and kissed me, saying that they'd stop by in the morning. My mom straightened up the towering stacks of research on my desk, chastizing me under her breath for working when I should have known better, and when she was satisfied, both at the guilt she'd laid and her cleaning job, she handed Jake an itemized list of precooked meals that she'd stowed in the fridge. And then, just like that, he and I were alone.

"I wrote a song for you," he said, as he sat on the edge of the bed.

Back when I was twenty-five and my boyfriend was a budding rock star, I used to think that this was the ultimate love letter: I mean, seriously, like the chick who inspired "In Your Eyes" wasn't totally psyched when Peter Gabriel penned that one. Could there be anything more romantic? Like a promise etched in a high school yearbook or initials carved into a tree. What Jake did was make music, and if he could make music about me, surely, it would have sealed our fate. Every few months, I'd ask him, "Write a song for me." He would always nod and swear that he would. Eventually, I grew too embarrassed to keep asking. I wasn't sure which was worse: the fact that I was quietly desperate for lyrics inscribed with my name or the fact that he never got around to writing them.

"Why now?" I asked, leaning back into my pillow, years after I'd lost my romantic idealism. "Is it because of the cancer?"

"I wrote it long before the cancer," he said. "You just weren't around to hear it when it was finally done."

"What took you so long?" I sat up and stared at him.

"I started it on the last road trip before we broke up. But you ended things before I could ever play it for you. And it's funny— once you were no longer there, writing it became the most critical thing in the world." He smiled slightly at the irony.

"You don't know what you've got 'til it's gone," I said wearily, my eyes drooping under their own weight.

"Something like that," Jake said. "Something pretty close to that exactly."

•   •   •

Dear Diary,

It's been nearly two weeks since Jake has been back; I'm sorry that I haven't written sooner. It's all been a little overwhelming, if I'm being honest.

The good news is that the doctors are really happy with my progress and recovery. And though there are no guarantees—after all, we still have a few more rounds of chemo—for the first time, they feel confident that I can beat this. Dr. Chin said that he doesn't want to get my hopes up, but it's too late. They're up. And maybe it's having Jake here or maybe it's just that my body is fighting back, but either way, like the nurse, Carol, said, I'm feeling like sunnier skies are heading my way.

Which, of course, brings me to Jake. It's strange, Diary. How you can live without someone for so long, and then how once he's woven his way back into your life, once he's proven himself invaluable, you wonder how you ever lived without him. Because that's what happened with Jake. I tried to take it slow. But Jake is like the quicksand in my dreams: Even if I try to fight it, I'm pulled in deeper. It's a strange thing for me, the collision of the two things that I can't control. This cancer and Jake.

To his credit, he's been nothing short of wonderful. Ned never could have done what he's done. Each morning, we change my dressing—the first few days, it was bloody and gooey and truly, fairly sickening, but he didn't flinch. My new breasts still look like a porn star's: swollen and engorged, and though I'm a little freaked out that I might look like a circus act for the rest of my life, Jake just smiles as he reapplies the gauze and tells me that with that cleavage, I'll certainly get the senators to do whatever the hell I want. Fly you to the moon, they would, he said yesterday. Just one look, and they'd be putty.

Of course, even if my boobs don't deflate, these senators would still most likely be terrified of them in their present state. You see, dear Diary, I'm currently nipple-less. And yes, it's as strange as it sounds. Where my small but pert breasts and rose-pink nipples once lay, now reside two hulking bald masses. But

none of this seems to faze Jake. He tells me that I'm beautiful,
even though I don't think it's true. I still try to wear my wig
around him as often as possible.

And it's not just in tending to my wounds that he's proven
himself. He's essentially been like a servant, which I realize sounds
like a strange term to use when describing an is-he-or-isn't-he
boyfriend, but at this moment, at this exact time, that's what I
needed. He indulges me in my Price Is Right *fixation, even*
hopping off the couch and rushing to the computer to frantically
look up an average price of a barbecue grill or lawn chair or
power drill just in the nick of time before the contestants place
their bids. He'll go to the grocery store when we're out of food,
he'll walk Manny when he needs fresh air. Last night, I was
so bored that I suddenly had a ridiculous urge to watch Top
Gun, *and he even ran out to the video store to grab the DVD.*
I watched him leave and thought that he'd be the perfect hus-
band to have around when I was pregnant. (If I ever could be, I
should note.) Pickles and ice cream at three in the morning? Yes
ma'am!

Sally, always the skeptic, is a little less enthused. "Remem-
ber that they call it 'winning you back' for a reason," she said
one afternoon when he'd run out to Citarella to pick up some
mint chocolate chip, right before I lit up a joint. "It's a challenge
at first for him, to see if he can pull it off. What really matters is
if he can keep his game face on once the thrill of the game has
worn off." Maybe you should write an article on that, I told her.
"Please." She sighed wearily. "Like I haven't a hundred times."
She then eyed me and said dryly, "Clearly, the advice doesn't
rub off on readers."

I should probably also tell you that Zach has called twice.
I returned his call the first time but got his voice mail, and I haven't

yet called him again. I know. I should. But Sally told me that he and Lila are still hanging out, and for whatever reason (and really, Diary, I'm not sure of the reason or else I'd try to explain it because Janice tells me that that's the real benefit of having a diary to begin with), I'm still pissed off about it. Any theories as to why? Yeah, I know. Me neither. I've asked Manny to contribute his brilliant thoughts, too, but he wasn't entirely helpful, either.

Sally told me that I wasn't being fair. That Jake was back in my life, and if Zach wanted Lila back in his, then who was I to begrudge him? She's probably right. No, she is right. But I sort of figure that I'm a charity case, so I'm allowed to take the help of whomever offers, even if it just so happens to be the ex-boyfriend who was the only person I ever truly loved. I'm not so sure what Zach's excuse is.

ROUND SIX

. . .

February

· SIXTEEN ·

I got to work early enough the morning of my first day back. Not as early as I would have liked to, and certainly not as early as I would have six months before, but 8:45 was pretty damn good for me right now. Jake wanted me to stay in bed with him. Don't get me wrong: I still had the physical desire of a dead whale and he'd only recently moved back in with me. Still though, I'd wake in the middle of the night and watch his chest rise and fall. And I'd gotten used to lingering in bed with him—sometimes, I'd smoke a joint so I could stomach breakfast, other times, we'd just lie around, spinning our worlds together after they'd drifted so far apart. At night, he'd pull out his guitar and sit cross-legged in the middle of the bed, the comforter puffy around his legs, and sing to me. I hadn't yet asked to hear the song he'd written for me, but I knew that I would one day. And I hoped that I would one day soon.

But this morning, my first morning back, I pushed back his hand from around my waist that tried to tie me to the sheets like an anchor and rose with a purpose. I, Natalie Miller, was going back to work. Regaining control. Getting back in the saddle. I tore the plastic from the dry cleaners off my perfect black Calvin Klein pantsuit, steamed up the mirrors in the bathroom from a long, hot shower, and even took the time to apply the earth-toned eye shadow that Sally insisted I buy during a recent venture to Sephora. The finishing touch was, of course, the wig. I secured it in place and gave myself a once-over. If you didn't peer too closely, you could barely see everything that cancer had changed about me.

The security guard to our building barely recognized me. In fact, he asked me for my ID, something he hadn't done in at least four years. I chalked it up to my brunette Farrah Fawcett locks and pressed the elevator button to the thirty-first floor. The office was just getting warmed up for the day. Junior aides were sipping coffee and picking at bagels in their cubes, and the phones were building a slow roar before reaching their fever pitch. I pushed open the door to my office, my revered office with the window view, the one that I earned from putting in countless and thankless late-night hours with and for the senator when everyone else had gone home to get some sleep or to see their kids or to catch the Knicks game. And what I saw was not my immaculate desk, piled high with pictures of diplomats with their arms slung around me and various charitable plaques that had been dropped by the office as a thank-you for Dupris's support. What I saw instead was Kyle with his feet propped up and his borderline tenor voice blaring into the earpiece on my phone. He waved me in, and I sat sulking on the leather chair that I'd bought at Pottery Barn until he finally hung up.

"Natalie. You look great! Welcome back." He offered a knowing and not entirely welcoming smile. More like one that a cunning boar might offer its next meal.

"Thanks. Now get out of my office."

"No niceties? Come on, Nat. At least a big hello for your friend Kyle. Not even a thank-you for bailing you out of the sea of collapsing cocktail tables at the Christmas party?" He swung his shiny Pradas back to the floor.

"Hello, Kyle." I sighed. "And thank you. Now will you please get out of my office? I'd like to get started on the stem cell campaign, and I have phone calls to make."

He nodded and placed his chin in his hands. "I see. I see. Well, the thing is, I'm not sure that this *is* your office anymore. While you were gone, the senator bumped me up a notch."

"Don't overinflate yourself," I said. "My name has been on that door for over two years now."

"Ah yes. But check to see if it's there now." He raised his eyebrows.

I stood up and walked to the door, swinging it toward me until I saw that, indeed, the gold "Natalie Miller" nameplate was no longer stuck to the outside.

"You're a fucking asshole," I muttered underneath my breath.

"Take it up with the senator," he said, smiling. "She'll be back in town next week. Until then, welcome to my cube. You know the one: toward the back by the water fountain? I'm pretty sure that you've passed it once or twice."

"Don't get too comfortable," I retorted, picking up my bag and slamming the door on my way out.

"IT'S A LONG shot, you realize that, right?"

I was on the phone with Senator McIntyre's senior aide,

Maureen Goodman. She had seven years on me and on paper, at least, we couldn't have been more different—she was a lesbian from Oregon—but I knew that both she and Senator McIntyre were vigilantly pushing for stem cell reform.

"I do realize that. But sometimes long shots bring in the best returns, right?"

I pushed my pointer finger into my left ear to try to block out the incessant noise that hummed in the background. It had been two and a half weeks since I'd been back on the job, and I was still stuck in Kyle's cubicle.

"Okay, if we're going to go after this, we're going to have to go after it hard," Maureen said now. "Make sure the senator is on-board, and then we'll start lining up names."

"She's already onboard. She wants this stem cell push done, and she wants it as much as anything this term," I said. "Let's fire up the big guns." I paused. "Look, Maureen, I'm willing to take a gamble and play the odds here," I said, as my voice got lodged in my throat. "I know that the president and his advisers are threatening to veto it. But let's at least make him turn it down, push away the hope for the people who could use it most. Let's put that on his lap, and rest easy knowing that we could have made a difference."

"Wow, spoken like someone who actually gives a shit," Maureen said, as we began hashing through which senators were on our side and which needed a bit more persuading. We narrowed it down to eight critical players, and we each took four.

"You're sure that Senator Dupris is willing to go to bat for this?" she asked one last time, just before we hung up. "It could end up as egg on her face."

"I'm sure," I said, and promised to e-mail her with my progress in the next few weeks. We had three months to draw out a majority. I didn't see how we could lose. And though I was indeed sure that the senator wanted to pull out the stops in pushing forward this initiative, I wanted to be doubly sure.

"Senator, I'm sorry to bother," I said, as I knocked on her door, which was already slightly ajar.

She looked up from an enormous stack of papers and told me to come in. On most days, even without the help of her on-call stylist and hairdresser, you'd call her beautiful. Once when we were stuck together on a long plane trip back from Europe, she confided that when she first started out, her looks got in the way. No one took her seriously, so she had to work twice as hard. Let that be a lesson, she said, Natalie. If they think you're dumb, you bust your ass and then when you knock them out, they have no idea where the punch came from in the first place.

Today, she looked worn, with dark circles receding into her pallid skin, a tiny fly behind her gigantic desk.

"I'm sorry to bother you, Senator." I took a step into her office. "But I just got off the phone with Maureen Goodman, Senator McIntyre's aide. She and I are prepared to give a full push to getting a stem cell research bill onto the floor, and I just wanted to triple-check that you were onboard. That you'd helm it up."

"I will." She smiled. "I'd love nothing better than serving that bill to the president on a silver platter."

"Fair enough," I said. "Consider it served."

"I CAN'T *NOT* go," Jake said. "And it's only for five days. Not even a week."

I didn't answer him. I sat back on the couch, inhaled my joint, and reached for the orange juice on the coffee table. To Jake's credit, he'd been kind enough to pick up the OJ. Fresh squeezed.

"Natalie, I know that I said that I was back for good. And

I mean it. But come on, every job requires some travel, and I have to go to L.A. This is a huge opportunity for us, playing on *Leno*."

I exhaled slowly, shooing the smoke away from Manny. I couldn't imagine that getting my dog stoned was what the ASPCA had in mind for his future when I adopted him.

"Nat, you won't even know that I'm gone. You're back at work. You're looking great, feeling even better. You're totally capable now."

"So you touched down just to be my nurse's aide? My own personal Florence Nightingale?" I sucked on my joint.

He sighed and rose from the dining table to come sit beside me. "No, I came back because I love you and didn't want to be without you. And a few days in L.A. and a short stint in Tokyo doesn't change that."

He was right. I knew that he was right. He was a freaking almost—rock star for God's sake. I could hardly expect him to stay at my beck and call when his future came clamoring. I stubbed out my joint and went over to the fridge. He was still waiting for an answer. Well, not an answer, really; he was obviously going to do *Leno*. A girlfriend who had nearly kicked breast cancer wasn't reason enough not to. And I say that without so much as a hint of sarcasm. It wasn't.

"Fine. Go." And I reached for a chicken breast.

"It's just for five days, Nat. *Five days*. And then I'll be back. Nothing's going to change."

"Nothing ever does," I said, as I walked into the bedroom with Manny to eat my dinner in better company.

· SEVENTEEN ·

I realize now that I've marked my time since my diagnosis by my chemo rounds. If I were cancer-free, maybe I'd mark it by the seasons or by my work milestones. I imagine that's what normal people do. If I were normal, I'd say that I was diagnosed back in September, that Jake came back in January, or that I shaved my head in late November. But instead, I say that Jake came back after my fourth round, and I cut off my hair on the cusp of my third. That's what it's like to live with cancer—it's hard to remove it from your life, even when you're talking about something else entirely.

So when I say that Sally's wedding invitation arrived just on the tail end of my sixth round, know that I'm not trying to overshadow her big day with my big disease. That's simply how things work now. Time, just like everything else in my world, revolves around my cancer.

It was fortuitous, I guess, that her wedding was ten weeks away. "I'm sending them early," she said. "That's the etiquette for a destination wedding. I wrote a story on it." If you're doing the math, this means that I'll be chemo-free by then, assuming things all go as planned. I was running my fingers over the calligraphy on the envelope, "Ms. Natalie Colleen Miller and Mr. Jake Spencer Martin," when the phone rang. I was so distracted by the invitation, that I didn't even bother to look at the Caller ID.

"Natalie? It's Susanna Taylor . . ." She paused. "The councilman's wife."

Crap, I thought, and dropped the invite on the mounting mail pile on my kitchen table.

"I'm sorry, I didn't mean to call out of the blue, but I spoke with one of your friends today, Sally Fisher. She asked me to call you again."

"You spoke with Sally? About what?" I stopped filtering through the mail long enough to register a look of confusion.

"Oh, she interviewed me for a story she's working on. We'd spoken a year or so ago and gotten on well, so she called me up again for something else. Anyway, I'm not normally this stalkerish, but Sally really thought that we might click." She laughed. "And she told me that you're not having the best go of it, so I thought you might be interested in joining the group for a gettogether in two weeks. We're meeting for brunch to celebrate the clean bill of health that one of our members, Olivia, just got. You'd like her. She's head of marketing at ESPN. Has balls made of steel." I heard her smile.

Goddamn it, I thought and felt my jaw clench up. *This is so my mother. When did Sally become my mother?* I inhaled deeply and unintentionally reached up to touch my necklace, as if the gold clover would grant me kindness, understanding, more compassion. I unwittingly touched it so often these days that Sally had deemed it the "portent of good karma." And then she made an *om* and pretended she was having some sort of spiritual awakening like all the celebrities claim they have during hatha yoga.

"Um, well, honestly, Susanna," I answered, as I tugged off my shoes and massaged the balls of my feet. "The next few weeks are a little crazy for me. You know how it goes—new term and all."

"I do, I do." I heard her thinking. "The thing is, Natalie, it's just brunch. If you hate us and want to flee down the street shrieking at the top of your lungs when we're done, you're welcome to. Honestly, it's just brunch."

I sighed. This woman should have run instead of her husband: She clearly wouldn't take no for an answer. "Fine," I said. "Just brunch. But other than pancakes, I can't promise that I'll get much out of it." At least she was forewarned.

We hung up, and I grabbed Manny's leash to head out for his evening walk. For February, it wasn't bad out. Crisp but not biting in the way that New York in February can be, when the wind whips through the buildings and leaves your cheeks burned with an afterglow. It was already dark, too late for the park, so Manny and I just wove our way through the streets, him lunging for discarded bagels on the sidewalk, me scolding him but only halfheartedly so.

I heard my name being shouted down the street, and Manny took off like a bolt toward it.

With a deep green scarf wrapped around his neck, tucked safely into his herringbone overcoat, Zach looked like he'd stepped straight out of a *GQ* shoot. And I mean that in the most delicious of ways.

"Natalie." He waved, as we drew closer. "Hey! I thought that was you. I'd recognize this guy anywhere." He leaned over and nuzzled Manny's nose. "How have you been?"

"Fine. Good, even. Only two rounds of chemo left. Hard to believe. Oh, and I've scheduled my nipple surgery for next week." I managed a half-grin. "Which is a good thing because I'm a little wary of these globes that I've been carrying around. Yahoo. Nipples here I come." It came out as unenthusiastically as I meant it.

Zach smiled. "No, I meant how have you been otherwise? Dr. Chin has kept me posted on your progress, so I know how well that's going. I always knew it would."

He did, I thought. *That was right.* "Oh, I'm doing well. You know, back at work, same old, same old." I didn't know if he knew about Jake, and I hardly wanted to bring it up. So instead, I beat him to the punch.

"How's Lila?"

"She's fine." He pressed his lips together into a thin smile, then waved me off. "I tell you what. In honor of your remarkable progress and overwhelming ability to kick cancer's ass, let's go to dinner."

I paused and looked down at Manny.

"Unless you have other plans," he added.

"Uh, no. Not really. But I can't take Manny into a restaurant. The pesky health department and all of that."

"Fair enough. So how about we order? Whatever you can stomach."

The electronic clock that pulsed on top of the bank on Seventy-second Street declared that the night was still peaking, just 7:05, so I figured why the hell not? Jake was in L.A., and I wasn't planning to work that night anyway. And besides, it was Zach. Really, though I didn't admit it to myself, that was selling point enough.

. . .

WE SETTLED ON pizza, and after two slices (and a joint—I always carried one on me), a glass of merlot, and a heated game of him versus me versus the real contestants on *Jeopardy!*, I could barely remember why I was mad at him in the first place.

Manny was begging from the bottom of Zach's leather couch, so I tossed him a crust and told him to scram.

"With that hair, you could practically be a supermodel," Zach said, reaching out to touch the long, winding strands.

"Yeah," I snorted. "As if." But he looked at me like he meant it, so I ran my fingers through the tips of my wig and wondered if it could be true. He stared at me a second too long, and I felt myself blush.

"Are you looking forward to the wedding? It should be fun, right?"

"You're going?" I asked. This Sally had failed to mention.

"Not sure yet." Then he went quiet. "Lila asked me to come along, but . . ."

"Wow. I didn't realize." I started twirling the ends of my hair.

"Didn't realize what? There's nothing to realize." He got up to clear our plates.

"Well, I mean, it seems like there's something to realize if you're flying to Puerto Rico to attend weddings with her." It came out colder than I intended.

"That's where the 'but' comes in." He sighed and walked back to me from the kitchen. "I didn't mean for it to get this far."

"So it's far? In that case, should I even be here?" I rose to leave, but he grabbed my hand and dragged me back onto the couch.

"It's not far. At least not to me. But that's part of the problem. Anyway, it seems to me that you have some entanglements of your own." My cheeks flushed like they'd been bitten by fire ants. I looked at my cuticles and started to pick them. "Why didn't you mention him?"

I shrugged. "Dunno."

"I thought that you weren't available. I thought that's what you said."

"I'm not. And I did." I sighed. "I don't know. Jake came back, and I'm lonely, and I loved him, and he promised to stay with me, which is all I ever wanted from him when we dated before, and so I just sort of agreed to it." I paused. "But we haven't been together *together* yet, so really, I mean it. I just don't feel available."

"So he gets a second chance but Lila shouldn't?"

I stared out his picture window. "It's complicated."

"It shouldn't be."

"This coming from the son of two shrinks who is presently hanging out with an ex-girlfriend and contemplating entangling himself even further though he suspects that he doesn't even like her? Thanks for your advice, but I'll pass." I got up and walked to the window, staring out at the skyline of the city.

"Where is he tonight?"

"In L.A. Playing Leno. They couldn't postpone. Then he's going to Tokyo for a few days since he's already on the West Coast. Shorter flight." I lowered my eyes so he couldn't see that I felt the sting of Jake's betrayal.

"But he wants to stick around?" He looked at me. "Is that what you want?"

I picked some dirt from under my thumbnail and raised my shoulders. "I don't know. Sometimes."

He sighed and got up to pour himself another glass of wine.

"You know, I didn't quite tell you the whole story with Natasha, my med school girlfriend. After I'd accepted my residency in

New York, she changed her mind. Decided that she *couldn't* live without me, even though I'd finally figured out how to live without her. We didn't get much time off, but whatever she had, she spent flying back and forth. Each visit, she'd whittle her way back in until after a while, I couldn't believe that I'd ever let her go." He took a sip from his glass and let it linger.

"This went on for six months: We were talking about moving to be with each other, planning our future, and eventually, I made my way to the diamond guy my brother recommended. I'd already bought the ring when she called me to tell me that she couldn't do it anymore. That she just needed to confirm that she definitely couldn't live without me, and it turned out that once again, she realized that she could."

"I'm sorry," I said softly.

"Don't be." He waved his free hand. "Even the second time around, I realized that she was right. But my point here is that sometimes people come back into our lives because it's what they think is good for them. And it has absolutely nothing to do with what's good for you."

◆ ◆ ◆

Dear Diary,

It's been a strange few days. To say the least. Jake called yesterday before he took off for Japan, and by all accounts, his stint on Leno was a tremendous success. We didn't talk about what that meant—what his record company did to promote bands who were considered "tremendous successes"—but I think that we both pretty much knew what it involved. The thing about Jake is that it's not that he makes promises that he has no intention of keeping, it's that he makes promises that get in the way of his other plans.

When he asked what I thought of the show, I told him that they were amazing. And they were. They played their new song, "Miles from Her," and even Leno came out and said that after this performance, he was buying the CD. What I didn't tell him was that I watched the show at Zach's. I know, I know. Who am I to call out Jake on his broken promises when I'm spending lingering evenings with my gynecologist who may or may not be dating one of my best friends? But I almost couldn't help it. No, that makes me unaccountable, so let me rephrase because Janice and I have been working on that: my taking accountability. Certainly, I could have helped it. Certainly, at any point in the evening, I could have gotten up, thanked him for the pizza and the company, and walked Manny the five blocks home. But what I mean by this, by the fact that I felt helpless, is that for the first time in a long while, I felt like I belonged in my own skin. I didn't worry about the pallor of my cheeks or the bulging shape of my new breasts that resemble flotation devices on a 747. In fact, I barely thought about them at all.

So like I said, Diary, it was a strange thing. Just before Leno came on, we were shooting the shit, I don't really even remember what we were talking about. Something on the local news, maybe. I couldn't believe that I'd stayed up that late, but with Zach, I wasn't even tired. It's like I wanted time to slow down, just so I wouldn't have to notice that the clock read an hour that meant I'd be wiped out the next day. But anyway, after the news and just before Leno, I got up to use the bathroom, and when I came back, he had that look on his face again—the one that I've seen from him before—the one where a guy is thinking something really intimate and personal and perhaps over the line and debating if he should open his mouth.

"Natalie. I have to be honest," he said. "I know that Lila is

*your friend, and I know you're with Jake, but the simple truth of
it is that I think you're amazing."*

I didn't know what to say back, so I just thanked him, sat
back down, and folded my hands carefully in my lap. But he
wasn't done.

"I know that you're going through a lot right now, and I respect all of that. I've seen enough cancer patients to know that
asking someone to make a big life decision right now isn't fair."
I nodded and he continued. "So I want to say, and then I'll
leave this alone, that what I'm doing with Lila is biding my
time. I know that makes me sound like an asshole, but I've told
her that I've given her all that I can, so I don't feel like I'm being
unfair."

I didn't ask him to elaborate, Diary, because we both knew
who he was biding his time for. In the face of his honesty, I didn't
know if I should grab Manny and run, or leap across the couch
and kiss him, but at that exact moment, Leno came on, so we
both just turned our attention to the TV and sat in a sort of
weird, anxiety-filled vacuum during his opening monologue.
After the Misbees played, I told Zach that I should go. He insisted that he walk me home, which was sweet and kind and
wonderful in the way that you want your boyfriend to be.

When we reached my door, he kissed my forehead and told me
to get some sleep. I watched him walk down the block, and when
he turned to look back, I thought to myself, "If something is good
enough the first time around, why would you ever let it go?"

· EIGHTEEN ·

N atalie." Senator Tompkins's aide, Brian, sighed into the phone. "You know that this is a risky thing to attach ourselves to. Our constituents are from the Bible Belt, and they're not sure how they feel about it."

"But it's the right thing to do," I replied, as I doodled on the list of names in front of me. Only three more to go, and with my new-found zeal for a cause I actually cared about, I was certain they'd crumble like stale cookies in an arid desert. (Not that stale cookies are often found in an arid desert, but you see my point.) "You know it, and I know it. Look at the national polls: People want to see funding for this research. If we get this bill to the president's desk, he's going to have to take a hard look at his policy. That's what our jobs are all about, aren't they?"

"I'll run some numbers and get back to you," he said. "I can't make any promises."

I hung up the phone and rubbed my eyes. Kyle was in D.C. for the day, so I was working from his (my) office. I surveyed the space. It's a funny thing, how you can return to the exact same place that you'd spent so much time and yet nothing looks the same. My senior year in college, I went to Disneyland with Sally, Lila, and two other sorority sisters. We wove our way through the crowds, past Mr. Toad's ride and beyond a live-action figure of Mickey. I looked back as we were exiting the gate to the park, and I remember thinking that it no longer felt like the most magical place on earth like it did when I was seven and my parents gave in to my relentless demands for a visit; now it was filled with whiney, dirty-fisted babies, sweaty, plump mothers, and struggling actors who donned Disney costumes while waiting for their big break.

My office was sort of like Disneyland, only without the ice cream stands and the carousels playing lullabies. I looked around: Kyle, like me before him, had chosen to cover the walls with his diplomas—Stanford undergrad, magna cum laude, Harvard Law—but nowhere in the room did he give any clues as to what he was really like. There were no pictures of his brother, the one I knew he had because he stood in the corner with a bored, blank expression at our last fund-raiser, or of his parents from whom our assistant, Blair, took repeated messages each week. There were only signs of what he'd achieved, not how he got there or who helped him achieve it in the first place. I stood up and walked over to his Stanford diploma, sticking my nose so close that it almost touched the glass. And from this view, the letters, the honors, the very name *Stanford*, all blurred together—none of it legible, none of it important. I pulled back from my blurry perch and looked at the diploma all over again. Only this time, the only thing I saw was the mark left from my hot breath and the way that with each passing second, the steam got smaller and smaller until you couldn't tell that I'd been there at all.

At that very moment, as I sat in rapt wonder gazing at arguably Kyle's greatest achievement in life, Zach knocked on the door.

"Hey, sorry to bother you." He poked his head in. "I know that you work at about a million miles an hour during the day and probably don't want to be interrupted. But I had a thought."

"No worries. Sit down," I said, retreating back behind my desk and waving my hand to guide him to the chair in front of it. "I've wrapped up most of my doable work today anyway. What's up?"

"Wow, listen to you. Three months ago, I didn't think that you'd ever wrap up work, like, ever." He laughed. "Okay, now don't read too much into this, but I have a few days off, and it's almost the weekend, and I know that Jake's away and Lila is out of town for work, too, and, well, I made a few calls and . . ."

I squinted up my eyes and shook my head. "Where are you going with this?"

"The question is really, where are we going together. Because if we leave here right now, we can be in L.A. by tonight and in the live studio audience for *The Price Is Right* tomorrow. Separate rooms, of course. I already checked out the Beverly Hills Hotel." He smiled slyly. "And to our luck, there are rooms available."

I exhaled and reached for my calendar on my desk, flipping through the pages because, surely, they couldn't really be blank. But they were. I scanned the stacks of papers on my desk, fighting the urge to create mindless busywork just for the sake of having mindless busywork to tackle. Then I pushed my chair back, bit my bottom lip, and grinned so wide that my eyes nearly filled with tears. And then I thought of a million personal reasons why

I shouldn't say yes. And then I realized that none of them mattered more than the fact that I didn't want to say no.

"I *CANNOT BELIEVE* that we're doing this," I said, as we stood in line outside the CBS studio on Beverly Boulevard, the crystalline Los Angeles sunshine bursting down on our backs. "This might be the most unlike me thing I've ever done in my life."

"Hey, you only live once, right?" Zach looked my way and smiled, his green eyes shielded by aviator sunglasses that made him look about one hundred thousand times hotter than he already was. As if that were possible. The line inched forward, and he placed his hand on the small of my back as if to guide me along. "Who do you think all of these people are, anyway?" We both swiveled our necks to check out the crowd.

They were just like every audience of every game show that I'd ever seen, which, by this point, was far too many for any self-respecting, Ivy League, thirty-year-old senior aide to a powerful politician. A crew of sorority sisters in their green Kappa Alpha Theta sweatshirts squealed behind us; a gaggle of senior citizens stood in front of us just below eye level. The rest of the line was filled out with midwestern housewives, a few uniformed sailors, and several men who appeared to be in a bowling league: Their matching shirts tipped me off. I was quite certain that Zach and I were the only two young professionals from New York. So when *The Price Is Right* staff started filtering through the crowd—this was how they assessed who would make their way to the podium down front (I'd read this online)—I debated wowing them into choosing sophisticated moi by playing up my hip New Yorker attitude. But I realized that dropping Senator Dupris's name on national television (sometimes Bob asks you what you do! I gasped in excitement at the thought) was probably a major no-no for the New York voting contingent. I pictured the white-haired Park Avenue set cringing in horror, *utter horror,* at the classlessness of it all. Perhaps the only time that my elevated status in life would do me no good. *That and keep you from getting cancer,* I reminded myself.

So instead, I told the interviewer, "This show is the only thing that made me feel normal when I was first diagnosed with breast cancer." I saw her face move from shock to horror to admiration all in a split second. "I'd sit on my couch and scream out the answers, and for an hour, my chemo and everything else that came along with it didn't matter. As to what I can blame my continued addiction to, I guess I'd have to say that Bob Barker is a hottie. Even if he's 857 years old." The interviewer chuckled and jotted down my name on her notepad.

"Nice work," Zach said, as she moved on to the nearly hyperventilating college crew behind us. "Play that cancer card when you need it."

"Why the hell not?" I shrugged and adopted the MC's voice. "Maybe *I'll win a new car!*"

It wasn't until we were seated inside the studio that I started to get nervous. I looked around and noticed that the space seemed much smaller than on TV. The room couldn't hold more than 150 people, which meant that my odds of getting called down were about one in fifteen. Despite the frigid air-conditioning, sweat began to pool in my armpits, so I tried to inconspicuously lift my elbows in the air to provide some ventilation.

I nudged Zach while the warm-up guy was telling painfully cringe-worthy jokes. "What if I blank out? What if I totally bomb?"

He laughed. "Well, this is assuming you get called. And if

you bomb, I'm pretty certain that no one we know will be watching."

All of a sudden, the lights went dark and spotlights started circling the audience.

"WELCOME TOOOOOOOO . . . *THE PRICE IS RIGHT*!" The MC's voice boomed into the overhead speakers. "AND NOW, HERE'S YOUR HOST—BOBBBBBBBBBB BARKER!!!!"

Zach and I stood up and applauded with the rest of the crowd, and I threw my fists in the air and whooped. I grabbed his arm in the excitement and thought that I might faint. But there was no time for that.

"LADIES AND GENTLEMEN, LET'S GET THINGS STARTED! JOANNE PORTER FROM PORTLAND, OREGON, COME ON DOWN! SEAN WASHINGTON FROM TUSCON, ARIZONA, COME ON DOWN! ADAM CARTWRIGHT FROM SAN DIEGO, CALIFORNIA, COME ON DOWN! AND NATALIE MILLER FROM NEW YORK CITY, COME ON DOWN! YOU'RE THE FIRST FOUR CONTESTANTS ON *THE PRICE IS RIGHT*!!!"

The cameraman rushed over and caught me midscream with my hands waving in the air, like I was doing some wild African dance. I looked over and saw Zach clutching his sides and literally doubled over in laughter. I kicked his shin and kept screaming and shaking my arms as I ran down the aisle, flipping the long locks of my wig behind my shoulders as I went. I was nearly out of breath by the time I reached the podium and landed in my spot on the end. Looking up to the stage, I saw Bob, skinnier than I would have thought and wearing far too much foundation and blush, but still utterly dapper. *Yum*, I thought. *Still on my list*. Before I even had time to respond to his hellos, the first prize was on display:

a patio set from some southern furniture supplier. *Shit. Patio set? I'm a New Yorker. We don't do patio sets.*

I breathed deeply though my nose and out through my mouth—Janice would have been proud—and tried to recollect the prices that I'd seen on the Internet when Jake and I played along. Joanne started the bidding with $1,050, and the audience tittered. Sean undercut her by $80 with $970, and Adam went even lower with $900.

"So, Natalie, what's it going to be?" Bob said into his pencil-thin microphone and cocked an eyebrow in my direction.

I swiveled around to the audience, just like I'd seen people do a thousand times before. "One dollar! One dollar!!! One dollar!!!!!!" Every last person in the crowd screamed as if by telling me the right bid, they'd actually be the ones to get the damn patio set. I caught Zach's eye and watched as his face crumbled into hysteria once again, and he wiped tears off his face.

I turned back to my microphone. "Bob," I said with the gravity of a funeral director, "I'm going to go with one dollar." The crowd exploded with volcanic applause.

"One dollar it is, from Natalie Miller of New York City," Bob said, as he winked at me. He swung his arm around and said, "Diana, just how much *is* that lovely patio set?"

With an all-too-white toothy smile, Diana pulled back the slab of cardboard to reveal that the actual retail price was $795. I heard surround-sound dinging, and the cameramen rushed over next to me.

"Natalie Miller of New York, New York, you get on up here," Bob said, just as I felt my breath leave my chest. But I made it to the top of the stage, where Bob put his arm around my shoulder and guided me to the right side of the set. "And now, Natalie," he said in a grandfatherly tone, "we are so thrilled to have you here today, all the way in from New York City! And we think you're going to be pretty thrilled to be here with us, too. Because, Mark, can you show her what's behind this curtain?"

"Gladly, Bob," the MC responded. "Natalie, how would yoooo-uuuu like to win . . . a NEW CAR?!?!?!" The lights on the stage flashed, and the music blared, and the crowd raised the decibel level even higher. And even though I absolutely didn't need a car, and in fact, a car would most likely be an incredible inconvenience to a New Yorker, I jumped up and down uncontrollably until my whole body was almost limp, and I'd nearly worked myself up into tears.

The game, it turned out, was one of my favorites. Out of a group of twenty numbers, I had to pick the two numbers that, when paired together, would give me the total price of the Ford Explorer. I'd played enough at home that I managed to win all six chances of picking numbers by correctly guessing the prices of various household cleaning products. When Bob walked me over to the numbers board, guiding me with his hand on my back just like Zach had done not two hours earlier, I felt my hands start to shake and worried that my armpits must have resembled Louisiana swamplands.

"I'll take the $197, Bob," I said, as I pointed to one of the numbers on the board. My stomach nearly rose through my throat, as the crowd clapped behind me.

"All right then. Diana, what's behind that tile, please?"

In an instant, the lights flashed and a dinging noise went off, and Diane whipped up the tile like a bullfighter would a cape, and I saw the picture of the back of the car. "AHHHHHHHHHH-HHH," I screamed, and jumped up and down in my Nikes. All that was left was to find the first two digits to the price of the car, Bob explained, and it would be mine.

This proved more difficult in real life than from the safety of my couch. With each guess, I was more sure that I was correct, and yet four tries later, I'd accumulated $256 in cash, but no front of the car. I turned back toward the audience.

"19482650179204," they screamed. *Ha!* I thought as I turned back toward Bob and shrugged. *I think I got the world's stupidest audience!*

"Okay, Bob," I said, my voice shaking, as he put his arm around me. "I'm going to go with . . . yes, I'm going to go with $21."

"Well, Natalie Miller from New York City, let's see if you just won a new car!" But the lights didn't go off and no dinging noises played, and within seconds, the audience started groaning. Diane had pulled off the tile to reveal more cash, and no front end. So Bob kissed me on the cheek—*he kissed me on the cheek!*—and congratulated me on my cash winnings of $277, and I was ushered backstage until I gained my chance at the Big Wheel. I felt my BlackBerry vibrate in my bag.

From: Goodman, Maureen
To: Miller, Natalie
Re: Reporter and stem cell story

Hey Natalie—

I tried you at the office, but they said you were out for the day. Lucky girl! I just got off the phone with a friend of yours—Sally Fisher. She's doing a big piece for the NYT Mag on the politics behind the stem cell bill, and she was referred to our offices. When I mentioned that we were working on this together with Dupris, she was surprised . . . she mentioned you were best friends but that she didn't realize you were helming the bill. Will this be a problem? I got the sense that the story would be positive, but you know journalists . . . one day they've

put us up on a pedestal, the next, they're happy to chop us
down. Thoughts?
—Maureen

I finished reading and Sean from Tucson wandered in. I could tell by the glum look on his face that he hadn't lived up to his armchair quarterback expectations, either. *Crap,* I thought. *Holy fucking crap.* So this is Sally's big story. We'd been so focused on my cancer, and on Zach, and on Jake, that really, we never discussed work anymore, both figuring it was the same old, same old. But this definitely was *not* the same old, same old. Not at all.

Before I had time to type a response, production aides swooped down and whisked us back onstage, marching us like penguins over to the Big Wheel. Bob didn't join us until just before the cameras started to shoot.

It was indeed a big wheel. Bigger—and it turned out heavier—than it looked on TV. Sean went first: His sorry winnings held the lowest value, and he managed to eke out a semidecent 70 cents. "I'll stick with that, Bob," he said, and moved over to the winner's perch.

I was next. I took a deep breath and pushed down on the wheel. *Damn,* I thought. *This is more of a workout than I've had in five months. Tick, tick, tick, tick.* The numbers slowly spun past me. *OH SHIT.* My eyes widened, as the wheel slowed down. *It's not even making it around one time!* Bob put his arm around me and told me to spin again, but all I wanted to do was crawl into the comfort of his arms and have him hold me. Instead, I pushed every last ounce of my weight into the wheel, and threw my arms down. *Tick, tick, tick, tick.* A little faster this time. Until . . . wait . . . hold your breath . . . it was perfect. Smack on the $1.00. I just won a thousand bucks!!!! I hurled my body in the air and started screaming, while Bob kindly bumped Sean from the winner's circle and escorted me into it.

Joanne from Portland, the only contestant who actually won her prize—new kitchen appliances—didn't stand a chance. She spun twice, and ha!, too bad for her, came out far over the $1.00 goal. I looked out to the audience and gave Zach the thumbs-up. I was going to the showcase showdown. The production assistants plopped us in the green room, and I frantically grabbed my BlackBerry.

From: Goodman, Maureen
To: Miller, Natalie
Re: Problems already

Hey Natalie—

I just got off the phone with aides from the Mississippi contingents' offices. We're already in deep shit. Evidently Sally called them, too—I mean, of course she would if she's a half-decent reporter—and they want to know what we're saying about them. Obviously, I told them nothing, but they said that if we even murmured a derogatory word about their senators, they'd unleash their "folder of secrets" (whatever that is) and happily feed it all—I assume background dirt on Dupris and McIntyre—to Sally. Well, this should be fun. Only not.

—Maureen

Holy Mary mother of God. I inhaled and exhaled and thought of Janice's soothing voice. Rationally, I knew that Sally was only doing her job. Irrationally, and this was the emotion that was winning out, I wanted to kill her. Well, not literally, but almost. I pulled up her e-mail address on my screen and started to type.

I wasn't sure why my hands were shaking, whether it was nerves from the imminent showcase showdown (my dream!) or whether it was because for the first time in our decadelong friendship, I was about to test its strength.

From: Miller, Natalie
To: Fisher, Sally
Re: Your story

Sally—

I know this sounds weird, but I'm writing from California. Yeah, I'm actually backstage at *The Price Is Right*. With Zach. Don't ask.

I just got an e-mail from Maureen Goodman, and she said that you're working on a story on the stem cell bill. Sal, look, I'm thrilled for you. You know that. You know that I'm the biggest champion of your work, but this piece could be really damaging for Dupris. For everyone who works for her. So I'm going to ask you a favor, and it's a big one. And please, this is off the record. (Sorry, I had to say it.) But it's to either (a) make sure that Dupris is cast in a good light in the article or (b) don't write it.

Gotta go. I'm up for the showcase showdown.

Nat

Just as I pressed Send, a production assistant grabbed my elbow and ushered me to a stage on the right and placed me in front of the "loser's" podium: the one who had accumulated the lowest winnings thus far. I knew that the loser was in a less strategic position because the "winner" got first dibs at which showcase to bid on. In nearly every case, he passed the first one to the loser. And in the cases when he didn't, you'd sit at home, mouth agape, and wonder if the idiot had ever seen the show. The second showcase was *always* more valuable than the first! Moron!

True to form, Adam from San Diego tossed the first prizes— new living room furnishings (circa: 1983), a new hot tub (not so helpful in NYC), and a new washer/dryer (ditto)—my way. I pressed out foreboding thoughts of Sally's exposé, squinted my eyes, and blocked out the screeches of the audience.

"Bob, I'm going to go with . . ." I stared at the hot tub one last time. "Yes, I'm going to go with $8,175." The crowd went bananas.

"All right, Natalie from New York City. Remember, you can't go above the actual retail price of your showcase, and the contestant closest to the price of his showcase will go home a winner. Should one of you come within $250 of the actual retail price, you'll take home *both* showcases." He winked at me, and I swooned.

Adam was lucky enough to land a themed showcase: what Barker's Beauties found at their local lost and found. My eyes widened when the lovely ladies emerged in bikinis and flip-flops. I already knew what was coming. The Beauties filtered through the navy steamer trunk and pulled out teeny bathing suits. ($200, I figured.) Next came a life vest . . . and stage left opened to reveal a speedboat. ($11,000, I calculated.) And finally, yep, there it was, a coconut. The stage-right curtain whisked open, as the MC shouted out "a vacation for two to Fiji!" (At least another $8,000, I reasoned.)

I looked over at Adam, and he had all of the signs of a novice written on his face. Perplexed, furrowed brows, wan, sweaty skin, frantic eyes pleading for the audience to guide him. *Sucker.* I smirked. *Don't mess with the showdown unless you're a seasoned expert.* Bob prodded him for an answer.

"Um, uh." Adam tried to buy himself time until the buzzer dinged in the background. "Uh, gosh, okay. I'll go with . . ." He looked out into the audience again. *Even they can't save you now, buddy.* "I'll go with $26,350, Bob." The audience groaned, and I let out a wide smile.

We took a break, and the makeup team bum-rushed us. I saw Bob getting his blush redone, and I grinned. I'm not sure that you can ever see a man get swathed in peach tones and ever want to bed him again. Yes, I'd have to tell Zach after this, I do believe that dear Bob was officially off my list.

The MC asked for the audience to settle down, and the Barker girls took their places.

"All right, Natalie," Bob said, moving into position next to my podium. "Let's see how you did. You bid $8,175. And the actual retail price of the showcase is . . . $8,235 . . . a difference of . . ." His eyebrows shot up. "Just $60!" He patted my arm. "Very good. Very good indeed. If Adam here doesn't beat that, you'll go home with both of these."

He moved over to Adam's perch, and the audience shouted out my name. "Now, Adam. You had the sun and fun package. And for that, you bid a grand total of $26,350. The actual retail price is . . . $22,540 . . ." Moans from the audience. "So, Adam, I'm sorry. You went over by nearly four thousand dollars, which means that Natalie here takes home both showcases!"

My legs started quivering, and my face contorted into all sorts of humiliating shapes (I'd know this when the show aired several months later), and I wondered if I'd ever had a moment as fulfilling as this. I jumped into Bob's arms the way that a sailor's wife might when he finally docked home after a year at sea, and started uncontrollably, mortifyingly, from-the-bottom-of-my-belly sobbing. It was Zach who rescued him from me (audience members who were friends of the winner were whisked onstage by production assistants), peeling me off, limb by limb, until I stood on my own feet and wiped the snot off my face, while Bob pretended that something almost entirely inappropriate (and if not that, then certainly terribly weird) had just occurred.

We waved good-bye to the camera, Bob asked everyone to spay and neuter their pets, and I stared up at the bright lights of the studio, the ones that surely would have made every pore in your body sweat if not for the arcticlike air-conditioning, and I figured, *maybe you can make your own luck after all.*

ROUND SEVEN

• • •

March

· NINETEEN ·

Two days after we got back, a week into my seventh chemo round and back in the discomfort of my cube, Brian returned my call.

"Natalie, I think we're in," he said.

I let out a whoop and grabbed the notepad on my desk, the one that held the list of all the senators who were about to change history.

"But there are strings."

"Aren't there always?" I said. This, after all, was politics. Twine was practically invented for it. I started doodling squiggly lines on the yellow pad.

"He wants Senator Dupris to back off her education push. It's not going over well down here, and frankly, if the bill goes through,

I think our schools might suffer. Vouchers aren't what our voters want."

"Brian, you know that I can't promise that. Education is her thing. It's what she ran on last year." Even as I said it though, I found myself agreeing with him. The senator's education plan really wasn't a solution. It was a false hope that parents might be able to land their child in a better school outside of their immediate district: It didn't address the real problem—that our teachers had no motivation to teach and the kids weren't learning.

But she sold it so thoroughly during the campaign that people actually bought it: She actually convinced them that something bad for them was really something good. It's amazing how easily swayed a mind can be if you have the tools to be cunningly persuasive.

"People run on broken promises all the time," Brian said. "And besides, I thought you said in our initial phone call that stem cell research was her big thing this year—that you guys were getting pounded from your voters asking for change."

I had said that. It was true. Our constituents *did* want public funding for research. But did they want it at the expense of their schools, even if the senator's solutions wouldn't really fix any-thing? I doubted it. Still, I promised Brian that I'd raise the subject with the senator. In doing so, I also raised the stakes.

THE FUNNY THING about chemo is that it lulls you into a false sense of security. You get used to the pattern of it—of watching the drip, drip, drip as it enters your bloodstream, of repeating the cycle of rehabilitating yourself every three weeks—so used to it that you feel like you own the chemo instead of it owning you. And any cancer patient can tell you, this? Is a mistake.

Which is how it turned out that Manny saved my life. Ironic, isn't it? Instead of being rescued by an alpha dog, I was saved by my rescue dog. I don't remember that part, of course, but pieced it together by what was told to me in the hospital. I woke up, and Sally, whom I'd listed as my emergency contact number when I was first diagnosed, was sitting by my side, listlessly flipping through *Cosmo*.

"What happened?" I said, tasting the stale saliva in my mouth.

"Neutropenia," she said, reaching for my hand.

I closed my eyes and tried to remember what Dr. Chin had told me about neutropenia, one of the complications that could arise. One of the complications that could kill you. *Neutropenia*, I thought—the absence of the necessary number of white blood cells. One in three cancer patients suffers from it. And without these cells, the ones that act like armor for your blood in the face of infection, you have no protection against bacteria and germs. You're essentially a walking time bomb, an open window for illness.

"How did I get here?" I asked her with my eyes closed, as I listened to the beeping of the heart monitor beside me. At least it assured me that I was still alive.

"You collapsed in your living room. Manny kept barking and barking until your neighbors insisted that the doorman see that everything was okay." She grew quiet. "Obviously, it wasn't."

"Fuck."

"They found you collapsed by the kitchen table. Manny was spinning in circles, going crazy. They called 911, brought you in, and then they called me."

"I don't remember any of this." I cradled my face with my hands. "Christ, I feel horribly ill." And then I remembered that I was supposed to be mad at her. That we hadn't spoken since I'd e-mailed her from backstage of *The Price Is Right*, and that instead of replying, she'd left a vague, but certainly not promising, message for me that I hadn't had the spine to return. I listened to her voice echo out from my machine and felt my stomach sink. I hated it, this feeling of wondering who was betraying whom. Me or her.

"They're treating it. They caught the infection in time." She started to say more but caught herself.

"We need to talk, Sal." I looked her in the eye. "We've been artfully avoiding each other, but clearly, we need to talk."

"Nat, I swear, I didn't know. I had no idea that this would be such an issue." She looked down at her hands. "But I can't . . . I can't just walk away from this. Not even for you." All at once, I felt exhausted, like the neutropenia really might kill me. Sally picked up on it. "Look, please, let's talk about something else. This isn't the time." She paused. "Where's Jake, Nat? I thought he was here in New York for this exact reason."

"He had to go back to L.A.," I managed. "Just for a night."

The Misbees had been so hailed on *Leno* that the label wanted to release an acoustic version of "Miles from Her" by April. Jake had halfheartedly tried to convince his manager to hold off until I was done with my chemo or, at the very least, to record the cut in New York, but Sony had already booked a studio and a producer in L.A. It had to be there. Within the next three weeks. That's *what* he told me. On Valentine's Day. That's *when* he told me.

I'd felt well enough to go out, so I pulled on my knee-high boots, a black lace skirt, and my movie-star wig, and we went to Bouley. It was nearly impossible to get reservations there—possibly New York's swankiest restaurant—during the year, much less on Valentine's Day, but when the maître d' heard that Jake was the one who wanted a spot, they found a way. This is how Jake's life was now: The fact that he was Jake Martin was usually enough to get him in or out of just about any situation.

At dinner, before Jake told me about L.A., I tried not to think about Zach. Instead, I thought about how people were turning and noticing us, but this time, it wasn't because I looked like a cancer patient. It was because my boyfriend was nearly a rock star. And I'll admit it: It was kind of cool. I saw women attempt to inconspicuously size him up as we ushered past, and I saw men lean over and whisper into their wives' ears when we raised our wine and drank a toast. I looked across the table at Jake and wondered, why doesn't this feel like enough? By anyone else's measure, at least at Bouley on that night, it looked like it should have been.

Now, in the hospital room, with an IV in my arm and my future looking noticeably cloudier than over that dinner, I felt like I should have stopped him from going to L.A. this time. Offered an ultimatum, although they never work. I know this because two of my girlfriends had threatened their live-in boyfriends with the line, "propose in X months or else get out," which is how they found themselves paying the bulk of their rent and living in a half-furnished apartment X months later. Still though, if not an ultimatum, then what? He came back to make things right, but when I found him faltering, was it now my obligation to make them right for both of us? I didn't know.

"He went to fucking L.A. again?" Sally said. "I *cannot* believe him."

"Sally, please. I don't have the energy. But he didn't have a choice."

She picked up her *Cosmo* and started flipping through it. Just so she didn't have to look me in the eye. "You always have a choice, Natalie. It's just that he didn't choose you."

• • •

Dear Diary,

I spent three days in the hospital, but I'm okay now. It's ironic, though, how I was cruising along, taking this cancer thing in stride, assuming that I'd tackle the odds (and everything else, really—Jake, work, you name it) without a problem, when it roundly landed me on my ass. And now, tack on Sally's big story, and everything has gone to pot.

When Jake got back, he was mortified. No, he was worse than mortified. His eyes welled with tears, and he asked me how this could happen—how he could leave one morning when I was by all accounts healthy (oxymoron, I know, but healthier, I guess) and return 36 hours later to find me laid up in the hospital, fighting off an infection that could conceivably end my life. I reminded him that I'd actually taken the day off from work that day, that I wasn't feeling well when he headed out to the airport, but he just said, "But you told me it was a cold. Nothing. How was I supposed to know?"

I didn't say this, Diary, but that doesn't mean that I wasn't thinking it. And what I didn't say was this: We have no way of knowing anything, but why the fuck is that somehow a justification for you leaving? I mean, if he's only sticking around for the times that I'm sick, because I am sick, well, then, that's not really much of an incentive to stick around at all, is it?

But as I said, I didn't say anything. I know. I KNOW. Look, Diary, should I have taken that moment to not so gently point out to Jake that he came back under the promise of taking care of me? Of being my alpha? Of course, I should have. Should

I have taken that time to say, hey, even with you around, I feel incomplete, worried that you already have one bag packed? Without a doubt. But the thing is this: Without him here, I worry that I won't just feel incomplete, I'll feel empty. God knows it was bad enough having my dog save the day just this once. Of having my dog be the one being whom I can trust completely. Even if Jake goes away now and then, and even if he's increasingly distracted with their new album and slightly in awe of his rising fame, isn't it better to take a chance on him than wait for my dog to wake up one day and find my cold, dead body splayed on the floor?

I know. You're telling me that it's not. That I'm finally answering the question that I've long been plagued by: Is enough truly enough? But the thing is, Diary, I'm tired. I'm 30 and I'm single and I have cancer and I'm tired. And if my not-so-perfect boyfriend wants to pretend that he's a martyr and occasionally wants to try to rescue me, far be it from me to tell him not to try.

And anyway, I should probably tell you that Zach and Lila stopped by my hospital room. Together. Days of Our Lives *was just finishing up, and I was contemplating a nap when they knocked on the door and came in. Lila brought flowers—"from us," she said, while Zach thrust his hands into his lab coat and looked at the floor like a second grader who had just been scolded by his teacher. After Lila had to rush back to work—she came on her lunch hour, which objectively, I know, is very sweet—he looked at me and shrugged.*

"What's that about?" I said.

"She told me that she thought we should visit, and I couldn't offer up a reasonable explanation as to why we shouldn't."

"So she has no idea? Doesn't know about dinner the other week or what you said? Or our brush with fame and fortune in

the game show world?" To be fair, I hadn't mentioned the trip to Jake, either.

"She doesn't want to hear it," he said. "Every time I bring up how I feel, or where we are or aren't going with this, she shuts me down." He sighed. "You know how she can be. She's like a train, and we're all just the tracks that she rides over."

I didn't think that I was in a position to judge, given that I was living with my quasi-boyfriend, so I just smoothed the sheets of my bed and told him that it was nice to see him. Even in these circumstances. He kissed me on the cheek and told me that he'd call this weekend to see how I was, and then he got back to his rounds.

He shut the door, and I stared up at Passions. *And it dawned on me that Zach and I, we were one and the same. Two people who didn't want to feel lonely anymore, so we tied ourselves to the closest anchors and let them bring us down. Sometimes, it's easier to sink than to swim.*

PS—I guess the good news is that Dr. Chin used my hospital stay as an opportunity to bump up my nipple surgery a few days. At long last . . . nipples. No more floating snow globes. I actually have semi-real-looking breasts. At least for a XXX star.

Sigh. And the better news is that at least this little setback got me out of that miserable, sure-to-be mope-filled lunch with Susanna Taylor and her gang of cancer-fighting superheroes.

· TWENTY ·

I cannot believe her," I said to Jake, over Sunday morning bagels and tea for me, black coffee for him. "I mean, how could she do this? She knows it's going to screw me." I leaned back into the cushions of our couch and sighed.

Jake bit into his poppy seed bialy and thought it over. "Nat, seriously. Do you hear yourself? You're asking her to choose your friendship over her big break, when really, you could choose just as well."

"I don't follow." I frowned, and wiped cream cheese from the corner of my mouth.

"Well, I just mean that you could say, 'Hey, you know what? I've put Sally second to my career my whole life, and this time,

I'm going to let her—*because of our friendship*, not in spite of it—go after this thing that she really wants.'"

I took a sip of my peppermint tea, mulled it over, and wondered if Jake had found some sort of enlightenment on his road trip, because he was just as guilty as anyone of putting people second to his career.

Sally and I had gone to lunch the day before. We artfully danced around the subject until it became clear that we had nothing left to talk about. When I asked her again to please stop, to please not dig deeper into this story, she squeezed her eyes shut and shook her head.

"Nat, you know that I'd do anything in the world for you. I mean, I feel like I've done everything I could for you as a friend. But there are limits. I have them, you have them. And well, these are mine. I've wanted this for *so* long. And not only does it suck that we can't see eye to eye, it sucks even more that you can't be supportive." She played with her straw so she didn't have to look at me.

"Sally, that's completely not fair," I responded, feeling my pulse race. "This has *nothing* to do with not supporting you, and everything to do with protecting my boss. You have no idea how ugly this is going to get." It came out condescendingly, even though I didn't mean it to.

The truth was that, just like the Mississippi contingent, I too had a "folder of secrets" on just about everyone in Congress—who they might have been sleeping with, what (ulterior) motives they had to vote why they did, which interns had gotten felt up more than once and by whom. As Sally probed deeper and deeper into each senator's reasons to back (or stymie) the stem cell bill, the two sides walked toward each other like medieval armies, only we were armed with our sordid knowledge of each other's histories rather than swords and cavalry. What she was doing was

exposing more than just the political divide on this particular issue, she was opening up a fissure into which we'd dumped all of
our dirty laundry.

She looked at me over her Greek salad and stabbed it with her
fork. "You know, Nat. Never, *never*, have I sat in judgment of you
while you've clawed your way to the top. *Never* have I made you
feel badly for forgoing your friendships or dating unavailable men
or making the choices that you've made that maybe I didn't agree
with. I stood by you all the same." She stopped, letting her eyes
wander as she searched for the right words until she found them.
"And now? I don't know. This feels like lousy payback. Like your
boss's ass is more important than mine."

"I didn't realize that you required payback. Forgive me. I
thought you were my friend with no strings attached." Overhear-
ing my raised voice, the couple next to us turned and stared.

"Everything has strings, Nat. Everyone has the point where they
know that they've been pushed too far." Sally sighed, and I thought
of Susanna Taylor and her philandering husband, of Zach and the
games Lila played with him, of Jake and his almost broken promises.
Sally interrupted my musings. "Please don't push me, Nat. Because
this time, I can't be held responsible if I push you back."

I STILL NEEDED to speak with the senator about the education
bill, not to mention Sally's story that wouldn't go away, but by the
time I got back into the office after recovering from my hospital
stay, Dupris was on vacation for a week in Aruba.

"Tough life," I said to Kyle, as we filtered through her mail,
tossing anything even remotely unworthy of her time into the assistant's bin. Blair was the one who would answer the letters to the
family in Buffalo who believed that the senator wasn't honoring

her campaign pledges or to the elderly couple in the Bronx who wanted to thank her for stopping by their church. The busier the senator got, the less time she had for the actual people who voted. Don't get me wrong—she still stopped and smiled for pictures on the street when people asked her to, and she definitely still shook hands with eager voters as she made her way to lunch at The Four Seasons. But this time around, her second term as a senator, she seemed more focused on pushing herself higher and less intent on actually getting things done. I'd recognized it only recently. I wasn't sure if it were because she had changed or I had, but it didn't matter really. I recognized it just the same. That's how it was with politicians: If you just noticed the shiny veneer on the outside, they'd always look perfect. So you had to peer closer, watch them when they didn't think they were being watched. Eventually, you'd notice the dings.

"It's not just a vacation," Kyle said. "It's a working vacation. She's down there with Andrews. He picked her up in his jet at Islip. Made it clear that she shouldn't bring along her advisers. Very hush-hush." Gerald Andrews, the head of the Democratic National Committee. I raised my eyebrows. The things I missed while knocked out at Sloan-Kettering.

"Yep, they're grooming her for the next ticket," he said. "Her star is about to blow out of the sky."

"Seriously? So the rumors are true. Can you imagine? The first female president."

"Can you imagine," he said, "what it would do for our careers?"

"I BOUGHT OUR tickets today," I said to Jake. He'd just come back from his publicist's office, and I'd just gotten in from work.

I sat on my plush white couch and rubbed Manny's stomach while Jake filtered through delivery menus.

"God, I'm starving," he said. "What do you feel like tonight? Do you mind if we get Chinese? I've been craving moo shu all day."

"Sure. But did you hear me? I bought our tickets to Sally's wedding today. We're taking the nonstop out of JFK at 9:00 A.M. I figured that this would give us nearly three full days down there."

"Sounds good," he said, as he walked into the bedroom in search of the cordless phone. I wondered if he'd even heard me. I probably could have told him that I ran naked through the subway that morning, fake boobs and all, and he would have had the same reaction: In this present moment all he cared about was his moo shu.

The only time that I got 100 percent from Jake these days was when we were dealing with my cancer. With the diligence of a schoolmarm, he reminded me to take my medicine. Because Dr. Chin encouraged a varied and colorful diet, Jake acted like my own personal nutritionist. And, of course, he asked me how I was feeling at least seventeen times a day, which I knew I should find endearing, but after about the ninth time, it grated. I know, I know. I should hardly complain. And it was true that he occupied not just the space in my apartment, but also a space in my heart. He could have been screwing groupies and snorting coke and engaging in entirely too much unhealthy debauchery, but instead, he chose to be with me. I suppose that this was at least part of the reason that I ignored the fact that he'd already broken his promise to me that he'd stay.

There is a moment in every relationship when one of the parties senses its imminent demise. There's a moment of incredible clarity, when your stomach drops with a heavy sense of dread, and you feel like control is slipping through your fingertips even as you try to hold on. The night I bought our tickets to go to Sally's wedding and the one when Jake was dying for moo shu—that was the night I had that moment.

I followed him into the bedroom. He'd just hung up the phone with Empire Szechwan and said, "They'll be here in fifteen minutes. That's what I love about Chinese—you order it and they're already at your door. I got you wonton soup. Figured that would go down easy."

"Great. Fine. But did you hear me about the tickets?"

"I told you that I did. I already said that!" He pulled his T-shirt over his head and threw it on top of the hamper. "So we're going? Are you two speaking yet?"

Sally and I had tacitly called an unsteady truce. Well, not really called a truce, but just stopped calling each other period so we didn't have to tackle this irresolvable subject all over again. Because we had tackled it all over again on the phone a few days after our lunch and ended up getting nowhere. I decided to treat her like any other journalist, so I barred access to Dupris. She snorted into the phone and told me that if I thought that the only way she could get information was from the source herself, then clearly, I underestimated her abilities as a journalist. And then I raised the stakes by saying that whatever she printed that wasn't directly from Dupris's mouth could be considered slander. To which she yelled that if I gave her damn access to the senator in the first place, legal action wouldn't even be an issue. We've endured a tense silence ever since. The truth was though, when I wasn't busy being angry at her, I realized that I missed her.

"Yes, we're still going. I'm her maid of honor for God's sake. So you marked it in your calendar? You told Sony and your agent and your publicist and anyone else who might urgently need you and page you back from Puerto Rico that you will be otherwise engaged that weekend because we'll be attending the wedding of my best friend?"

"Correction: best friend to whom you're no longer speaking. But yes. For God's sake, I'm not that disorganized." He paused and examined his skin in the closet mirror. "But you know, sometimes things are out of my control. I mean, if they absolutely, absolutely need me, I have to be somewhere."

"It's not like you're the president, Jake," I said, turning around and walking back into the living room.

"Natalie, give me a break," he said, plodding after me. "You know that I'm trying my best. And I have every intention of coming to Sally's wedding with you. Why are you flipping out?"

"I'm not flipping out at all," I said, as calmly as possible to indicate that I wasn't flipping out even though I very clearly was. "But it seems to me that you're already offering up excuses, and the wedding is still five weeks away."

"I'm not offering up excuses of any kind. Jesus Christ. I was just saying that sometimes shit happens, and I don't have a choice."

I grabbed Manny's leash to take him out for a walk. I was out of pot and wasn't hungry anyway.

"No, Jake, that's where you're wrong. Me getting cancer? True enough, I had no choice. How you treat the ones you love? Well, there, you always have a choice," I said, as I slammed the door.

. . .

Dear Diary,

Jake and I had a fight. A pretty big one too. Sort of like the old times. When he'd get back from a long road trip, and we'd reacquaint ourselves with each other, and we'd finally ease back into things, and then he'd announce that he had to leave all over again. And I'd simmer in my own anger, pretending that I didn't care that he was off to Madrid or Amsterdam or even fucking Tucson, as if anyone actually wants to go to Tucson, until I couldn't pretend anymore and would finally explode. Usually after a particularly crappy day at work. I mean, after days like those, even Tucson sounded like nirvana.

This time, I know that not speaking with Sally and this whole shit-show with her article is weighing on me. But I also know that, like what Zach once said, if something didn't work the first time around, it's probably not going to get much better the second. Especially because the second time, you're haunted by all of the things that went wrong before.

So you look for hints, for signs, even if they're not quite lying on the surface. But Jake is slipping; I can feel it. I think he thought that he could rescue me: It was romantic, it was idyllic, it was the way to win me back. But after all that faded, after the heady rush of my diagnosis and his knight-in-shining-armor entrance, we're left with just the two of us. Me, the cancer-laden jockey gripping the reins, and him, a budding rock star who is dying to break free and gallop.

But that's not really the reason I'm writing. I'm writing because I contacted Ned. Yes, you read correctly. Ned, the guy who ditched me on the day that I was diagnosed with Stage III cancer. Ned, the weaseliest weasel who ever weaseled. (And that's saying a lot considering the current standing of both Brandon and Dylan.) I'm sure that you thought that I wouldn't bother including him in my chronicles, since I already knew why we broke up. Namely, that he's the lowest scum and most spineless *amoeba to ever have inhabited the planet. And this is true. But I promised myself that I'd track them all down: the five loves in my life, and as I round the corner to the end of my treatments, I wanted to see this through. If only to let his spineless ass know that I'm back with Jake.*

Anyway, it turns out that Ned did accept that transfer to Chicago. I know this because when I called his secretary in New York, she told me that he was no longer in that office and passed me a 312 number.

I called Ned at his office from my cube in the back of my own office, but he wasn't there, so I left a message. I heard his voice on the recording, and I felt my blood almost literally boil. Maybe six months wasn't enough time for me. Maybe this was a mistake. But I tempered myself as much as nearly possible, and I'd have to say, Diary, that I left a relatively downright dignified message, even if the undertones of my voice did not-so-subtly imply that I thought he was pond scum. Oh well, I can live with that.

It's funny, isn't it, Diary? That thin line between love and hate? How you can go from seriously contemplating spending the rest of your days with someone, only to discover that the next day, you'd be totally content should he encounter the un-fortunate circumstances of having all his fingernails ripped out simultaneously. Weird how that can happen, but it happens all the same.

Ned didn't call me back, which I guess isn't surprising. He might have been smart enough and funny enough and just hand-some enough to eke out the persona of a desirable man, but he was never particularly courageous. Maybe I don't have to ex-plain that to you, dear Diary, since he left me at my lowest mo-ment rather than stick out some hard work during hard times.

So maybe I'll just let Ned go. Not try to pry too far into that one because it's too recent to see objectively, and really, what else do I need to know? He left me for some chick in Chicago. Maybe that's the way to close the door to that chapter. Let sleeping (scummy, small-penised) dogs lie.

ROUND EIGHT

· · ·

April

· TWENTY-ONE ·

If I hadn't experienced it myself, I'd never believe it to be true. But on March 28, the day of my last chemo treatment, I found myself unsure what I would do without it. The chemo and its patterns had become so ingrained in my life that I literally worried how to move past it. Strange, isn't it? How life can play that trick on you?

I said good-bye to Susan, the receptionist who checked me in each time; hugged Mary, my nurse, good-bye as I got up to leave; and gave all of the staff who had nurtured me back to health (I hoped) gift certificates to Bloomingdale's. It was odd to admit, but I would miss them. And it was odder still to admit that I was sad. Whoever would have thought that the one place I'd find solace from my loneliness would be at the chemo ward at Sloan-Kettering, where the staff not only had championed my well-being, but also had grown to be my family.

I raised this with Janice the following Tuesday.

"It's very normal for patients to become attached to their care-givers," she said. "They're the ones who looked after you like no one else could. They're literally the ones who saved your life. If you weren't grateful, it might be strange."

"That's true," I said, nodding in agreement. "But don't you think something's wrong with the fact that I feel like they're the only people I can rely on?"

"I don't know. Do you think that something's wrong with it?" Janice's doublespeak was now second nature to me, so I barely took notice.

"Well, yeah. To be honest, I do."

"So what's the solution?"

I knew that she wouldn't tell me the solution because she never offered her own advice, a trait that I found as annoying as I did endearing. "If I gave you my own advice," she once said when I begged her to actually just lay out a course of action for me, "then it wouldn't be organic to you. You'd have less incentive to follow through. And that would defeat the whole point of our sessions." I supposed that she was right, but it would be helpful neverthe-less.

"I'm not sure," I said, mulling it over. "I guess that I could trust in the people in my life more, give them a chance to prove that I can rely on them." I thought of Sally and the crossroads we'd reached. And I thought of Zach, minus that inconvenience known as my second-best friend, Lila, and his mint chocolate chip ice cream. I thought of Susanna and how I should probably return her messages.

"That's certainly a good start," Janice said. "What else?"

I looked around her office, at her silver-plated picture frames with photos of her gleaming family and just-handsome-enough husband and wondered how they'd all come out so normal. I noticed her equestrian awards on the wall behind her desk, and the books on her shelf, at least half of which had nothing to do with medicine.

"How do you find that balance?" I asked, changing the subject entirely. "The one between caring too much about your patients and the one where you get to have a life of your own?"

"This isn't about me, Natalie. Let's focus on you."

"Janice, please. This is about me. And I'd like to know how you find that balance. I always seem to be off-kilter, putting too many eggs in one basket while ignoring the other one entirely. But I'd like not to do that anymore."

She thought about it for a minute and took a sip of her coffee. "How do I find that balance? For me, it's not so much a struggle. I think if you give too much of yourself to any one thing—work, marriage, even your cancer recovery—you're bound to lose sight of the other parts of yourself that need nurturing. Like a tree. If you just focused on bringing out the blossoms, you'd never see the gorgeous leaves or the age-old roots or the bark that holds all of its scars and tells its history."

"So I should be more like a tree?" I asked.

"No." She laughed. "But you should water every part of yourself that is thirsty." She looked at the clock. "Our time's almost up, and you still haven't answered your original question."

"What was that? I don't remember."

"You were answering the second part of your question. How you can come to rely more on the people in your life."

"Oh," I said, thinking it over. And then it hit me. "I suppose that it's not just about relying on the people who have proven themselves, but cutting out the ones who haven't. Because they taint it for everyone else. After all, if one person can sink me, who's to say that the others won't, too? Or at least that's the excuse I can tell myself when I push them away."

Janice smiled and rose to lead me out the door. "That, my dear, is what we call progress. That's what we call progress, indeed."

"THANKS FOR MEETING me," I said, gingerly taking a bite of a currant scone and wiping the butter off my fingers with a napkin.

"My pleasure. I was so thrilled when you called." Susanna Taylor waved her hand and took a sip of her tea. She paused to let the hot water go down. "I know that this isn't easy for you."

"The cancer?"

"The whole thing," she said. "Calling. Asking for help. Juggling the job. Feeling alone." She smiled when she saw my eyebrows rise. "No, I haven't been stalking you. I've just been there. So I know. That's why I started the support group to begin with."

When I got home from my session with Janice, I sat at my desk and turned Susanna's card over and over again in my hands. I'd been thinking about calling her the entire cab ride home, but when I was faced with actually doing it, I tried to come up with all the reasons that I shouldn't instead. Finally, I realized that if nothing else, she was a link to Sally, a link that could perhaps help bring us back together. So after twenty minutes, I picked up the phone and dialed.

Today, Susanna set down her porcelain saucer, the kind that my mother inherited when my grandmother passed. "So how's work going?" she asked.

I stared down at my own teacup and shrugged. "Okay, I guess." I looked around the café, which had been designed to evoke a quintessential British tea shop. Wire-backed chairs with lavender seat cushions, blooming floral wallpaper with paintings of the English countryside on top. The scent of butter wafted in the air. "I'm not sure that your husband missed much when he lost the election."

"Try telling him that." She snorted. "But I take it this term isn't running as smoothly as the last?"

"It's not that." I shook my head and sighed, choosing my words carefully. "It's just that . . . well, it feels like we're doing all this work, and I'm not sure how much it matters."

"Hasn't it always been that way?" she asked. "I mean, I've never been in politics—I was a lawyer before I quit to focus on fund-raising—but that was always my impression. A lot of self-aggrandizing bullshit. I never understood why anyone would want to get involved." She took another sip. "Why did you?"

"A million reasons, probably," I said. "Mostly, I'd say, because I wanted to be president."

"Wow, lofty goal. You mean, become president so you could change the world for the better?"

I watched a mother clench the hand of her young son and guide him down the front steps to the café. "No," I replied, still staring. "I mean become president for the sake of becoming president." I shook my eyes from my daze. "Well, maybe that's not entirely fair. There was a time—and this was so long ago that it's hard to remember—but really, there was a time when I thought that it was about being a *good man*." I circled my fingers over the rim of my cup and thought back to fifth grade when my history teacher, Mrs. Roberts, talked about Abraham Lincoln, George Washington, about *good men*, and how my ten-year-old heart swelled because I felt like I could be one of those people. A really good man. "And Dupris used to inspire me to be that. In her first few years, it felt like maybe we could really change the world. But now, I mean, it sort of feels like you fight the fights to win them, not because the fights really matter."

I ran my hands over my face. The senator had been deflecting my requests for a meeting for weeks now. I still hadn't told her about the exposé, and according to Maureen, who'd allowed Senator McInytre to speak with Sally, the article would indeed be explosive. And Sally had been right: Just because I kept Dupris directly out, it didn't mean that she hadn't been discussed.

The senator and I would bounce by each other each morning: Kyle and I would bring her up to speed on the news headlines, the latest maneuvers by various senators, and whatever gossip floated our way. But I needed to sit down with her—I made this clear—to go over the intricacies of ensuring the votes for the stem cell bill, the very one that was causing me so much angst, but she kept waving me off. Finally, I had Blair pencil me in. I mean, literally, pencil me in. I couldn't believe that this was what it was coming to—that the assistant had to write in a slot for me two weeks down the line, but ever since Senator Dupris had gotten the secret nod as the next in line from the DNC, she was virtually AWOL.

Susanna Taylor saw me staring into my teacup, as if the leaves could read my fortune. "Sally called me back to ask me a few more questions about my thoughts on the stem cell bill," she said, as if reading my mind. "I'm sorry that you two are at such odds. I know how much she values you."

"I'm just so lost," I said, as my voice caught in my throat. "About Sally, about who's right, about life." I glanced down at my breasts and shook my head. "About all of this."

"It's funny, isn't it?" she said, but I looked at her blankly, so she just continued. "How the thing that cancer changes the most isn't your breasts or your hair or anything at all on the outside." I felt my eyes rush with tears. "What it changes is everything else instead."

I glanced down and saw fat, heavy drops land on my lace placemat. "I'm sorry, I'm sorry," I said, wiping my cheeks, apologizing for displaying my too ripe vulnerability to a woman I barely knew.

"Natalie, it's okay," she said, as she reached across the expanse of the table and clutched my right hand, holding it until I met her eyes. "You have to know . . ." She paused and took a breath. "What you have to know in all of this, *through* all of this, is that no matter how lost you are in this maze of this hell and confusion, that in the end, I promise you, you will be found."

AFTER MY LAST round of chemo, Dr. Chin called me back in to run the usual battery of tests: MRI, ultrasound, you name it. He took a look at my new breasts and declared them nearly healed, though he said that the scars wouldn't recede for a few more months. I flipped my hand and told him that I didn't mind them anymore—it seemed somehow appropriate that I bore literal scars from this all. Battle wounds, really. I wouldn't get a Purple Heart or a Medal of Honor, but I'd been to hell and back, and there's simply no way that you can come out unscathed. If this was the damage of war, so be it.

And besides, I'd nearly gotten used to it, my new chest. My boobs were much perkier than my old ones, and despite the fact I'd asked for the same size as before, these were rounder, firmer, fuller. I'd turn to look at myself in the mirror, and though it took me a while, I'd recently come to admit that they were indeed a nice pair. A fine rack, as Kyle would say. Maybe this summer, I'd even sport some cleavage.

Because Sally and I had retreated to our respective corners and in spite of the fact that I was still less than happy with my parents, my mother came up for my last visit with Dr. Chin. She met me in the lobby of my apartment building, a cashmere scarf knotted perfectly on her collarbone, her highlighted hair languidly toppling over her crisp Italian wool blazer. Before I could even say hello, she pulled me close to her, and I could taste her Jil Sander perfume.

"I'm sorry about Australia," she said in my ear. "We shouldn't have gone." Since they'd returned, my parents and I had kept up a guarded facade. Me, pretending like I didn't feel abandoned. Them, pretending like they hadn't left me adrift. They called diligently, dutifully, and I returned their messages with updates on my health and my progress. But the void remained nonetheless.

I tried to pull back from my mother's embrace, but she wouldn't let me break free. So I tried to remember the last time I'd heard my mom apologize for anything. And I realized that I never had. And then I realized how closely our cloths were cut.

"Thank you," I said, when she finally released me.

"Can you forgive us?" She held open the glass door to my apartment building and raised her right arm to hail a taxi.

"Come on, Mom," I said, scooting into the back of the cab and wondering how Sally's last-minute wedding preparations were going. "There's no time to hold grudges when you've seen how fragile things can really be."

She slid in next to me and grabbed my hand. She didn't let go until we landed at the hospital.

We sat in Dr. Chin's office, just as I had with Sally nearly seven months back when he delivered the potential death sentence, and we waited. I'd been sick since the night before, but this time, it wasn't from the chemo. It was from my nerves, which were fraught with anxiety, with fear, really. With the fear that after all of this, it wouldn't be enough. That even though I felt like I'd earned a slot in that 56 percent of survivors, it would turn out that earning it, deserving it, had nothing to do with it at all. I sat in his office, my stomach plugged full of Imodium, my palms sweaty and my fingers shaking from the adrenaline, and I supposed that this was true: that getting cancer, that beating it or succumbing to it or defying the odds of it, had nothing to do with worthiness or deservedness or who you were as a person. It just happened, and nothing I could or couldn't do would change that. I reached for my lucky charm around my neck and hoped that today, it would grant me good fortune.

Dr. Chin came into his office holding my chart, and before he even sat down, I started weeping. It began with a trickle from my left eye that I wiped away, but snowballed into heavy, purging sobs. The truth of it was, I wasn't even sure why I was crying. It was over. The worst of it was over, I told myself. Unless, of course, it wasn't.

Dr. Chin cleared his throat and offered me a tissue. Then he smoothed his hands over the manila folder in front of him and waited for me to compose myself. So I blew my nose, dabbed my eyes, and waited for my verdict. I knew it before he said anything. His grin belied the news.

"Natalie, I have only good things to report," he said. Never in my life have I seen my mother cry, but then she started in, too. "You have licked this thing. Knocked it out of the park. We ran through your tests, blood work, and scans, and I could not be happier to declare you officially in remission. We couldn't detect a cancer cell around. I'd like to put you on a radiation schedule to ensure that we maintain your progress, and then other than that, all we need is to see you every three months for a checkup."

I heard the enormity of what he said. I heard it first and then I absorbed it, and after the relief washed over me, and after I thanked him over and over and over again for saving my life, for giving back to me what I didn't know was possible to lose, I clutched my mother's hand, and we walked out of there. Just as I was about to close his door, I turned back to him.

"Dr. Chin, what do most of your patients do once they learn that they're cancer-free?"

"That's a good question, Natalie. And I feel like I should answer it by saying that they go to Disneyland." We both laughed, and he continued. "No, really, I suppose that they go about finding the lives that they want to live, rather than the lives that they think they should be living. If nothing else, beating cancer gives you that second chance."

BECAUSE SALLY AND I weren't speaking, Lila threw me an "I Kicked Cancer's Ass Party" on Saturday night. She invited everyone I think I knew in the city. People I hadn't spoken to in months, people who might not have even bothered to call when I was sick. But it didn't matter. I asked her to. The only one who wasn't there was Sally. And really, as I looked around, hoping to make out her face, I realized that even in a room packed with people, I somehow felt lonely without her.

My mother had taken me shopping for the occasion. "It's your coming-out party," she said. "We have to find you something fabulous."

"Actually," I said, plunging my hands into the pockets of my jeans. "It's my coming-back party."

It was one of those afternoons in early April in New York where you can't imagine living anywhere else. Pink blossoms dotted the trees, and candy yellow daffodils tried to poke their necks out of the soil of the planters that lined Fifth Avenue. The smell of spring hung in the air, and to me, it was the smell of hope. My mom, who I'm quite certain hadn't eaten ice cream since 1965, treated us to cones along the way. I had mint chocolate chip, and I thought of Zach and wondered if he'd be there tonight.

As we rode the escalator to the top floor of Bergdorf Goodman, I watched my reflection pass by on the mirrored walls. I literally looked nothing like I had six months back. It wasn't just that I was twenty pounds thinner or that the hair that hung from my head wasn't my own or even that my new breasts protruded ever so slightly more than my old ones. It was more in my eyes. Behind the fatigue and the wrinkles that had seemingly appeared over-night, there was new light—the light that turned on when I be-came a survivor. I watched my eyes over and over again as I climbed to the sixth floor. I could barely believe that they were mine.

"This would look great on you," my mom said, as we cruised through the designer racks, pulling out dark jeans and a cashmere shell.

"Too boring," I said, placing it back.

"Sweetie, you could never be boring," she said. "No, these are classic. Refined. So you."

"Screw refined. Screw the old me," I said. "I'm ready for fun."

That's how I ended up in the dressing room with two Pucci print dresses and a leopard-print mini. I stood naked in front of the mirror, just like I had at my bridesmaid's fitting, and stared at my body, so foreign, so different from when I started. I stared until my mother called from in front of the curtain and asked me if I were okay, and then I double-blinked my eyes, snapped out of it, and remembered Susanna's wise words: that my body was just a vessel. What it carried inside of it was what really mattered.

In the end, I settled on the second Pucci. The bold-patterned, bright pink, yellow, and green Pucci. When Kyle saw me in it at Lila's apartment later that night, he said that he didn't recognize me, I looked so different. I smiled and told him that was the point entirely.

Jake had to meet me at the party, and he wouldn't show up until well past 10:00 anyway. He had a prescheduled dinner with his manager, but I didn't mind so much. I wanted to get ready by myself, to transform myself from cancer victim to cancer survivor in the solitude of my own presence. I zipped up the back of my dress and thought about how it might feel to break free of Jake and find that I wasn't broken. That there are worse things in life than walking away from someone whom you once loved, and that if you're granted a second chance and choose to embrace it, you better run like hell toward it or else it keeps getting farther and farther away.

Jake hadn't yet arrived when I saw Zach across Lila's living room. Lila had outdone herself: She'd put sparkling white Christmas lights around the door frame, decked out the windowsills with flowing vases of calla lilies, and even pasted together a collage of pictures from my past. "It's a tribute to who you are," Lila said, when I saw it and misted up. I lingered over a picture of Sally and me at our senior year formal and wondered how things could ever have gotten this far.

Zach's face glowed under the hue of the lights. I gave him a small wave and a weirdly shy smile, and he moved toward me and leaned down for a kiss. A cheek kiss, that is. Lila was hovering in the kitchen. A buzz-kill at best.

"So I guess this means that, as your doctor, I should suggest that you kick your pot habit," he said.

"So I guess this means that as your patient, I'll need to seek another doctor."

"I was going to suggest that anyway." He smiled. "I think perhaps we've breached some sort of ethics at this point."

"Nothing's happened," I reminded him. "Separate hotel rooms and all of that."

"Oh, but the possibilities." He raised his eyebrows and grinned. "Maybe if I dress up like an old guy with too much makeup on? I know how you like that look."

"Anyway," I said, looking down at my manicure.

"Anyway," he said back.

At that very moment, Lila rushed over and pulled me into a gaggle of college friends who had taken the train down from Boston to celebrate. As I walked past Zach, I turned and I reached out to grab his hand.

"It occurs to me," I said. "I don't think I ever thanked you for the mint chocolate chip ice cream. You saved my life that day, you know."

"I'm pretty sure that you saved it all on your own," he said, squeezing my fingers until Lila dragged me away, and I was forced to let go.

LATER THAT NIGHT, after I'd toasted to my newfound health, after I'd kissed my last well-wisher good-bye, and after Jake and I fell onto each other, slightly tipsy on both champagne and life, in the cab ride home, I let him take my hand and lead me into our bedroom. I felt his breath on my neck as he leaned in and unwound my zipper, and I felt the cool rush of air over my nearly naked body as my dress fell to the floor.

I moved to turn off the lights, but he placed his fingers on my waist and pulled me back toward him.

"You're stunning," he said. "Right now, exactly as you are. You're stunning."

My eyes welled, and rather than answer, I simply smiled and led his hands to my breasts. He kissed my lips, and then he kissed my neck, and then he kissed the part of me that wasn't even part of me six months earlier: the replacement breasts that I had come to think of as my own. I inhaled when he moved his lips over them, waiting for something to take over me: joy, rage, passion, *something*, but nothing came. Mostly, I was just lost in my thoughts, in my consciousness, as his fingers next explored my body, as mine then explored his, and finally, when I opened myself up to him, and we made love for the first time in nearly three years.

When it was over, he pulled the crisp sheets over our bare selves, kissed my forehead, and told me that he loved me. And I told him it back. What I didn't tell him was that I thought that sex would mystically alter something between us, magnetically pull us back to where we needed to be. And now that it had happened, I knew that sex couldn't change anything: It never did. Not with anyone before Jake, and not with him now. We were still running on empty. *I* was still running on empty. The only question that remained was, was I strong enough to find the right fuel to fill me up?

*   *   *

Dear Diary,

Well, you're never going to believe it because I could barely believe it myself, but Ned did indeed get back to me. True, he didn't call because I think that might have been too hard, but he did e-mail, so I'll at least give him some credit for having one ball, if not two. It was interesting to read what he wrote, what he had to say. Both for himself and about us.

Dear Natalie, he wrote.

I was surprised to hear your voice in my mailbox, but not nearly as surprised as the fact that I'm writing. I didn't think I would, but it turns out that I have some things to get off my chest. I hope you know that I tried to stay in touch with you when we first broke up. I'd feel terribly embarrassed if you didn't know that. (Diary—note from me here. How annoying that he's concerned about saving face! As if walking out on me shouldn't have been embarrassing enough! But I'll let him continue.)

I got your message about you wanting to talk about our relationship. I didn't have the energy to call, because I'm worried about what you might say. I first want to tell you, Natalie, that I can't take you back. (Diary, me again. Can you believe that he has the nerve?) In case that's why you were calling. I mean, I don't know if it was, but I thought I should just put that out there. When you get calls from ex-girlfriends saying they want to talk about your relationship, that's pretty much the logical assumption. If it wasn't, then I really apologize for making that leap.

Anyway, having said that, I guess I should clarify why not. Natalie, I'm happy. I mean, really, really happy. I think that maybe I didn't realize what happiness was until now. And I don't mean to rub it in your face or anything. Because God knows that you've had your share of rough times, but I do hear that you've beaten the disease, so I definitely want you to know that I'm thrilled for you. (Diary—how nice of him, no?) But it's just that my happiness is so plentiful that I can't even imagine going back to where we once were.

So where were we, Nat? I don't know. I suppose that we were in a safe place that hovered somewhere between ambivalence and true fulfillment, and rather than try to make it anything that it wasn't, we closed our eyes and called it love. I don't think that you ever knew that I wasn't happy. At least, not until I made the decision to tell you about Agnes. I admit now, my timing was horrible, and again, I apologize. But in the end, weren't we both better off?

Happiness is an amazing thing, Natalie. It keeps my life revved, it keeps me from being lonely. It's shown me that love is much better than you thought it could be. It's much better, no, it's much different, from what we had. What I have now is what it should be.

I hope this doesn't sound like I'm gloating. I'm not. I just wanted to express how I feel, in case that's why you were calling. I have to get back to work, but before I go, I want to say, Nat, that I hope you find this same happiness. That I'm sorry for everything that you've gone through. And that if you can find it, this light, this happiness, it's enough to make you look back and realize what you were missing.

Please don't hate me, Natalie. I wish you everything that I have.

Best,
Ned

So that was it, Diary. My first instinct was to call him up and declare that he should in no way flatter himself, that I'd sooner poke skewers through my eyeballs than take him back, but really, I figured, what was the point? He was happy, and I guess, for that, a teeny, tiny, teensy part of me is happy, too. Until he walked out on me, I thought he was a decent guy. So I probably shouldn't begrudge him much. He was right: I didn't realize that he was as burned out on us as I was. Funny. Maybe if we'd actually talked about it, something would have changed.

So anyway, Diary. I've tracked them all down. Opened up my past and survived the whirlwind that it brought. It's almost poetic that Ned wrote me just as I wrapped up chemo. It's like I can take all of my history, all of the knowledge learned, and toss it aside now. Or put it to use in places it could better be served. Like in restoring my friendship with the one friend who matters. Or forgiving my mother for not always being perfect.

You know what, Diary? I'm ready to start fresh.

· TWENTY-TWO ·

What do you mean, she's not in the office today?" I barked at Blair, even though I conceivably knew that it wasn't her fault.

"Natalie, I'm sorry," she said, as the blood drained from her face. "She decided to take a last-minute trip to D.C."

"Shit." I said. "But I scheduled this meeting with her two weeks ago. I absolutely have to talk to her this week, and I'm out of the office Thursday and Friday. I can't switch that—I'm in Puerto Rico for a wedding."

"Andrews wanted to talk to her in person." Blair made a face. "You know how it is."

"I do indeed know how it is. Christ. Okay, put me down for Wednesday. Any time, I don't care. But I need thirty minutes.

Minimum. If she wants me to get this stem cell bill done, she's got to give me thirty minutes." I cleared my throat. "And I have a few other issues to talk to her about." Namely, Sally's story.

Blair tapped her free hand on her desk and clicked onto the senator's schedule on her computer.

"How about eleven? I can switch out a conference call, and you get in. Will that work?"

"Blair," I said. "You're the greatest. Remind me of that the next time I'm about to have a breakdown."

"I will." She smiled. "You better believe it."

I stopped by the watercooler for a glass, trudged back to my cube, and picked up the phone to call Maureen, Senator McIntyre's assistant, my comrade-in-arms in nailing down the senatorial votes.

"I've locked mine down," she said. "Texas was wavering, but I pinned them down on Friday. Of course, I had to promise an open-ended favor in return, but it seemed like a fair price. Next time they want to drill for oil in Alaska, the senator might have to agree not to call them fucking short-sighted assholes on live C-SPAN. We can live with that."

"I'm one short," I replied. "Senator Tompkins. But I have a bargaining chip; I just haven't been able to put it in play yet. Dupris is never here anymore, and with my chemo treatments, I haven't been able to shadow her on the road."

"How are you feeling, by the way?"

"Better," I said. "Good, even. It's amazing how great you can feel when you don't have thousands of poisonous cells and chemicals chasing through you. In fact, I'm heading to the Caribbean this weekend."

"Shut up! Natalie Miller's taking a vacation?"

"I swear to tell the truth and nothing but it." I laughed. "Actually, my best friend's getting married down there. I figured it was a good excuse and all." I wondered if it were fair to call Sally my best friend anymore. I'd sent her an e-mail after Lila's party. A white flag waving in the wind to say that I was sorry, and that even though we stood in separate corners on this issue she was still the truest person I knew. And that I was still honored to stand up with her at her wedding. I hadn't heard back.

"I've never been so jealous of anyone in my life. I swear, I think the last vacation I took was when Clinton was in office." Maureen sighed into her phone.

"We were in college back then, Maureen." I picked up a pen to start doodling.

"Exactly. But who's counting?"

"THIS DOESN'T HAVE to be our last session, you know," Janice said, as she tapped a pencil on her desk. "I see plenty of patients long after they go into remission. Many patients discover that a lot has changed for them, and it helps to have someone to talk to."

"I know." I nodded. "I'd like that. To come back. But just not every week. I'd sort of like to see how it feels to be on my own. To muddle through some of this stuff and rely on my own instincts for a while."

"Fair enough. Though you're not on your own. You have a wide net to support you, and of course, you have Sally and Jake."

"Sally still isn't speaking to me," I said, shaking my head.

"Isn't her wedding any day now?" she asked, furrowing her brow.

I nodded. I wasn't even sure if she wanted me there after the way we'd left things. True, I'd e-mailed to apologize, but as Jake pointed out after he read it, I'd hardly apologized at all. I'd only asked to move on. Never once did I retreat from my corner or tell her that I understood why she had to do what she was doing or that in everything in my life, her friendship was the thing that mattered most.

"So where do you go from here?" Janice asked me, scribbling a note to herself in my file. "Lose a friend and chalk it up to fate?"

"I'm not sure that I believe in fate," I said, fingering my necklace. "Well, it's not that I don't believe in fate, but I firmly believe in your opportunity to manipulate fate."

"So what does that mean for you, right now?"

I sighed and stared out her second-floor window, wondering if the early spring sun were strong enough to sink under your skin and warm you from the inside out. "I suppose that it means that for the first time, I have a decent perspective on what matters. And that if I don't do something about it, it might not by mine for much longer."

"Ah." Janice smiled. "You might have uncovered the secret of life. How does it make you feel?"

"I think that's giving me a little bit too much credit." I grinned. "But how does it make me feel? I suppose it makes me scared because, ultimately, I have no one to blame my failures on but myself." I watched a pigeon land on her windowsill and wished that I'd could take back everything I'd said to Sally. "But I suppose that it also liberates me. I mean, just like I have to own my failures, I can also own my successes. And at least try to turn my failures around rather than try to outrun them."

Janice smiled. "Well, no wonder you don't want to see me each week. If all of my clients were as well adjusted as you, I'd be out of a job."

"Trust me, Janice. I might be well adjusted now, but if you'd gotten your hands on me a year ago, I'd probably have provided enough sessions to buy your horses a new barn. Funny how cancer can do that to you—knock off your psychosis when, arguably, it should really make it much worse."

"Sometimes it does," she replied. "It's all about how you choose to perceive it."

When our hour wound down, she came out from behind her desk and gave me a hug. I smelled her perfume and felt the silk scarf that was draped around her neck, and I thanked her for helping me find my way.

"Good luck," she said, as I was slinging my bag on my shoulder.

"It's not about luck," I said, as my four-leaf clover poked out of my crewneck sweater. "It's about making your own good fortune."

· TWENTY-THREE ·

On Wednesday, the day before Jake and I were set to leave for Sally's wedding, the senator was running late, which threw my schedule even further off-course than it already was. Blair dropped by my desk at 10:00 and said that the senator was in a chopper on the way back from Albany. She'd have to bump our meeting to noon. And would I mind terribly if it were more of a walking lunch? Dupris hadn't shown her face in New York in three weeks, and Andrews's public relations advisers wanted her to get out among the people. Hand-shaking, baby-kissing, and all of that.

Fine, I said. But I need thirty minutes.

You'll have it, Blair said. I promise.

Our noon meeting was pushed to 12:30, then 1:00. Finally, at 1:15, the senator flew through the door with two briefcases on each arm.

"I'm famished," she shouted. "Blair, can we get some lunch?"

"You're due for a walk-through, Senator," Blair replied. "Andrews wants you out among the people during lunch hour. It's prime time for a photo shoot."

"Christ, fine," she said. "And I hear that Natalie needs to talk to me? Tell her to grab her stuff—we're leaving in five. I'm about to devour my own hand. Make a reservation at The Four Seasons for 1:30."

Shit, I thought. *I needed thirty minutes, not an entire afternoon.* I still had to get Manny to the kennel and stop by the boutique on my corner for some beachy T-shirts and run to the drugstore for enough sun block to deflect even the hint of a ray touching my skin. And, of course, I need to get back to both Maureen at Senator McIntyre's office and Brian at Senator Tompkins's. *Shit,* I said out loud.

I grabbed my bag and yellow pad with my list of pro and con names and made a dash for the elevator, where I caught up with the senator just before the door clamped shut.

"Natalie, how are you feeling?" she said warmly. "I haven't really had a chance to catch up with you since you went into remission. We're so, so happy for you."

"Thank you, Senator. Actually, I'm feeling great. Maybe even better than before." I put on a grin to assure her that this was so. "But really, I need to speak with you about a very pressing matter."

"Of course," she said, as the elevator touched the bottom floor and her cell phone rang. She held up her finger to me. "Just give me a second. Walk with me. We're going to The Four Seasons. I hope you haven't eaten."

I had, in fact, eaten. I'd gone down to Ben and Jerry's for some mint chocolate chip about an hour before, but it didn't really matter to the senator. Lunch, it was.

"Fine, I'll look out for them," I heard her say into her phone, as she snapped it shut. "Photographers. Andrews has tipped them off. He wants some shots in tomorrow's paper. So smooth out that beautiful hair of yours, Natalie. So what were you saying? Oh yes, pressing matter. What is it?"

Unconsciously, I raised my free hand and ran it over my wig.

"It's the stem cell bill. The one you asked me to babysit until we were sure that we had enough signatures to push it through . . ."

She and I were now weaving our way through midtown lunchtime pedestrian traffic. A taxi just to our right was leaning on his horn and my voice drifted away under its clamor.

"I'm sorry, what? I couldn't hear you."

But before I could repeat myself, we were encircled by a mob of people. As she always does, the senator pulled out her dimpled smile and professionally whitened teeth, shook hands, and murmured how kind they all were for their support. Eventually, the crowd parted much like I imagined that the Red Sea once did, and we made our way past.

"I was saying that there's a snag in the stem cell bill," I told her once we were in the clear.

"Which is what?"

"Well, there are two snags actually," I replied and thought of the *New York Times* exposé. Maureen had sent me an e-mail saying that the Mississippi contingent started leaking Sally all of the dirt in their "folder of secrets." I'd worked for Dupris long enough to know that, undoubtedly, her secrets were best kept that way. I cleared my throat. "The first issue is Senator Tompkins. He's the last signature that we need. But he wants to go in for a deal."

"Of course." She sighed. "Harry always plays hard to get. What is it?"

"He wants you to back off your education push. He doesn't think that it's going to be effective, and his voters aren't loving it. In exchange, he'll support the research."

"No way," she said, as we crossed Fifty-seventh Street. "Find someone else to give us that last vote."

"There is no one else, Senator." I pulled out my pad from underneath the crook in my elbow. "Maureen and I have spent every waking second talking to lobbyists, aides, even assistants to aides. Tompkins is it. No one else is moving from their position, and he's the only one who is flexible."

"I'm not letting him put me in a position to have to choose," she said. "It's like *Sophie's Choice*—how can he ask me to drop one for the other?"

"Because this is how it's done." I sighed at her melodrama. "You know that." I hated it when she pretended to be so pious as to not recognize the negotiation tactics that played themselves out on the Hill every day. And it's not like she hadn't done this very thing before herself. In fact, she'd had me orchestrate this very thing before.

"Well, I won't back off education. In fact, I'm going to bolster my campaign for it. You tell him that."

A wave of nausea overtook me, and I had to pause to regain my breath. "Senator, with all due respect, the stem cell bill can make a difference, a tangible difference in voters' lives. By backing this, you could conceivably save hundreds of thousands of people. What could be more worthy than that?"

She flipped her hand to the side. "Education is where I'm at, Natalie. Andrews wants it; I want it." A bus blew by us with an ad for Susanna's not-for-profit on the side, complete with her picture.

Dupris watched it pass. "Isn't that Councilman Taylor's wife?" She snorted. "I can't believe she showed her face in the town again. I wonder what happened to her?"

"What happened to her is that you made me apologize to her at the Christmas party. Or have you forgotten?" I muttered. "And what further happened to her is that she turned out to be a decent person. A *good* one, in fact. Who's trying to make a difference."

"Oh, Natalie." Dupris's heels clicked on the sidewalk as she started walking again. "Don't take things so personally. I was just asking! No offense was intended."

I felt my pulse quicken and clamped down my jaw. No offense was ever meant by the senator unless she'd sent one of her minions to do the offending and thus fall on their swords for her. Like I might have done with my best friend.

"Anyway, where were we?" she continued. "Oh yes, the stem cell bill. Sorry, my hands are tied."

I stopped in the middle of the street, which forced her to turn and look back at me.

"Well, I guess that brings us to the second thing," I said in a tone I used to reserve for my mother. "And that's an enormous exposé that's coming out about the machinations of politics. A cover story, in fact. The *New York Times Magazine*. Oh, and it's taking its cues from the stem cell bill. Why certain people are voting one way, why others are voting another." I smiled sarcastically. "You know, just a nice little piece on how pure all of our intentions are." I saw her eyes widen. "And it just so happens that I've spent the past month trying to keep your nose out of it, trying desperately to protect your image from being smeared, when it seems to me that you're doing a fine job of smearing it all on your own."

I saw her mouth drop, and I thought that I had her. Instead, she took a step toward me and for an instant, I was certain that she was going to slap me. But she lowered her voice, grabbed me by the elbow, and said, "Why didn't you tell me about this ages ago."

"Because, Senator, you prefer the don't ask, don't tell policy. You know that you do." She looked at me and clenched her jaw. "I was trying to keep you above it," I said.

We walked the block in silence.

"I have to think about this, Natalie," she said finally, just as we approached the steps of The Four Seasons. "Sit down and talk it over with Andrews and figure out how I'll do the least damage."

"Of course," I replied dryly, stopping at the stairs.

"You're not joining me for lunch?"

"No, Senator," I said, just before I spun on my heels. "I'm pretty certain that I just lost my appetite. Besides, I'm headed for sunnier skies."

· TWENTY-FOUR ·

There were no skies more sunny than those off the coast of San Juan. Jake loaded our suitcases into the back of the cab while I pulled on my oversized, Jackie-O glasses and read the driver the address. Sally had told me that the hotel was smack on the beach, just a literal stone's throw from the airport, so when we pulled into the resort's driveway, with its skyscraping palm trees and mammoth lion sculptures, I'd barely even had time to check my voice mail; the ride was less than five minutes. I was just about to key in my password when I saw Sally standing at the imposing marble entrance. I'd left her a message the night before, hat in hand, tearfully explaining that nothing mattered more to me than her forgiveness. And saying that if she'd still have me, there was nothing I'd be more proud to do than stand up beside her at her wedding.

"Hey," she said shyly. "You're here to watch me become an honest woman?"

"Sally, you're long past an honest woman. Sorry, there's nothing I can do about that."

"Sshh," she mock whispered. "Don't tell Drew." I pulled her into a tight hug, as Jake paid the driver and went to check in.

"Sal, I'm so sorry." I choked on my words. "I can't . . . I mean, I just didn't . . . I'm sorry. I should never have asked you to do what I did." She shook her head on my shoulder telling me to stop, but I wanted to finish. "You have been nothing but an incredible friend to me. And I'm sorry that I can't say the same. I'll make it up to you."

"Hey." She pulled back and wiped away her mascara. "We don't keep score. There will be no making up. Only moving on."

"Fine." I smiled. "To moving on." I raised my hand in a mock toast.

"Oh, you said it, sister. There is waaaaay too much of that going on already." She nodded toward my fake cocktail. "So here's the dealio," she continued, as she readjusted her ponytail and linked her arm in mine, as if our friendship had never taken a plunge from which it might not have recovered. "I have, like, a zillion things to do before people get here. Honestly, when I planned this, why didn't it ever occur to me that throwing a wedding where 150 people show up for three days and expect a nonstop party would be totally exhausting? Anyway, I digress. I have a zillion things to do, but you, my dear, should make your way down to the beach with that rock star boyfriend of yours, order some rum punch, and show off your size zero body and perky breasts."

"Size two and counting. I've been eating like a cow. No, correction, I've *eaten* about ten cows. I can't stop."

"Okay, so go get your size *two* ass down to the beach and vegetate. I have to have dinner with our families tonight—please shoot me or else I might shoot Drew's mother first—but I'll try to swing by your room later. And if not, we're doing manicures in the morning. And hair and makeup for Saturday is at noon."

"Don't worry about me," I said. "Jake's promised to show me how to windsurf."

"If I didn't have my own wedding to attend," Sally said, raising her right hand to her forehead and pretending to faint, "I'd drop dead. Because the day that Natalie Miller cuts loose in a bikini, turns off her BlackBerry, and hits the waves to surf a big one is a day that hell just about froze over."

"This just might be that day," I said before I kissed her on the cheek and went to find Jake at the front desk.

WINDSURFING, IT TURNED out, was not so much my thing. Jake had been helpful enough, but my postchemo arms didn't have the strength to keep the sail aloft, so, more or less, I went nowhere. With the exception of the occasional times I went flat on my ass and belly-flopped into the ocean. After an hour, we gave up, and he returned to the room to nap, and I fell asleep on a beach chair with one hand grazing the sands below. The shouts of three teenage boys tossing the football in the waves woke me up, so I rubbed my eyes, pulled on my cushy hotel robe, and made my way to our room. The air was so cold inside, I felt as if liquid nitrogen had been shot through my veins.

Jake was lying on top of the sheets in the dark, still in his bathing suit, his hands tucked behind his head. I flipped on the lights.

"Have a good nap? I checked out the seafood buffet menu. I think we should definitely hit it tonight."

"Actually, I didn't sleep."

"Is something wrong?" I felt my stomach drop.

"Sammy called." Sammy, the Misbees manager. Jake didn't even need to keep talking. I knew what was coming next. But I let him keep going anyway. He swung his legs up in the air and rolled himself upright. "The thing is, Nat. They need me in London."

I blinked and started picking my cuticles.

"They need me in London," he repeated. "And I don't know what to do."

"Of course you know what to do," I said quietly. "You just don't want to do it." I stood in the doorway, unable to move.

"No, truly. I don't know what to do." He said it with enough conviction that I believed him. "I promised you something. I promised you that I'd be here not just for Sally's wedding, but I'd be there for you. But London . . ." His voice trailed off. "We got a call from the Rolling Stones. The Rolling *fucking* Stones, Nat. They want me to come and record a song with them. And then maybe have the band open up on their summer tour. I mean, the Rolling Stones for Christ's sake."

"I get it, Jake. It's the Rolling Stones. You don't have to say their name ten more times for me to get it." I took a few steps forward.

"I haven't said yes yet. I wanted to talk to you first." He folded his hands in his lap and reminded me of a five-year-old who's been caught pants-ing the girls in the playground.

"But you're going to. Say yes," I sniped, as a I dropped my robe and reached for dry clothes in my suitcase. "We both know that you're going to, regardless of what I say. Because really, what could I say that would be enough? That I was counting on you to be here for this? You already know that's true. That I was counting on you to live up to your promises? I think you already know that's true, too." I considered it for a moment. "You know, Jake,

I didn't ask you to come back. You came back on your own. I didn't think things could be different, but you asked me to believe that. So I did."

"It's just Sally's wedding," he said. "It's not the end of the world. This is my fucking career, Natalie."

My eyes flashed, and I threw his damp towel to the floor. "No, Jake," I said. "That's where you're wrong. It's not the end of *your* world. But that doesn't mean that your world should be a part of mine."

"Natalie, I love you." He flopped his arms helplessly.

"That's not enough."

"What would be? Tell me what would be enough so that I can make this up to you."

I thought about it. I really did. I zipped up my sweatshirt and moved to the window, staring out at the rhythm of the lapping waves, the kids darting in and out of them. I thought about Colin and about Brandon and about Dylan and about Ned. I thought about how what might have been enough six months ago wasn't nearly enough anymore. I thought about second chances and how easy it is for them to get tossed aside like misplaced Post-it notes. I thought about how I once would have given anything to have Jake come back, but now I knew that what happened the first time wasn't a mistake because it had already repeated itself. The first time out, in a relationship, on a baseball diamond, on the Senate floor, you can blame naïveté. You can say that you didn't know how to do it any differently. But the second time around, there's really no such excuse. You should know better now. And I hoped that I did.

"It's not about making it up to me, Jake," I said finally. "It's about doing it right the first time so there's no space in between you coming back and me asking you to leave."

"I don't want to leave, Nat. I don't. Please don't ask me to leave."

"But you do, Jake. You do. You just don't want to admit it yet. And besides, it's not like I'm not asking. We're both already gone. You wanted to come back and rescue me. Fine. I wanted it, too. But it turns out that no one can save anyone else, and you certainly can't save me."

He got up and moved to the window, curling himself around me, and for a few last lingering moments, we just looked out at the beach without words.

"I can hear your heart beating," I said to break the silence, just like I used to when we were lying in bed, before cancer ever hit, before we came undone and then later tried to undo the damage.

"What's it saying?" he said back, just like he always used to. This was our thing.

"It's saying 'I love you.' "

"You know what they say—'a heart can never lie.' " And then he pulled me tighter so that the thumping of his heart literally echoed in my ear. I don't know how long we stood there, watching the sun go down on more than just the water, but all of the sudden, I felt claustrophobic, so I untangled myself from Jake and grabbed the room key to get some fresh air.

I was almost out the door when Jake called me back.

"Nat, what if I say no to the Stones? I'll do it if it will make the difference."

My eyes filled with tears because this was the moment, the one that you either seize or shy away from when you're going to make your own fortune. I took mine and clutched on. And then I shook my head no to his plea.

"So what do you want from me then?" he said, desperation filling his voice. "What is it that you want?"

"It's not about what I want *from* you, Jake. It's what I want *for* me."

"So who saves you then?"

"I do, Jake. I save myself." And I closed the door behind me.

It wasn't until after I got in the elevator that I realized that I'd never heard his song. The one he wrote for me. And then I realized that it didn't even matter.

I DON'T KNOW why they call them rehearsal dinners, when nothing much really gets rehearsed. Mostly, guests get tremendously shit-faced, the members of the wedding party give obscenely random toasts, and, inevitably, one, if not more, of the parents of the bride and groom breaks down and shares embarrassingly long speeches and intimate details of the bride's or groom's childhood.

Sally and Drew's rehearsal dinner was no different. Since you have most likely sat through dozens of other similar events, I will spare you the painful details. But what I should probably fill you in on is the fact that as we poured into the rented restaurant in Old San Juan, a quintessentially perfect Caribbean restaurant, complete with open-air sides, stucco walls, and bright flowering trees that gave you the sense that you were still outside, I did not see Zach in sight. I suspected that Sally knew something about his absence, but she was a virtual tornado all day: part bridezilla, part Tasmanian Devil, so it didn't seem fair to bring up my crush in the midst of her spiral. The only downtime we had was our manicures at the spa, and since Lila was a fellow bridesmaid, and since this was supposed to be girl-bonding time, I guessed that it wasn't entirely appropriate for me to inquire about the status and location of her is-he-or-isn't-he boyfriend. Especially since I didn't really feel like explaining why mine was homeward bound.

I knew that I had no right to be disappointed. I knew that Zach was coming as Lila's date, and I further knew that this not only gave me no right to be disappointed, but made me a fairly lousy friend to boot. But I was disappointed all the same. My newly svelte figure afforded me the luxury of donning duds that I could not normally pull off, and to be honest, I thought I looked pretty damn fine that evening: my bright pseudo-Missoni crocheted dress clung to all the right places, and even though I didn't grow them myself, even I had to admit that my breasts were one of my better accessories.

As these things tend to happen at rehearsal dinners, Lila had a wee bit too much to drink. It wasn't so much her fault: The waiters were passing around rum-laden cocktails at such a clip that I feared that even Sally's thirteen-year-old niece was a little tipsy from her virgin margarita. Osmosis and all. So when we pushed back our chairs from the buffet dinner and toasted our final toast to the happy couple, Lila nearly fell over. It was both fortuitous and regretful that I was the one to steady her before she toppled to the adobe-tiled floor.

"Fucking asshole," she slurred, as I held her elbow and righted her.

"Excuse me?" I said. "I was just trying to help. What's the problem?"

"Not you." She waved her hand in front of her face, as we followed the crowd out through the door and onto the street. Jessica, a college friend, had suggested an after-party at a bar, the Blue Parrot, down the block, and I was considering retiring to my king-size bed and pile of *Cosmo*s, but Lila was dragging me with her at the moment. Literally almost dragging: She was half-bent over, pulling at my arm, and more or less stumbling over the cobblestones as we walked.

"Lila, slow down. You're going to trip and break your neck." I pulled back my arm, the one without which she truly might have fallen to her peril. Stilettos, 100-proof rum, and unpaved streets do not mix. When she stood upright, I asked her again, "What's the problem?"

"Men. They're the damn problem. Fucking men," she said, as she plopped down on a concrete stair leading up to a storefront.

"Zach?" I asked. "Is something wrong with Zach?" *Oh please let there be something wrong with Zach!* I secretly prayed.

"Asshole," she muttered.

"What happened?"

"Dunno. Dunno, Natalie. Things were okay, not great. Okay though. A warm body and all of that. He said he'd been telling me how he felt for a long time but that I wasn't listening. As if I don't listen! I listen, Natalie, don't I listen? That's *crap!*"

I didn't think it was the right time to point out that she was, in fact, among the worst listeners I'd ever encountered, so bad that I sometimes wondered if I were having conversations with myself when she and I were chatting, so I just nodded and kept my mouth shut.

"Anyway, we're done." She sighed. "Done. Split. Kaput. Over. Finito. I think he's already into someone else." She kicked off her heels and started rubbing her feet, and I felt blood rise in my cheeks. He'd obviously never mentioned our trip to Los Angeles, nor my brush with fame on a game show.

"You'll be okay, Lila. You will be. You didn't love him."

"True," she said, as she wagged her pointer finger in the air. "Very true, my brilliant friend, Natalie. But . . ." Her voice trailed off. "He was someone, you know? He was *someone*. He filled in the empty spaces." And then she started to cry.

Crap. I am a terrible, conniving, underhanded person, I thought as

I rubbed her back. Though maybe I should have already known this, given that I aspired for a lifelong career in politics.

"Maybe Zach didn't want to be someone who just filled in empty spaces," I softly suggested, trying to erase my momentary lapse into self-hatred. "Maybe that wasn't enough."

"It's true. I know. We didn't love each other. Not anymore anyway." She wiped the mascara from her eyes. "But still. It sucks. I hate fucking weddings where I'm single."

"Well, have you checked out two of Drew's groomsmen? Not bad, I'd say. Not bad at all."

"Yeah, I noticed." She laughed. "If I recover from the hangover that this rum is going to leave, maybe I'll hit that situation tomorrow night."

"That's the Lila I know and love," I said, as I coaxed her shoes back on and pulled her to her feet.

"What about you, Nat? Now that you gave Jake the old heave-ho? I'll take one, you take the other? You're looking remarkably great these days."

We started walking down the street toward the Blue Parrot, my second-best friend and me.

"No," I said, thinking of Jake's heartbeat, wondering if he'd already made it to London. "I think a warm body isn't enough for me anymore. I think I'd rather hold out until something is so big, so encompassing, that I'll have forgotten what just enough feels like in the first place."

"You're lucky, you know."

"Not really." I mulled over my past six months and figured that Lila was still too toasted to make much sense.

"No, I mean, I know that you haven't been lucky and that your life recently has been relative shit, but when you say that—about finding someone, about getting more than enough—I hear it in your voice. The hope. The belief that you will. Maybe that's what I'm missing: Once you make the decision to settle for anything less than that, it's easy to lose sight of something better."

I thought about my diary and of the paths that I'd stumbled down, bruising myself along the way. It dawned on me that I still had one entry left to write: one about Jake. And then I realized that I didn't need to bother because I already knew what he'd given me, why we'd ended, and what was left to still chase down. It was that hope. Because now that I'd caught wind of something better, there wasn't a chance in hell that just enough would ever be just enough ever again.

· TWENTY-FIVE ·

W hen we met at the spa for hair and makeup the next morning at noon, Lila practically had an IV of coffee and water plugged in.

"Christ, what do they put in their rum around here?" she muttered, as she pushed her black sunglasses back on her nose after kissing me hello.

Sally was remarkably calm for a bride who was seven hours out from her big moment. "We slept in separate rooms last night," she joked. "And I hope this isn't a sign, but it was the best damn night's sleep I've gotten since we got engaged."

Sally's mom, her future mother-in-law, and Drew's younger sister, Lacey, joined us in front of the mirrors, and the stylists got to work. I'd told Sally that I didn't need them to do anything to my wig, that makeup would be just fine.

I was done first, and when Ricardo, my makeup guy, twirled me around in the mirror, I almost didn't recognize myself. His artistry brought out my deep blue eyes, which normally faded into my pale skin; the strokes of his brush highlighted my cheekbones that now protruded more so than they used to. The light bounced off the charm on my neck, and I wondered if I'd ever been so beautiful.

"Holy crap," Sally said, when she turned to look my way. "You've never looked better."

"Good Lord," Lila agreed, as she nursed her bottle of water. "You're definitely landing one of the groomsmen looking like that."

We passed around tiny sandwiches and cookies, and the rest of us, Lila excluded, sipped wine and Diet Coke. Those three hours weren't so much about making ourselves more beautiful as they were about marking time before everything changed. Not changed for the worse, but changed nevertheless. When your best friend gets married, you're so filled with love and joy and hope for her that you really don't stop to mourn the fact that life is moving on. And I don't mean mourn in a bad way. But marriage changes things; it's undeniable. It ushers in the next chapter and throws the state of equilibrium in your friendship slightly off-kilter. Until you readjust and find a different, not worse, but different, level of equilibrium on which to operate. It wasn't unlike my cancer.

So for those three hours, we sat and absorbed the moments, and I wondered how I almost so cavalierly risked it all. For a wishy-washy politician. Or maybe because I didn't know how not to put it on the line for the wishy-washy politician.

Sally gave us our bridesmaids' gifts—pearl earrings—and I

gave her one of my own: a framed picture of us from over a decade past, a month after Sally plunked down next to me in our freshman year creative writing seminar and asked if I had an extra piece of gum. "It's amazing how life works," I said aloud at some point. "How fate and how faith and how destiny just all come together. How if you hadn't sat down next to me or if I'd decided to go to Princeton, how we probably wouldn't be here right now."

"You know, I almost didn't ask you for the gum that day. I remember thinking that I looked so lame trying to make conversation. Funny looking back on it now, right?" Sally said, before her stylist asked her to pucker her lips and stay quiet. "What a tragedy that would have been. But I guess that's how it works. Life dishes it out, brings you together, pulls you apart, whatever. It's up to you to figure out the intended course."

I smiled at myself in the mirror. *Good fortune,* I thought. *I'm pretty sure that I already have it.*

THE PHONE WAS ringing as I unlocked my door, so I dropped my bag by the bed that the maids had already made up and lunged for it.

"Natalie," Senator Dupris said over the line. "I'm sorry to call, but Blair has sent you repeated e-mails, and you haven't responded."

You're not sorry to call at all, I thought before I spoke. "Sorry, Senator. No BlackBerry service down here."

"Hmmm, yes, I see. Well, I know that you're on a vacation of sorts, but I need your help crafting a statement. Some research assistants from the *New York Times Magazine* have been hounding our office about my position on the stem cell bill, and I'd like to finesse a statement about my stance."

I sat down on the floral-patterned comforter and leaned against the decorative pillows piled against the headboard of the bed. "And what is your stance, Senator? I'm afraid that I don't know." I took in my breath, knowing that in her answer my future was held. Even if she wasn't aware of it.

"Natalie, dear. You do know my stance. It hasn't changed since Wednesday. I'm sorry, I know how important this was to you." She broke the news in a sorrowful tone, though I knew her well enough to know that she wasn't regretful in the least.

"Senator, please," I sat up on my bed, making my plea. "Hear me out. This research, what they're doing in the stem cell field, it is unprecedented. It's opening up paths in medicine that doctors didn't even realize existed—offering potential cures to Parkinson's, Alzheimer's, cancers, and a litany of other diseases. Who knows what they can accomplish? To refuse to negotiate with Tompkins, not to mention refocus your energies on education, is effectively closing the doors to these paths, and it sends a signal to the president that we're okay with his refusal to fund these ventures. Quite simply, there's nothing more important than this. At least not right now. Nothing." Maybe I should have added that there was nothing more important to me, but I left it at that. The truth of the matter was that my vote, other than when I pulled the lever to cast a vote for the senator, didn't much matter.

I heard her pause and for a second, I thought that she might reconsider. That she might see beyond her faceless constituents and raw ambition, and instead just see me, someone who might need this research one day not too far in the distant future.

"Natalie. I understand your position. I do." She exhaled. "It's not that I don't care about stem cell research, because you know that I do. But I'll reiterate exactly what I said the other day: I'm not backing down from education. Period. It's going to be my legacy. Andrews firmly believes so, so I'm standing behind it."

"But your education package is shit!" I cried, though I couldn't believe it when I said it. I stood up and looked in the mirror: My cheeks were flaming red, despite the immaculate makeup from just an hour before. "It's shit, Senator. It's not going to make one fucking bit of difference for the kids who are still trapped in crappy schools and for teachers who don't have the proper resources to provide adequate education. You *know* it. It's shit, and yet you're crushing something potentially life-changing because it's the goddamned party line."

I heard her inhale sharply and compose herself. "Natalie, this is my decision. I'm here for the long run. I'm in it to win it. And so, this is what I have to do to come out on top." She paused. "So I'd like to get back to crafting this statement. Put your feelings aside and let's move on."

"What if it's not about winning?" I asked, ignoring her request and moving closer to the mirror to stare myself in the eyes. "What if this has nothing to do with coming out on top? I thought for you, this was about making a difference."

"It's not up to me, Natalie. I don't have a choice." I heard her take a sip of her coffee.

Before I spoke, I thought about Mrs. Roberts's fifth-grade class in which she spoke of *good men*, and I thought about Susanna Taylor who actually was one. I thought about Sally and how I'd almost pushed her away. I thought about all of Dupris's other broken promises, I thought about Jake's, and then, finally, I thought about mine.

"With all due respect, Senator," I said quietly, "you always have a choice."

I heard her start to balk, but I'd already made my way back to the desk, where I placed the cordless phone back where it belonged. Namely, hung up.

I sat on the cushy bed and stared at my shaking hands, wondering if I'd regret it, but as I examined the deep lines in my palms and traced my fingers over a scar from a paper cut I'd gotten when I was ten, I felt no remorse. So I took the phone from the cradle once again and dialed Sally's room.

"You want scoop? You want exclusive scoop on the senator?" I asked her. "You've got it."

THREE HOURS LATER, Sally was the first one who saw me. And she gasped. She was standing near the beach, and when she caught a glimpse, she broke into a glowing smile and ran over, grabbing her veil as she went so that it didn't get caught in the rosebushes that lined the brick path.

"Do you mind?" I asked. "Because if you do I absolutely won't go through with it."

"Mind? Why would I mind? You look amazing."

"I don't want to ruin your pictures." I shrugged. "You'll have them for a lifetime."

"How on earth could you ruin my pictures? If anything, you'll only be standing me up." She hugged me, as the photographer called us into our places.

I wasn't planning on doing it, on leaving my wig behind, when I got ready that afternoon. But once I clicked good-bye to Dupris, I sat on the floor and stared into the mirror until it was time to pull on my dress. Sally and Lila were right: I did look amazing. Better than I might ever have looked. It didn't matter that my head was covered in nothing more than light peach fuzz, and it didn't matter that my arms were still too skinny and that my nipples were still slightly unnaturally pink. What mattered was that beyond all of this, I saw what I was truly made of. And that was hope.

So after I zipped myself into my light-blue, tea-length gown, the one that once hung on me like a used burlap sack, the one that I could barely stomach to look at back when I was but a skeleton of my old self, I decided that wearing hope, my hope, was accessory enough. I closed the lid to the toilet and sat down, brushing out the strands of the wig until they were shinier than they'd ever been. Then I grabbed its travel bag, tucked it in, and put it away for safe-keeping. It had given me enough, but now I was ready for more.

I DIDN'T SEE him until after I'd walked down the aisle. As Sally's maid of honor, I was in charge of (a) ensuring that her train and veil didn't run into any snags, (b) holding her bouquet when she clasped Drew's hands and pledged herself to him, and (c) maintaining and overseeing any and all last-minute crises once we were under way. So it was easy to see how I overlooked him in the seats as I walked by. And I was so damn focused on walking to the beat of the slow Puerto Rican music that I didn't make much eye contact with the guests anyway.

I was fiddling with Sally's train while the judge was explaining the difficulties of marriage when I first saw him. Four rows back and to the left. I felt someone staring and, at first, merely assumed that it was another guest who wondered what on earth Sally was doing with a bald chick in her wedding, but then the gaze didn't move. So I finished adjusting her dress, stood upright, and looked over.

And there he was. Zach. How I hadn't noticed him before,

I didn't know, because once he smiled and gave me a little wave, it was nearly impossible not to keep staring.

Sally and Drew said their vows and kissed the way that people do who are starting out their lives together and let out some whoops, and when I handed her back her bouquet and pulled her into an embrace, she said with a smile, "Surprise."

"I don't get it. He's not with Lila anymore."

"I know. He called to say that he didn't feel right coming down with her. He felt bad that he was canceling at the last minute, so wanted to speak with me directly." Drew tugged at her to walk down the aisle, so she started speaking quickly over her shoulder. "I told him to come anyway. That it might end up being worth it, even if things hadn't worked out as originally planned."

"Aha." I grinned.

"Aha, indeed," she said, as the quartet broke into a salsa, and she took off down the aisle toward her married life.

THEIR RECEPTION WAS big and boisterous and busy. A thirteen-piece band played from the stage on the patio, spotlights created dancing shadows from the palm trees, and candles flickered on the orange silk tablecloths. Guests leaned into one another to make themselves heard over the din of the music and celebration. Not only was I required for postceremony pictures, but as the maid of honor, I also had to play semihostess, meeting and greeting family members, old friends, and random people whom I'd never see again after that night.

By the time I had the chance to grab my name card—Table 2— off the place-card table and make my way to the bar for a drink— piña colada, nonvirgin—the band was already on its second set, and the dance floor was full of New Yorkers and Iowans (Drew's home state) who were making wholehearted attempts at Latin dancing without much luck. I surveyed the ballroom, looking for the only person who mattered. But all I saw was a sea of pulsing limbs moving to the music, and Lila over in the corner, pressed up against one of those handsome groomsmen. *Good for her,* I thought. At least she knows what she's getting into.

I didn't much feel like dancing, though I knew that I had plenty to celebrate, and Sally had already told me that dinner wouldn't be served until 9:00. Party first, eat later, she said, when we were getting our nails done the day before. So fill up on the hors d'oeuvres at the cocktail hour, she'd advised.

I grabbed three miniquiches and headed toward the sign that read EXIT. Pushing open the side doors, I felt a cool, salty wind blow in from the ocean, and I made my way down the stucco stairs to the beach. The sun had long since set—Sally and Drew timed their vows so that the glow of dusk would hover over them during the ceremony—so mostly, other than a few lights provided by the resort and the bulbs from the security station, the sand was covered in darkness.

I left my shoes by the concrete's edge and walked toward the water, the cold beachy grains sticking to my soles as I went. Plunging my feet in, I stared up at the night: Plane lights blinked overhead as they made their way to the nearby airport. I looked up and thought of my grandmother who hadn't been able to beat back the same cancer, of whether or not she was looking down on me, and of whether or not I'd made her proud. I'm not sure how long I stood there just gazing up at the sky. I heard the echo of the band behind me and the rush of the waves in front, and it was hard not to be hypnotized.

So when I heard my name, it was easy to think that I was dreaming. But when I heard it again, I turned toward it.

"Natalie," Zach called, and I saw him moving closer.

"Hey," I said softly.

"Hey yourself," he said back.

"Lila told me what happened. I didn't think you were coming."

"I wasn't sure if I was. But I called Sally Thursday night, and she convinced me. So I hopped on a flight early today."

"Lila was pretty wrecked," I said, as I circled my right foot in the sand.

"I've noticed that she's recovering just fine," he said dryly. "But enough about her."

"But enough about her," I agreed.

"I thought it was a rule that no one could be more beautiful than the bride." He leaned down to roll up the hems of his pants as the water lapped on his feet.

"Really? I've never heard of that one." I grinned.

"Oh yeah, it's true. Friendships have been known to be lost over that sort of thing."

"Hey, when you have it, you've got to flaunt it," I said, raising my hand to pat my invisible hair. "After all, haven't you heard? Bald chic is in this year."

"Too bad yours will be growing back." He looped his elbow in mine.

"Well," I considered. "Maybe I'll keep it short anyway. Maybe it's the start of a whole new me." I paused and glanced sideways at him. "You don't look so bad yourself."

And it was true. In fact, in his crisp blue suit and perfect pink tie, I could barely believe that I'd managed not to throw him down on the beach and climb on top.

I took a few steps backward and sat down in the sand, sweeping my dress underneath my legs. Zach followed and plunked down beside me.

"So," he said.

"So," I said back, staring out across the vastness.

"You no longer have cancer."

"I no longer have cancer," I agreed.

"Knocked that fucking disease right out of the park."

"I did indeed."

"So I guess that this no longer makes you unavailable?" We both kept gazing out on the rolling water.

"I guess that as of this moment, I am, in fact, officially and totally available." I smiled.

"In case I should be interested."

"On the off chance that you know someone who's interested." I smiled wider.

We sat there until the band stopped playing its set. Zach wrapped his arm around me and pulled me close enough that I could inhale the crisp smell of his skin. We sat, and we stared out into the ocean and listened as the waves ushered in the sea of change. At one point, I put my head on his shoulder, and he ran his fingers down the nape of my neck where tendrils of hair used to lay. And then I realized that we'd come full circle. That after six months of horror and of fear and of, in many ways, liberation, we sat on the beach, miles away from the lives that we'd come to occupy, and once again, just like back on the night in his living room when he made me a chicken and I smoked too much pot, he let me lean. Of all the things that were beautiful there in San Juan—the tide, the stretch of beach, the love that was rising up inside of me—this was what I found most breathtaking. He let me lean.

When the music stopped, he helped me up, and we turned to head back inside.

"Hold on," I said, and let my feet sink into the cool sand. I reached up to the back of my neck, undid the clasp on my four-leaf-clover necklace, and clutched it tightly in the palm of my hand. Then I took a step closer to the waves and with every ounce of strength in my body, I hurled it out into the vast sea.

"What was that for?" Zach asked. Rather than answer, I stood on my toes and leaned closer to him, pressing my body against his and tasting the salty aftertaste of beer on his lips. Finally, I pulled back, interlocked my fingers into his own, and walked toward the hotel.

"Who needs a good luck charm?" I said. "When you've figured out how to make it all on your own."

REMISSION

· · ·

July

· TWENTY-SIX ·

*D*ear Diary,
     I know, don't hate me. It's been over three months since I've had time to write. The thing is ever since Sally's wedding, I've barely had a chance to catch my breath.

     We'll start off with my health. I had my three-month appointment with Dr. Chin this week, and the news was smooth sailing. It was strange going back there. I missed it at first—the order that it provided—but now, it was like revisiting high school. And what I mean by that is as I walked down the sterile corridors, the halls brought back nothing but skeletons, memories of a time I'd rather leave behind and a person who had nothing to do with me at all.

     I swung by Janice's office while I was there, too. She was out to lunch, so I wrote her a note.

Janice,

     I was here for my checkup and wanted to say hello. Really, what I wanted to tell you is that you were right:

that we're not so different from trees after all. What I really needed was some water, and happily, I've quenched my thirst.

Thanks again for all of your support. I'm sure that I'll see you soon.

Love,

Natalie

Work? Well, that situation isn't quite as robust as my health. When I got back from Puerto Rico, Senator Dupris called me in.

The senator asked me to sit down and wondered if I'd had time to think about "the incident." She even formed quotation marks with her fingers. I told her that I had, indeed, had time to think about it, but that I didn't have much to say. She attempted to furrow her overly botoxed brow, and said, "Natalie, rethink this. You've been very loyal right up until 'the incident' (there go those fingers again), and if you apologize, of course, I'm prepared to move beyond it." I told her that was very big of her, and she agreed. But then I told her that I had no such plans to say I was sorry because, in fact, I had no regrets whatsoever. That I'd gotten into politics to truly make a difference, and it seemed to me that I'd clearly lost sight of that. She peered at me like she didn't understand, so I sat up in my chair, looked her in the eye, and said, "With all due respect, Senator, I followed behind you because you were my mentor, someone whom I wanted to emulate, but now you're hardly a role model, and you're certainly not mine."

She curled up her lips like she'd just sucked on a lime, and I stood to leave. "I appreciate the opportunity," I said. "I've learned a lot, and much of it I enjoyed. But I can't follow blindly behind anymore, not when I've finally learned how to see."

So now, I'm trying to figure out my next move. Susanna

Taylor has asked me to come work with her, so I'm mulling it over. Maybe I can get back to where I started—to being a good man. I think I'd like that.

Oh, other news. My hair is growing back! It's strange: It's coming back with curls. I told my mom about it, she said that my grandmother had hair like Shirley Temple, so we laughed that maybe this was a sign from above.

I'm sure that you're reading this and are thinking, cut to the good stuff. Give us the real skinny, ergo, Zach. Okay, so I will. That night, the one on the beach when I put my head on his shoulder and stared at the stars, we stayed up talking in his room until the sun came up. And then we went out on the balcony and watched day break over the horizon. And not to get entirely too cheesy, but I couldn't help but think it was somehow symbolic.

When we got back to New York, I broke the news to Lila. Diary, it's entirely understandable that she didn't take it so well. But three days later, she sent me an e-mail saying that if she couldn't have him, she was happy that someone she loved could. And anyway, that gorgeous groomsman just moved here last month, and Lila's been absolutely glowing.

As far as Zach and me, there's not so much more to add, other than I feel like I've finally met my alpha. We talk about our future sometimes. Dr. Chin says that I might be able to have kids—we'll wait and see—so I'm hopeful that I can. But even if the chemo has withered my ovaries I think we'll be okay. "We'll adopt," Zach says. "Or just live with a hundred dogs. Either way, we'll make it." I know that he's probably right.

We also sometimes talk about the past. About my cancer, about how without it, we might never have found our way toward each other. We occasionally talk about my remission, about how I need to outwit the disease for five years until we can exhale and feel like I'm truly not on borrowed time. But as Sally says, studies show that positive attitudes extend the life spans of cancer survivors. So I try to focus on sunny skies.

Oh, before I wrap up, I want to say that Jake left me a message three weeks ago. I e-mailed him back because he was on his way to Tokyo, and it seemed like the simplest thing to do. For more than one reason. He wrote me the next morning and said that he was happy to hear that I was healthy. And happier still to hear that I was happy. Then he said that the real reason he was calling was because that song he wrote for me, well, they were releasing it as a single. He said that he regretted never playing it for me, so should I one day flip on the radio and hear "Letting Her Let Go," to think of him. I didn't think he was being selfish to ask, in case you were thinking that, Diary. I suspect he just wanted me to know that he finally came through on one of his promises. I guess he thought that it counted for something. And I suppose that it does. I haven't heard the song yet, but I'm sure that when I do, I will indeed think of Jake. And then I'll think I'm so glad that sometimes promises are broken, that sometimes promises aren't enough.

"It's strange, isn't it?" I said to Zach last night. "Who'd ever have thought? Cancer didn't just change my life. It gave me one instead."

He didn't answer. Rather, he stretched out beside me on his rich leather couch and slung his arm around my waist, pulling me into him. "That's the thing about second chances," he said after a while. "If you learn from your mistakes and spin the wheel right, you just might win the whole damn house."

PS—Zach and I are headed to Fiji next week, thanks to Bob Barker. I wrote him a thank-you note, and he sent an autographed headshot back to me. Sometimes when I'm feeling lost I'll take it out of my desk and smile. The price is right, indeed.

· ACKNOWLEDGMENTS ·

If I were to thank everyone who has ever nurtured my writing and my aspirations, this would undoubtedly turn into the world's worst and never-ending Oscar speech. So, with as much restraint as I can muster, I will limit my thank-yous to those who have helped me along the way with this specific project.

That said, I must first thank my indefatigable agent, Elisabeth Weed, who offered to represent the book less than twenty-four hours after receiving my e-mail, and whose endless passion and efforts have earned both my gratitude and friendship. And I have nothing but sincere adoration for my crackerjack team at Morrow: my editor, Lucia Macro, who has been a tireless cheerleader, and Samantha Hagerbaumer and Tavia Kowalchuk.

Before anything else professionally, I am a magazine writer, and I must, must, must thank the countless editors who have sent work my way over the years. Every time you call or e-mail or pick my brain, I am both flattered and amazed, and with all of you (okay, with 95 percent of you), it's been a true pleasure.

I would be nothing more than a solitary writer sitting in a lonely office if not for my friends at FLX. You are my home away from home, and I am constantly touched by your support and loyalty. Specifically, the NST Fiction group. To say that I literally would not be writing this without you does not say it clearly enough. Specifically, heartfelt thanks to Lauriana Hayward, Rachel Weingarten, Tricia Lawrence, Marie Karns, and Diana Burrell. To my early readers: Michelle Kroiz Winn, Andrea Mazur, Shannon Hynes Salamone, Todd Shotz, Randy and Tamara Winn, thank you for printing your own three hundred–page copies without complaint, but more importantly, thank you for your feedback, your enthusiasm, and your friendship. I am many times blessed. And a big shout-out is reserved for Caryn Karmatz-Rudy who helped hone my fiction skills and encouraged me to keep at it for reasons none other than the fact that she's a rock-star.

This book touches on sensitive, painful subjects, and I'm humbled by the women who shared their stories with me. I cannot even hope to have done justice to the insidious disease that is breast cancer, but I also hope that I haven't misrepresented it by too much either. For the women who have stared down cancer, you have my admiration for your courage. Thank you for allowing me to tell this story, as a way of working through my own grief, when breast cancer robbed me of a dear friend. And a big, hearty thank-you is sent out to Dr. Pamela Munster at the University of South Florida, for advising me on medical facts and treatments.

I must reserve my final thanks for those who are forced to tolerate me on a daily basis. Should I become a best-selling author, I will, no doubt, prove to be even more insufferable, and yet they love me still. Mom and Dad, thank you for bestowing me with the confidence, creativity, and freedom to ever dream of making it as a writer. And to my family: my husband, Adam, for becoming and being the man I needed, and to my children, Campbell and Amelia, for whom my heart beats every day. For you, everything and always.

A+

AUTHOR
INSIGHTS,
EXTRAS, &
MORE...

FROM

ALLISON
WINN
SCOTCH

AND

WM

WILLIAM MORROW

Some people call this a "cancer" book, but that's not quite how you see it, is it?

Well, certainly, it is a book that deals with cancer. That's unavoidable. But I see it as something so much more universal than that: I really see it as one woman's journey to find the life she should be living. And so many of us, who hopefully *haven't* been touched by cancer, can relate to that . . . questioning whether or not we made the right decisions, assessing whether or not we're happy in our current state, figuring out how we can make improvements in who we are and what we offer to the world. What I love most is when readers tell me that they didn't feel like the book was about cancer; rather it is about one woman's experience as she tries to find her way, and that her disease was just a catalyst for her path to self-discovery, because that, truly, is the message that I set out to write.

Natalie has the spirit of a survivor. Where did you get the inspiration for her courage and her willingness to grow and learn, in the midst of her illness?

Through both my research for the book and in my career as a magazine writer, I've spoken with a lot of women who have battled cancer. I've always walked away with the impression that these women are *incredible* and that their courage is unmatchable. And I hoped, should I ever be faced with something as equally horrid, that I'd be able to meet the challenge with the same strength. I really wanted to inject some of the tenacity that I'd culled from speaking with survivors into Natalie and her story.

The topic of cancer is obviously one that many men and women have been touched by and one that is terribly serious. What writing styles did you employ to make this a book that readers can readily engage in while facing this serious topic?

Oh, I love this question because whenever people ask me about the book, I reply, "Well, it's about a young woman who gets cancer . . . but it's funny! Really!" And it is! When writing the book, I wanted to be sure that it wasn't a weepy sob-fest, so inserting maudlin prose and plotting was never an option. Instead, I exposed Natalie to semi-absurd, yet still realistic, situations that left her off-kilter: becoming obsessed with the *Price is Right,* tracking down ex-boyfriends as a way of passing the time, learning how to smoke pot to blunt her physical pain.

The *Price is Right* sections seem to be among readers' favorites. Are you a fan of the show and is Bob Barker on "your list?"

Ha! Well, I only wish that I had time to catch the show these days, but unfortunately, you know, there are these little things called *work* and *motherhood* that take precedent. But as a kid, yes, I was a huge fan of the show. When I was twelve or so, it was my fantasy to spend my eighteenth birthday—that's how old you had to be to go on—on the show. Fortunately, I outgrew the obsession when the time came! So, no, as much as I adore Bob Barker, he's not on my list!

Why did you choose to include diary entries in addition to writing the book in first person?

Part of it just sprung up from instinct and another part was very intentional. When the book opens, Natalie can be seen as a very cold, calculating person, and I wanted to give readers a way to crack her shell, to see behind her facade and realize that even though she may be ambitious and cutthroat and not particularly empathetic, she was also just a young woman who had very honest and tangible emotions and fears. The diary entries allow readers to tap directly into her mindset, and, I hope, help readers understand what was going on behind her wall.

Did you know the ending when you began writing the book?

I had a general idea, in that I always intended for Natalie to make a recovery. But how she got there wasn't entirely set in stone. In fact, when I first started writing, I hadn't planned on having Zach as the second love interest. Ned was the guy whom I figured would duke it out with Jake. But as I began to craft Zach's character and his scenes, I implicitly knew that he would be a better match, and so that, of course, altered the arc of the book. I also only realized that the book would end at Sally's wedding when I was about halfway through. I know! It seems like a crazy way to write, but it's a process that works for me: going about it chronologically and seeing what comes out in the wash.

How much of the book is based on real life?

Honestly, I get this question a lot, and the answer remains the same: just about none of it. Sure, as a writer, I had a good time dotting a few elements of my real life into the book—I do have a dog named Pedro (à la Manny), I did get married in Puerto Rico—but 99 percent of it sprung from my imagination and my love and understanding of these characters. So those ex-boyfriends that Natalie tracks down? They're not mine!

Have you ever gotten back in touch with your exes in the way that Natalie does? Do you think that's really a good idea?

I'm someone who has always tried to maintain a positive spin on break-ups and the people I've dated, so for me, it wouldn't be so weird to maintain contact with an ex, and thus, I didn't find it strange or even unrealistic for Natalie to track them down. I do think that there's a lot to be learned from our personal history, and certainly, I believe that if you don't take the time to gestate and ruminate on the reasons that something—a dating relationship, a job, whatever—went wrong, you're bound to keep repeating yourself in a very damaging cycle. So while I wouldn't suggest that everyone start googling their prior loves, sometimes, a little reflection on the past is a good thing.

How do you think the title, *The Department of Lost and Found*, relates to the story?

Well, clearly, it's metaphorical, as the book is not about a literal Lost and Found! But for me, again, getting back to the first question, this is a book about a woman who had lost focus on her life and her priorities, and when she's stripped of all the elements that she once deemed important, she has no choice but to take a naked and honest look at herself. When she does that, she discovers that what she was chasing down might not have been the thing she should have been chasing at all. And in that sense, she truly finds herself and her calling.

What do you want readers of this book to walk away with?

Well, I really think it's about understanding your own personal options. What I loved most about Natalie's journey is that she comes to recognize that how you live your life and how you embrace your experiences, regardless of what those experiences might bring, is always a choice, and that no one has control over how you react to these experiences other than you. You can choose to get bogged down in misery or you can choose to find a way to crawl out of it, and I really try to live my life by this philosophy: take what you're given and turn it into something incredible because the alternative just isn't an option.

Debbie Winn

ALLISON WINN SCOTCH is the *New York Times* bestselling author of *The One That I Want* and *Time of My Life*. She lives in New York with her husband, their son and daughter, and their dog. Her next novel, *The Song Remains the Same*, will be released in 2012.

Allison Winn Scotch